DEAD SPACE

SIU SERIES
BOOK 2

TOBY NEIGHBORS

Dead Space (SIU Book 2)

Copyright © 2026 by Toby Neighbors

ISBN: 978-1-968189-19-8 ebook

978-1-968189-20-4 print

Mythic Adventure Publishing, LLC

Idaho, USA

ALSO BY TOBY NEIGHBORS

End Times

The Four Horsemen

Surviving Wormwood

Wizard Rising

Magic Awakening

Hidden Fire

Crying Havoc

Fierce Loyalty

Evil Tide

Wizard Falling

Chaos Descending

Into Chaos

Chaos Reigning

Chaos Raging

Controlling Chaos

Killing Chaos

Elder Wizard

Lorik

Lorik the Protector

Lorik the Defender

We Are The Wolf

Welcome To The Wolfpack

Embracing Oblivion

Joined In Battle

The Abyss Of Savagery

The Vault Of Mysteries

Lords Of Ascension

The Elusive Executioner

Gryphon Warriors

Regulators Revealed

Avondale

Draggah

Balestone

Arcanius

Avondale V

Third Prince

Royal Destiny

The Other Side

The New World

Luck Holds

Zompocalypse

Spartan Company

Spartan Valor

Spartan Guile

Dragon Team Seven

Uncommon Loyalty

Total Allegiance

Kestrel Class

Jump Point

Gravity Flux

Modulus Echo

Zero Friction

Planet Fall

Charter

Jack & Roxie

My Lady Sorceress

The Man With No Hands

ARC Angel

Battle ARC

Broken Crucible

Hidden Kingdom

War INC

Carthage Prime

Cronus Team

Skandia Seven

Mercurial

Magnificus Prime

Incursio

Merlin Appears

Runners

Survivors

Infiltrators

Resistance

Conquest

Occupation

Extraction

The Signal

Battle Orders

Base Of Fire

Hard Site

Recall

Evade

Assault

Space Fever

Staying Alive

Fractal Cut

Blast Zone

Action Zone

Covert Infil

Armor Brigade

Havoc Squad

Thunderbird

Ghost Tactics

Quantum Combat

Infinite Threat

Shadow Threat

Evolving Threat

Lingering Threat

Latent Prowess

Gravity Masters

Gravity Storm

Daughter of the Night

Supernova

Artifact

Blood Moon

Renegade

Juggernaut

Retribution

Independence

Sons of Perdition

Iron Man

Brutal Planet

Hell Flyers

Foray

Conspire

Siege

Colossus

With Pete Garcia

Apocalypse One Percenters

**CHAPTER
ONE**

THE RESTAURANT HAD an excellent view of outer space. Detective Becky Nash was wearing her best gown. It was black and made of a thick, stretchy material that hugged her curves. Her hair was in long braids that had been pulled up into a carefully formed bun on the top of her head, almost as if her hair were a work of art on display. She looked like an Egyptian princess, but she felt out of place.

"What do you think?" JD asked.

"This is impressive," Becky said as her date settled into the seat opposite from her at the little table.

They were on top of a three-story building that was part of the cityscape on the enormous interstellar ship *Colossus*. It was the first colony ship to leave the Sol system. Their destination was Secundo, a vibrant world that would be a new Earth. There were nearly half a million passengers and crew on board. The upper level, called Topdeck on the ship, was covered with a huge, transparent dome. A grand arch with lights hung over the center section and - during the ship's daytime hours - mimicked the sun. At night, the arch was dark and the city lights came on. There were all sorts of amusements and pastimes to keep the passengers busy on, but there were businesses and administrative spaces, too. The ship was a new beginning and there was a lot of infrastructure still being hammered out in anticipation of reaching the new world.

"Good," JD told her. "I was hoping to impress you."

"You don't have to do that," she said, unable to hide a grin.

"It's all worth it to see that smile."

It was their first date. Becky met JD, which stood for Julius Descarte, after he had saved one of the most prominent men on the ship from an assassin. It seemed crazy to think that on the colony ship, there might be contract killers, but there were plenty of people who wanted to see the colony project fail. Julius was in the right place at the right time. He had acted selflessly and had come close to getting killed himself. His right hand was still wrapped in a bandage, but he didn't seem bothered by it.

"You're pushing pretty hard," Becky said.

"When I find something I like," he said with a nod, "I don't hold back."

"You don't really know me."

"I know you're a police officer," he said. "I know you're good at your job. I know you're beautiful."

Becky felt her cheeks flush. The restaurant had dim, romantic lighting and her skin was a dark shade of brown. The embarrassment didn't show, but she felt it just the same.

Nine decks down in the Special Investigation Unit HQ, Dave Bannon and the rest of the SIU team watched what was happening in the fancy restaurant. The ship had the latest surveillance cameras that covered ninety percent of the ship's spaces. Dave had one in the restaurant displayed on their big wall screen. He had zoomed in on the couple. Around the main image were several more from other cameras that showed the restaurant and the surrounding area.

"I don't like it," Dave said. "He's too aggressive."

"Smooth too," Jeopardy said from her desk.

"Just keep watching," Sergeant Flint ordered.

A week had passed since the plot to kill Everett Goddard had been foiled. Shortly afterward, Beck and Dave had cornered the assassin, who then took his own life. At the same time, Jeopardy Bess and Logan Keys were both injured by the assassin's roommate, a woman named Evie Norada. They were still trying to piece everything about the case together. Evie had clearly been a contract killer in her own right. She stabbed Logan in the back and took down Jeopardy with a throwing knife to her thigh before the police woman could shoot her. The follow-up investigation had revealed nothing. The pair of assassins had cleaned out their berth before the SIU were on to them. With both of the suspects dead, there was no way to question them.

Sergeant Flint had taken point on the investigation, which shifted from the perpetrators to the victim. Everett Goddard was an economist with a background in international banking. He was in charge of the Colossus banking system, which was no small matter. Every person on board the massive ship who had exchanged their finances for the digital currency on the *Colossus* was currently working, either on the ship itself or in some capacity for the other passengers. There were teachers, bartenders, personal trainers, janitors and skilled tradesmen, all working with the passengers. There were others who worked on the ship's systems as adjunct crew members. There were also those whose entire focus was on the colony. It was not only a vibrant world to inhabit, but also a chance to test long-held beliefs about what was possible in a wide range of sciences. Agriculture was extremely important. The colony would need to plant, grow and harvest their own crops. With nearly half a million people on the new world, it was important that the land be managed well. Farmers would be utilized and their crops coordinated, so that there was more than enough food to feed everyone on Secundo.

The investigation into Goddard wasn't fruitful. The man had a few personal issues, but nothing criminal. His fiscal policies were moderate but fair. The *Colossus* banking structure was clean. With the bank president an investigative dead end, the SIU squad turned their attention to the people around Goddard. It didn't take long for several red flags to appear in conjunction with Julius Descarte.

The *Colossus* had a massive, ship-wide information network. There were warehouse-sized compartments that were filled with servers to allow the passengers and crew access to an entire world of information. Earth's history and collected knowledge were traveling with the colonists. But there was also a private databank that was reserved for the ship's senior officers and law enforcement professionals. It had the personnel files for every person on the ship and each passenger's complete history was available. For instance, Everett Goddard had been arrested in college for possession of a controlled substance. No charges were filed, yet the SIU team knew where he had been arrested and what the controlled substance was. There were notes in the file from the arresting officers and the prosecutors who eventually decided not to file charges against Goddard. They knew where he was born, where he grew up, what his parents did, where he went to school and even what grades he made. With a few clicks, they could discover his work history and professional associations. None of it was very interesting. Everett Goddard was a man who loved money and enjoyed both speculation and manipulation of it. But he wasn't a criminal.

Julius Descarte, on the other hand, had a very thin file. They knew where he was born and what he did for a living, but almost nothing else. There were no school records, no arrest records, no professional memberships, not even the normal, varied work history that most people accrued. And what was listed seemed generic at best. It was more than enough to make a seasoned detective's intuition tingle. He was supposed to be a consultant, but there were no records of the companies he had consulted for. He had tax records, yet even those left more questions unanswered.

The companies listed were almost all what law enforcement personnel considered gray. The companies were subsidiaries of larger companies, with little or no direct link to any products or services. There wasn't even any listing of the business leadership. They were a name and an Employer Identification Number, which was usually registered to a country with little or no oversight. In other words, they were shell corporations, the type usually set up to launder illicit funds.

To make matters worse, Julius Descarte was listed on the manifest with a wife and two children, which gave him a berth with two separate bedrooms. His speciality was listed as *Vital*, which earned him a berth on level three and meals in the VIP dining room. There wasn't supposed to be a difference in amenities, yet the VIP passengers who had paid exorbitant fees to book passage expected a high quality of living. The final straw in the investigation was the fact that Julius Descarte had no work assignments. Everyone on the ship was supposed to have some sort of work assignment. Some researchers and specialists worked from their berths. Others were involved in Colony planning, including a think tank whose job was to help plan contingencies for emergency situations that might arise on the new planet. To have no work listed was more than just a clerical error, especially with all the other factors involved.

Jeopardy got up to walk Stu, her black-furred police dog, and Sergeant Flint turned his attention back to his detective on the date with the suspicious character who went by the name Julius Descarte. The server had brought JD and Becky wine and a single plate with some type of fancy pre-meal appetizer. Flint was no foodie and his attention was on the man sitting across from Becky Nash.

"So, what is it you do exactly?" she asked him.

He waved a hand dismissively. "That's boring. I'd rather talk about you."

"That's all we've done," she said.

"What can I say?" he chuckled as he swirled his wine. "I live a rather boring existence."

"That's hard to believe, especially given the way we met."

"I've never done anything like that," he admitted.

"Good. It's a miracle you weren't killed."

"Don't I know it," he said. "I had plenty of time in the med facility to think about my life. I think accepting passage on the *Colossus* was the best decision I ever made."

"Why's that?"

"You mean other than meeting you?"

"Come on," Becky said, turning uncomfortably in her seat. It made the tiny microphone hidden in the lining of her dress rumble with static.

"I'm serious," he said. "But I think I can make a real difference on Secundo. Back on Earth, it was all about the money, you know."

"What do you do, exactly?"

"It's consulting, mostly. Maximizing profits, prepping organizations for future expansion … like I said, it's really very boring stuff."

A pair of servers came with plates of colorful food. They were set down before the diners and the appetizer was removed. More wine was poured, and one of the servers explained what was on their plates.

"Slow braised salmon, with purple cauliflower mash, and a citrus foam," the server said. "Paired with a sauvignon blanc from White Oak Cellars. Enjoy."

The servers walked away, and Becky picked up a fork. "It looks delicious."

"Yes, it does," JD said, never taking his eyes off his date. "So, delicious."

Back in SIU headquarters, Dave Bannon grunted irritably. "I don't think he's talking about the food."

CHAPTER
TWO

DAVE BANNON and Sergeant Flint weren't the only people snooping on the date. Much further down in the ship, Crank had hacked into the ship's surveillance feed. From his desk with his laptop humming quietly, he had a clear view of his boss. Behind him, Nova, Slash, and Fever were watching. Normally, Crank would have spied on his boss alone. He was a voyeur by nature. It wasn't simply his deviant mind, but he felt safer at a distance. It was better to spy on other people than to risk his well-being by going out and interacting with people. Perhaps his demented view came from associating with violent individuals who flew into a rage at the slightest provocation.

Whatever his motivation in most circumstances, he was spying on his boss because, for the first time in recent memory, he absolutely disagreed with what JD was doing. It was reckless. Posing as a legit businessman was one thing. Going on a date with a cop was something entirely different and the three lieutenants who served JD alongside Crank agreed. They didn't like being close to the police, even if they weren't called that on the *Colossus*. The ship didn't have police, but rather 'LEOs'. It was merely a matter of semantics, but the law was the law in Crank's mind. And no matter how he dressed up and talked sweet, JD was still head of the Ghetto Kings. You could take a thug out of the hood, but you couldn't take the hood out of a thug. Crank knew that sooner or later, his boss would slip up and say something that would get them all in trouble. Maybe he was being paranoid, but why take the risk? JD had at least twenty different women on the *Colossus* alone who had traded their bodies for passage to Secundo. It was one of Crank's many responsibilities to keep up with them. At a moment's notice, they could be called up to JD's berth for whatever activities he desired.

"You always want what you can't have," Nova said.

"That's not funny," Slash said. "JD is playin' with fire."

"Boss knows what's what," Fever said. "My guess is he's just getting some easy intel. They ain't got no reason to suspect him of anything."

"Pigs are always suspicious," Slash said.

"At least he ain't done nothing to be in trouble for," Nova said. "Not yet."

Crank knew that wasn't true. Even if JD couldn't be tied to the criminal activities of his crew yet, just being on the ship under false pretenses was a major violation of the ship's charter and bylaws. JD, if he was found out, could face severe criminal penalties, including solitary detention in the ship's brig for the duration of the voyage to Secundo and back. Four years of solitary would make a person crazy. Crank spent more time alone than anyone he knew, and there were times when he caught himself having a conversation out loud with himself when no one else was around.

"She ain't bad looking," Nova continued. "I like them braids she's sporting."

"How many honeys are on this ship, Crank?" Slash asked.

"Two hundred and eighteen thousand, three hundred and sixty-four," Crank said, pulling the number from memory faster than if it was written on paper and sitting in front of him. "One hundred and ninety-seven thousand are classified as single according to the ship's manifest."

"You hear that?" Slash said. "One hundred and ninety-seven thousand honeys on this ship alone. Even if half of 'em are butt ugly, you can't tell me that there aren't more good lookin' women on this ship than a man could taste in a lifetime. Ain't no reason to go sniffing around some cop. JD's losing his mind."

"Maybe he just feels the need to push the boundaries," Nova said.

"Fine, just so long as them boundaries don't push back," Slash said. "We had it pretty damn good back home."

Crank didn't disagree. He had used his computer hacking skills to get everything he wanted in life, from money to friends and even physical protection. The idea of leaving had been a hard sell, but the truth was, Crank wouldn't do anything without JD. At least, he had never thought that he would. JD had been more than a shot caller to the computer genius. He had been a protector and, if not exactly a friend, then at least a friendly benefactor. Yet Crank was no fool. He knew his skills were invaluable to JD and the Ghetto Kings. Just because hacking came naturally to Crank didn't mean that his contribution to their criminal enterprise was any less valuable. They were on the *Colossus* because of him. While Crank had no desire to be in charge, or to face the threat of violence that always hovered around the man on top, he also didn't want to get rolled up with him because JD was pushing his luck dating a cop.

They watched as the fish course was followed by the main course.

"What they eating?" Fever asked.

"Prime rib," Crank said.

"He goes down, we all go down," Slash said. "Y'all know that, right?"

"He would never talk," Nova said.

"Ain't got to," Slash said. "They's a trail."

He pointed at the computer in front of Crank. He wasn't wrong. There was a trail, but not one that led to him, or to Crank certainly. It all led back to a user on Earth. Crank had been that user, although he had been smart enough to create a fake identity and didn't log in from his apartment. If they followed the trail, it would lead them back to earth, and far from Crank or the Ghetto Kings. Nor had he set up their fake identities and boarding passes at the same time. There were firewalls and different IP addresses for each of the GK gang leaders. He had put less effort into the women they insisted he make room for. They were the real threat. If one of them got collared, they would almost certainly sing. While they knew almost no GK business, they knew who the five men were. Their testimony would tie the gang leaders together. Which was why, despite all he knew and believed about JD, Crank had invited the others to his berth. Just in case it became necessary to cut ties with their fearless leader.

"That true?" Nova asked.

Crank shook his head. "We're all insulated," he assured the trio. "If they try to follow JD's trail, it's a dead end."

"Says you," Slash replied. "I don't trust nobody when it comes to computers. They ain't no way to destroy the evidence."

Crank knew that wasn't true either. It was a common misconception, one that the authorities liked to promulgate and which made for a handy plot device in Hollywood movies, but it wasn't the truth. The authorities had capable people, yet none were as good as Crank. But he didn't attempt to reassure the three lieutenants. If he had learned anything from JD, it was that fear was a very useful tool, especially when it came to manipulating others.

"He won't get caught," Fever said. "He gets back, we'll let him know."

"We tell him he can't have that cop, and he'll just want her that much more," Nova said. "Better to ignore it."

"It's our lives on the line," Slash said. "He made big promises.

We can't just hope he doesn't throw it all away on some fine piece of—"

"We shouldn't say anything," Crank said. "We can make our contingencies quietly."

"Our what?" Nova asked.

"Our plans in case JD gets pinched," Fever said.

"What are you on about, Crank?" Slash said.

He was a scary man. Slash was muscular and had a deep, resonating voice that always sounded angry to Crank. But it was his eyes that scared the hacker the most. They were dead eyes, as if they had seen so much evil there was no hope left in them, no expectation of good at all. Slash also had a reputation for being a brutal killer. Crank preferred to stay as far from Slash as possible, but if things went south with JD, the remorseless killer would be useful if Crank could manipulate things the way he hoped to do.

"We know the plan," Crank said. "That part doesn't change."

"Be a lot of heat if JD gets fingered," Nova said. "How you suppose we do this deed while the law is huntin' us down?"

"They won't be," Crank said. "Because if that occurs, we'll be ready."

"You keep sayin' that, but it's starting to sound like you're tryin' to reassure yourself instead of us."

"Look, it won't take much to put a few false clues in places where the law can find them," Crank said. "It's all about misdirection. We point the authorities toward something that's not us. In the meantime, we focus on integrating into the new world's financial system. It's still just a hustle we've done a thousand times on the street."

He was in murky waters. The truth was, Crank had done very little on the street. He had been useful to JD in getting dirt on others, which the gangster then used to blackmail or control those people. But Crank had never done anything personally.

"Still seems like we traded money on Earth for money on

another planet," Nova said. "And it'll be decades before Secundo is anywhere near as modern as Earth."

"That's not the point," Fever said. "On Earth, we were forever locked out of the system. Didn't matter how much money we made. We could never get access to what we really wanted. Them doors was always gonna be closed to thugs like us."

"And Secudo is going to be different?" Slash asked.

"Yes," Crank replied. "Vastly different. We'll be top dogs on Secundo. We'll be the old money, and we'll be in charge of the boy's club. Our thug life is over after this one last gig. We do this right, and we'll have the means to shape Secundo in our image. Nothing will be denied to us… ever."

"I COULD SEE you back to your cabin," JD said.

"That's considerate," Becky said. "But I'm down on eighteen and that's way out of your way."

They had just reached a bank of elevators, and after pressing the down arrow, Becky had turned. She found JD moving close to her. They were alone in that area, and Becky's back was to the wall. It went against her protective instincts to let him maneuver her into that position, but she pretended not to care.

"I don't want the night to end," he said.

"It always does."

"Doesn't have to," he urged. "We could go back to my place."

"I'm flattered, but that's way too fast for me."

"Come on, a little music, a little wine… we don't have to do anything you don't want to do."

"I have to work early tomorrow," she said. "This was wonderful, really, but I think I should head to my cabin and get some sleep."

"Duty first," he said with a grin that was somewhere between friendly and outright ridicule. "Can't blame a man for trying."

"I can, but I won't this time," she said as the elevator dinged and the doors behind her slid open.

Becky turned and found that the elevator car was empty. She stepped in and turned toward the controls, but JD beat her to them. For a split second, she felt afraid. Julius Descarte was suave and handsome, but she didn't actually feel any attraction for the man. In fact, it was difficult for Becky to let her defenses down with anyone. She had seen too much evil in the world, most of it carried out by seemingly normal, mundane people. At every turn, she questioned JD's motives. Even if the date wasn't an undercover operation, she wouldn't have felt comfortable alone in the elevator car with him.

"What are you doing?" She asked.

"Heading down," he said, with another ambiguous grin.

Becky stepped back into the corner of the elevator. JD waved his cufflink device at the controls and pressed the icon for deck three. *Approved,* a computerized voice said. The doors closed, and Becky waited for the attack. It didn't come. Instead, JD stood on his side of the elevator and watched her.

"You don't trust me," he said.

Becky shook her head. "Don't take it personal," she told him. "It comes with the job."

"Am I a suspect or something?"

"No," Becky lied.

"But you don't trust me," he insisted.

"Want to know how many rapes I've investigated that took place on elevators?"

He laughed. It wasn't a joke and Becky certainly didn't think it was funny. Nor was his laugh an uncomfortable one. It was almost as if he reveled in the idea. She felt a chill run down her back and she suddenly wanted to get as far away from JD as possible.

"I'm not going to rape you," he said.

"Oh, that's not what I'm worried about. But, there's always the possibility that you might try."

"Sounds like you're the dangerous one. Should I be afraid?"

"Only if you try something you shouldn't," Becky said.

The elevator reached deck three, and the door opened. "Last chance for romance," he said.

"Thank you, but no," Becky said.

JD stepped off the elevator and held the door open with one hand. "How about a second date then?"

"I'm pretty busy," she said.

"I'm not going anywhere for at least two years," he replied.

"Alright," she said. "Message me."

"I will," he said. "Count on it."

She stepped to the controls and scanned her cufflink. He stood back, watching her. She might have felt flattered under different circumstances. She was dressed up in her best outfit and had worked for over an hour on her hair. It wasn't easy doing all that she normally did before a date when the shower was restricted to one minute of water flow. Still, she knew she looked good. She wasn't a voluptuous woman, but her dress showed off her curves and revealed more of her skin than any other outfit she owned. But his look wasn't appreciation of her beauty or even simply lust. There was a gleam in his eye that made her feel like he might lunge for her throat. It was like being close to a large, predatory animal. It made her nervous and angry at the same time.

Without looking away from JD, she pressed the icon for deck nine. *Approved,* the computerized voice from the elevator said.

"See you around," JD said.

Becky flashed him a smile as the doors closed, then she sagged back against the far wall. From her tiny purse, she retrieved an earpiece and inserted it.

"Dave?"

"I'm here," Bannon said. "That was a feisty little exchange."

"I'm so glad you heard it," she said. "I was afraid you might lose signal on the elevator."

"No, we're reading you loud and clear. And I've got updates. Your date is not who he says he is."

"I got the same feeling," she said.

"Nash, Bannon, sorry to break this up," Sergeant Flint interrupted. "But duty calls."

"This guy is up to no good, Sarge," Dave said.

"That may be, but he'll have to take a back seat for now. Nash, I need the two of you to check on a missing person."

"Wonderful," Becky said. "I'm heading to the office now. I'll change clothes, and we can get started."

"At least the food was good, right?" Dave asked.

"Sure," Becky said. "The food was wonderful."

Ten minutes later, she was out of the skin-tight dress and in bluejeans, sneakers, and an oversized sweatshirt that hung low enough to hide the pistol on her hip. Beside her, Dave Bannon wore tan pants and a golf shirt with a lightweight jacket that was baggy enough to hide his sidearm. Together, they looked like passengers on the ship and nothing about them drew much attention. Becky had even undone her hair and pulled the braids back into a single ponytail.

"Jasper Hezron," Sergeant Flint said. "He's a passenger stationed on deck thirteen. Part of the maintenance crew there, but also taking classes part-time. He's caucasian, twenty-six years old, five-eleven with brown hair, blue eyes, no tattoos or scars."

"How long has he been missing?" Becky asked.

"Just missed his third shift. Hasn't responded to messaging from his supervisor, who also checked with the university. He hasn't been in class for three days either."

"Great, and I suppose his cufflink isn't pinging."

"It was for about twenty-two hours in his berth. Now it's gone dark," Flint said.

"Suicide?" Becky asked.

"I doubt it," Flint said. "He's assigned to berth 14342, along with a Mason Boland. Go do your thing."

"Sure," Becky said. "He's probably just wandering around lost."

"It's a big ship," Dave added.

"I'll coordinate from here," Sergeant Flint said. "Make me proud."

"Anything for you, Sarge," Becky told him.

They left the SIU office and made their way to the closest elevator. Dave had a map of deck fourteen pulled up on his cufflink. It was a wide device, almost six inches long, that served as both a locator and proof of identity. Passengers used them to get on and off the elevator or into their berths. Law enforcement had larger, more powerful devices, including a touch screen on the upper side as it wrapped around their forearm.

"Looks like we need to go up and circle around to the far side of the ship," he said as he tapped the up arrow on the elevator control.

They went up to deck one, what the passengers called Topdeck, and took the public transport train. It was like a subway car, only inside a tunnel that was just outside the ship's artificial gravity. Most people called it the tube. The Colossus was eight miles long and two miles wide. Getting around quickly on the ship required circuitous routes. On the far side of the ship, they exited the Tube and took another elevator down to the fourteenth floor.

Dave led the way. The main hallways were wide with three colored sections and conveyor-like people movers built into parts of the deck. While Dave navigated, Becky kept her head on a swivel. It was most likely that Jasper Herzon wasn't involved in anything shady, even though good policing techniques required that Becky be fully conscious of dangerous possibilities. Someone might have taken Herzon and locked him in a storage room. Worse still, he might have been killed and his body disposed of in any number of ways. That seemed unlikely to Becky, but she had already worked her first murder case on the ship … and she wasn't the type of cop to take things for granted.

There were people coming and going. It was 2300 ship time, but the crew members worked in shifts, and it was easy to forget what time it was on the vessel with no real day or night. The lights in the wide corridors of the ship never went off. As the pair of Law Enforcement Officers made their way through the connecting passageways, they saw several hundred people going about their day. In Becky's mind, it seemed impossible that a person could get away with murder on the crowded ship, but she had to try and think like a criminal. If a person was desperate enough, they would try anything.

"Here it is," Dave said, pointing at the door that was like hundreds of others they had passed. The only difference was the number printed on the outside, 342. Dave tapped the icon on the door's control panel that served as a doorbell.

"One sec," a voice said over the intercom.

"Someone's home," Becky said.

"Probably the roommate," Dave replied.

They both pulled out their bifold ID wallets. Inside was a picture ID of each of them with their name, rank, unit, and a few other vital statistics printed on it. The other side of the wallet contained their badge. It wasn't exactly necessary. Their cufflinks had all the same information, but the people who created the law enforcement systems on the *Colossus* felt it prudent that the SIU have traditional IDs with badges. Unlike the patrol officers who wore black jumpsuits with the acronym LEO on the back, and the usual items on their thick utility belts that marked them as cops.

"What?" A man with short, spiky hair asked as the door slid open.

"I'm Detective Bannon, this is Detective Nash. We're looking for Jasper Herzon."

"Good luck with that," the spiky-haired man said. "That dude is a complete flake."

"What's that supposed to mean?" Becky asked as they stepped into the narrow domicile.

It was just like her own. Two bunks built into the wall, a narrow table, a row of lockers, and the bathroom facility in back.

"Sure, come right in," the spiky-haired man said. "I don't know where he is. Jasper is not a reliable person. Maybe it's being on the ship, but that dude can't keep time straight, much less be where he's supposed to be when he's supposed to be there."

"When was the last time you saw him?" Dave asked, as Becky looked around their shared berth.

"I don't know, a few days ago."

"What's your name?"

"Mason Boland," he said.

"This your bunk, Mason?" Becky asked.

The recessed bunks had privacy screens that could be pulled to block out light and noise so a person could sleep. They worked well on light, not so much on noise. Becky knew because her roommate snored, and it tended to keep her awake.

"Yeah, that's mine. I was just chilling."

There was a strong odor of synthetic tetrahydrocannabinol, and Mason's eyes were dilated. The synthetic drug was supposed to work quickly through a person's system. The idea being that someone high could come down relatively fast, if needed, and could still function in normal society without the drug affecting their mental capacity for long periods of time.

"Do you often vape THC?" Dave asked as Becky knelt down beside Jasper's bunk.

"Sure, when I can. I work in the dining hall. It's boring."

Becky understood the urge to self-medicate. If not for her job, the tiny accommodations on the humongous ship would bother her more. If she was required to be in the same space on the same deck - day after day - she would struggle with feelings of claustrophobia.

She reached out and checked the lower bunk's privacy screen. It was locked. She looked at the controls.

"Any chance your roommate is in his bunk?"

"I don't think so," Mason said. "It's been like that for days."

"Could be a malfunction," Dave said.

Becky knocked on the outside with her knuckle. There was no reply.

"Can't you just open it with a master code or something?" Mason asked.

"We can," Dave said. "But there's no cause to do that yet."

"Privacy laws," Becky said as she stood back up.

"You want to show us his lockers?"

"Yeah, okay, it's these ones."

Dave looked pained at the man's poor grammar but didn't correct him. Instead, he checked the locks. The lockers were also secured. Becky stepped into the bathroom. It was dirty, with towels and clothes dropped carelessly on the floor. She pressed one side of the mirror to access the storage behind it. The mirror swung on hidden hinges. Inside, she found the usual items from a pair of men living in shared space. Toiletries, mostly, and some medicinal creams that she checked the names of.

"Those are mine," Mason said. "I don't use it anymore."

Becky stayed clear of the dirty-looking caps on the tubes of medicine. She didn't find anything of interest that would give her a clue as to where Jasper Herzon could be.

"Did you and your roommate argue?" Dave asked.

"Sure, sometimes."

"What about?"

"You know, normal stuff. He didn't like me vaping, didn't like it when I left clothes in the bathroom, stuff like that."

"Did the arguments ever get heated?" Becky asked.

"No, not really. He would get worked up, and I would ignore him."

"You didn't want to knock his lights out when he was on your case about something?" Dave asked.

"Nah, man, I ain't violent like that. I just let it roll off me, you understand. They're just words."

"Did he ever get violent with you?" Dave persisted.

"No, he was pretty uptight, but he didn't go all macho on me. He's a short guy, not very athletic. I don't think he would ever start a fight with anyone."

"Looks like we're done here," Becky said.

"Tell me about his friends," Dave said. "Who did he spend time with?"

"He had a pretty good gig up on Topdeck," Mason said. "I'm sure he had friends, but they didn't come around here much. I don't remember seeing him with anyone in the dining hall either."

"Where did he work?" Dave asked.

"The Engine Room," Mason said.

"I thought you said he worked on Topdeck?" Beck said, turning to face the spiky-haired Mason.

"He does. The Engine Room, it's a club up there."

"Oh, that's right," Dave said. "I've seen it."

"Wait, I thought he was part of the janitorial staff," Becky said. "That's what Sergeant Flint said."

"He was. But then he got hired as a bartender up top. I know he was trying to get an official work change assignment."

"That's helpful," Dave said, patting the man's shoulder. "Thank you, Mason."

"Yeah, sure," the spiky-haired roommate said.

"He was right, you know," Becky said just before stepping from the berth. "You should clean up after yourself and stop vaping that crap. It smells like death."

Mason looked shocked, but didn't say anything. Dave just shook his head and stifled the laugh that Becky's remark evoked.

"What?" Becky said when they were in the hallway outside room 342. "You know I'm right." That got Dave laughing. "Did you see the creams in his bathroom? That guy had something funky going on."

"No doubt," Dave said. "I need a shower."

"My guess is the Engine Room won't be much better," Becky said.

"Let's go find out."

CHAPTER
FOUR

LOGAN KEYS HAD to get out. The doctors still had him on IVs and the best he could do was wander back and forth in the medical center's single hallway. The *Colossus* was full of young, healthy people for the most part. They had all undergone basic medical screening before being accepted. So the med center was mostly empty. Logan shuffled through the hallway, pulling a rolling stand with his IV drip hanging from the metal pole.

Getting stabbed was a new experience. As a kid, he had suffered plenty. Plus he had been shot twice since becoming a law enforcement officer. None of the wounds he had endured growing up or since joining the police force had come close to the pain of his recent stabbing. The female assassin had been quiet. Not even Stu had sensed her presence back in the berth she had shared with Filo Manns. Perhaps the small space already smelled of her scent, but Stu, in the bathroom, gave no warning. One moment, Logan was talking about the assassination attempt with Jeopardy, the next, he felt cold all over as an awful pain spread through his body. He knew he was in trouble when his knees buckled. In all the fights he had been in, both in the ring and in the street, his knees had never buckled. He went down sometimes, usually in a strategic move to improve his position. He had never before felt so weak.

What made it worse was knowing that Jeopardy was in mortal danger and there was nothing he could do to help her. Things had gone blurry after that. His next solid memory was waking up after surgery. The entire attack had seemed like a bad dream until he tried to move. The slightest movement sent lightning bolts of pain shooting through his entire body. It was the kind of pain that took your breath away and left you panting and weak.

All his life, he had been strong. Suddenly, without warning, he was weak. And not just a little bit, but helpless. He needed help to do everything. A med-droid fed him for the first few days of his recovery. He was pumped so full of pain killers he felt like his body was stuffed with foreign matter. When he could move, it didn't feel like himself anymore. That was slowly changing. He had weaned down from the pain meds and was moving more, but he still felt like he had suddenly become an elderly person. There were times when just walking down the hall in the med bay left him feeling exhausted. His head ached and he had to refrain from turning or bending his upper body. Forgetting about his injury caused deep, throbbing pain that could only be alleviated by strong narcotics. His bowels felt as though they were full of cement, and his head was stuffed with cotton, yet he was determined to get out of his room even if it killed him.

"How long?" He asked.

"You realize we can't help you with pain management if you leave," the med tech said.

"I'm aware. How long until I can go back to my berth?"

"You'd be going against doctor's orders."

"They say all I need is time."

"True, but your wound is right by a nerve bundle," the med tech explained for the hundredth time to his unruly patient. "The scar tissue—"

"I know, I know," Logan said. "It could leave me in pain for the rest of my life."

"We might need to do another surgery."

"Pass," Logan said. "You've cut on me enough. That's what got me into this fix."

"Please, Mr. Keys, just go back to your room and relax."

There was no use shouting at the man. He was just doing his job … and it was a pretty thankless one. There were droids that could scrub the blood and piss off the floors, although humans were still needed to do most of the intricate jobs of tending wounds and post-surgical care. Logan understood that everyone was different. Some people might be overjoyed to be ordered to lie down and relax. But Logan wasn't built that way. He needed to push himself, which was why he worked out twice a day, and often stayed active in the night until he dropped into bed totally exhausted. Anything less left his brain too much energy to dig up his past and there were things he preferred to never think about again.

Most police officers have trauma from the vile crime scenes they were tasked with working. While the rest of the world could look away, a police officer had to look, no matter how heinous the view was. Those memories stayed with a person and could even drive them crazy, if given the chance. But Logan wasn't terrorized by what he had seen on the job. The horrors in his mind went back further, to when he was a child, and he was forced to do things that no human being should ever have to do.

"I wish it were that easy," Logan said. He slowly turned and started shuffling back toward his room.

He hated everything about being in the med bay. They had taken his clothes and refused to let him have his own things other than underwear. Of course, bending over to put on a pair of socks was out of the question. But he could probably get into a pair of jeans without too much trouble. Once he had them on, he would happily sleep in them. Nothing could be worse than the papery gown that didn't close in the back. Not that Logan was modest, but he felt like an invalid without proper clothes. No matter how hard he willed it, or how many treks he made up the hall and back to his room, he wasn't getting better fast enough.

Halfway back to his room, the main doors to the med center slid open. Logan felt a slight thrill. Just outside the med bay, he saw Jeopardy giving Stu the order to sit and stay. The doctors had allowed the police dog in to see Jeopardy on the night she was brought in. While he was in surgery, the doctors had removed the knife from Jeopardy's thigh. It hadn't nicked the bone or cut through any vital arteries. They removed it, cleaned and sutured the wound. She was walking the next day and allowed to leave the following day, before Logan was even fully cognizant. She had gotten rid of the crutch they sent her out with, but he noticed the slight limp in her walk.

"Hey there," he said. "I thought you weren't coming by."

"I just left HQ," she said. "Becky wrapped up her date."

"How was it?" Logan asked as Jeopardy turned and walked slowly beside him back toward his room.

"Boring," Jeopardy said. "She got him telling a few lies, mostly about his family. I trailed him using the surveillance cameras back to his berth."

"You think he lied about the family just to get a few friends on board with him?" Logan asked.

"It's possible, but I doubt it. This guy isn't just dodgy Logan, he's creepy."

"Man, I've got to get out of here."

"Don't rush it," Jeopardy said. "Sarge had to pivot to a missing persons case."

"Oh, no," Logan said. "Not again."

"Seems more like someone slipped through the cracks. No reason to think it was foul play, not yet anyway," she told him.

Logan settled into a chair. His back was still sore, and he hated to admit that he was tired, although that was the truth.

"Any updates?" Jeopardy asked.

"They still don't want me to leave."

"Then you shouldn't."

"I'm going crazy in here."

"I've been thinking about that. There's no reason why you can't work while you're here."

"How?"

"Monitor the ship's network. Check surveillance footage. Run background checks."

"You're not selling it," Logan said.

Jeopardy chuckled. "It's something. At the very least, it will keep your mind occupied."

"Sure," he said. "You've got me over a barrel here. What else can I say?"

"You can say you won't rush your recovery," she said.

"I'm not used to polishing a seat with my backside."

"We all go through seasons in life. This will be a short one in the grand scheme of things."

"Doesn't feel short. Feels like I've been trapped in this room forever."

She put her hand on his. For a moment, neither spoke. Logan didn't want the moment to end. They hadn't crossed any lines that would require human resources to get involved, but he felt certain they would at some point.

"I have a proposal," she said at last, removing her hand and stepping back.

"I'm all ears," he replied.

"You don't have a roommate."

"Correct."

"But you'll need someone around once you are released to help care for you. Why don't I move in for a while? It'll be me and Stu, actually. He has his own crate."

"You want to move in with me?"

"I want to give you the option of getting out of here sooner by having a caregiver in your berth," she said.

"That sounds great to me," he said.

"It's just platonic," she warned him.

"I understand," he said, although he was pretty sure she felt the same way he did.

"Alright, I'll put in the paperwork. In the meantime, I'll have a computer brought to you. Make sure you keep your comlink on during your shift."

"Yes, ma'am," he replied. "And Jeopardy… thanks. This means more to me than you know."

"As soon as I get confirmation from logistics about the room change, I'll let the doctors know."

Logan sat back in his chair, ignoring the pain. He watched her leave, and for a good while afterward, he had a genuine smile on his face. His first since waking up after the attack. Things were finally starting to look up.

THE ENGINE ROOM was a club at the far end of Orion Boulevard on Topdeck. The building it was located in was actually a warehouse with divided sections, which were rented out to various businesses that required space for the goods they would be selling over the two-year journey. The *Colossus* had lots of warehouses that were loaded with goods for the colony, and others that held food, medicines, and spare parts for the ship. But the businesses on Topdeck had to pay for storage of their goods, and the building at the end of Orion Boulevard was one such place.

Only the Engine Room wasn't full of parts or gadgets or supplies for a retail store. It was instead a club with a retro grunge theme. The staff wore flannel and thick leather boots. The music was of the shouting variety, with lots of reverb in the guitar, and very little coherence in the lyrics being sung. It was a change from the pounding dance music in most clubs, but had the same dark corners and shady looking passage ways leading to back rooms where who knew what could be taking place.

Becky had been in all sorts of bars. She had seen things that stuck with her long after she had forgotten the name of the place or why she had been there. It always surprised her how foolish people could get. Alcohol made people abandon their inhibitions and often do things they regretted once the buzz of inebriation faded. And yet, for some reason, they continued to drink, often as an amusement. She understood the people who drank to forget the horrors they had endured. But as a pastime, drinking was way overrated in her opinion.

The Engine Room had a long bar at one end with the typical mirrored wall lined with hard liquor. Although loud music was pumping through the speakers, no one was dancing. Instead, they hovered in clusters, usually around tall tables, and shouted to be heard over the music. The bar was busy. A disheveled-looking man in his forties wore a ragged tee-shirt with a band's album cover on the front. Below the shirt was an apron over well-worn jeans and round-toed boots.

"What are you drinking?" He asked Becky as she leaned over the bar.

"I'm not. I'm looking for someone. Does Jasper Herzon work here?"

"No," the man said, and turned to a woman with long, dark hair next to Becky. The woman shouted her order, and the bartender started making it.

"I heard he worked here."

"Sorry," the bartender said, setting a glass full of dark liquid on the bar and holding out a digital scanner. The girl with dark hair waved her wrist at the scanner, which lit up as it accepted her digital payment.

Dave got into the conversation. "Do you know Herzon?"

"Look, I'm working here," the bartender said.

"So are we," Becky said, showing him her ID. "We need to find him."

"Good luck," the bartender said. "He flaked out on me two days ago."

"What's that mean?" Dave asked.

"Means he didn't show up for his shift, which I had to cover solo, like I'm doing right now, which is why I can't talk. I'm too slammed."

They waited while he worked his way down the bar, filling orders. The club had a few waitresses. They wore flannel shirts, but tied them at the bottom just above the top of their faded blue jeans with rips and tears down the legs. They gathered up trays of drinks and carried them to the tables.

"What's the difference between a bar and a club?" Dave asked.

"On paper, a club has members," Becky said. "Used to be a way to get around municipal laws against bars, per se, I suppose."

"This place has a specific type of clientele," he said.

He wasn't wrong. All the people looked the same. Tee shirts, flannels, jeans, heavy boots that weren't quite workwear, and certainly not fashion footwear. They seemed beat down and worn out, yet Becky knew better. They were all exceptionally lucky to have gotten onto the *Colossus*. Their dire attitude was part of the outfit they wore.

Becky Nash was a student of people. It always amazed her how tribal people were. They sought out people who liked the same things, dressed the same way, talked with similar vernacular and, in general, sought the same things. They weren't really tribes, but there were people in groups across a wide spectrum, from gang bangers to bible thumpers, and from academics to conspiracy theorists. The scariest people were those who had no tribe, no friends, no desire to fit into a societal category. Even contrarian groups gave people a sense of belonging and made them hesitant to commit atrocities. It was the loner with no empathy, no moral compass, who wanted to watch the world burn.

"It takes all kinds, I suppose," Becky said.

"Here comes the bartender," Dave said. "Let's find out who our guy was spending time with."

"Copy that," Becky said.

The bartender frowned as he saw them. Becky leaned over the bar and shouted, "Club soda with a twist."

The bartender's frown deepened. "You'll have to pay for it," he said.

"I got it," Dave told him.

The bartender held up the payment scanner. Dave Bannon paid for the drink, which didn't cost much, but added a generous tip using his cufflink.

"Thanks," the gruff man behind the bar said as he fixed Becky's drink. "But I can't help you with Herzon. The guy ghosted me. I had even put in for a work transfer, but he didn't stick around long enough for it to go through." He set Becky's drink in front of her and she took a sip. "Now, I'll have to cancel it."

"What about his friends?" Dave asked. "Who was he spending time with?"

To his credit, the bartender paused, thinking for a moment. He nodded. "There was someone. A girl. I don't know her name, but she wore her hair in braids. Not like yours," he told Becky, "Just two thick ones and a black beanie. She would hang at the bar when Jasper was working. They talked a lot. I'm pretty sure they were a thing. Does that help?"

"It does," Dave told him.

"Good, that's all I've got."

He headed back down the long bar, and Becky set her drink down. They made a fast scan of the club. There were no women with braided hair and beanies, so they headed out. When they were outside the club, it took a moment to adjust to the quiet.

"What now?" Dave asked.

"Now, we find out who the woman was," Becky said. "You search the security footage. A woman with two braids and a beanie shouldn't be too hard to find."

"What about you?"

"I want to talk to logistics," she said. "Let's make sure the bartender isn't leading us on a wild goose chase. It's possible that Herzon put in for a change of domicile and it just hasn't hit the system yet."

"Good idea," Dave told her.

"Why, thank you, detective," she replied. "Let's get a few hours of sleep and take another run at finding Herzon in the morning."

**CHAPTER
SIX**

NOT EVERYONE DESPISED THE NIGHT. While most of
the ship worked between the hours of 0700 and 2300, some of the
crew and a few passengers worked through the night. It was tradi-
tionally called the graveyard shift, although Titus didn't know why.
As a person who didn't enjoy the company of others, he preferred
working at night when most other people were asleep. The *Colossus*
never slept, but most of Topdeck shut down after midnight and
didn't reopen until midmorning. Titus enjoyed being on the upper
deck after it was mostly deserted and the big overhead arch
lighting was off. During the day, the transparent dome reflected the
arch lights, creating a sort of dull white sky. But at night, a person
could see the stars.

The *Colossus* was moving fast, nearly the speed of light. Titus
could do the math to calculate how speed affected time, but he
didn't bother. In fact, he understood a timetable that no one else on
the ship was even aware of. There were big countdown clocks in
various places on the ship that showed how long it would take
them to reach their destination. But Titus knew they would never
reach it. He was on board to ensure that was the case.

As he made his way down the dark street, walking behind the

big machine with spinning bristles that cleaned the walkways, his mind drifted to his highest priority. He had been hired because of his technical expertise. It was sheer irony that he had been brought on board the *Colossus* as a general laborer when he was, in fact, a highly trained and accomplished specialist in his own right. But there was little need for bomb makers in the colony of a new planet.

Since coming on board the *Colossus,* he had been gathering his supplies for the package he was making. Bombs were like any other mechanical device. Assemble the right components in the right order, and the result was inevitable. A combustion engine needed spark, compression, fuel, and air. A computer needed electricity, circuitry, and programming. A bomb was no different; it needed power, detonation, and fuel. The trigger could be configured any number of ways. He would use a simple digital timer, which he had bought at one of the gourmet cookery retailers on the ship. Power would come from batteries. He had brought his own batteries to ensure they were good. It was easy enough to pack batteries and detonators inside common items. His had been an old-fashioned alarm clock. People rarely used them anymore, but for the heavy sleeper, certain precautions were mandatory. His alarm clock was a wide, blocky device with a speaker and charging capacity for his phone and tablet computer. It didn't work, but no one had bothered to unpack it and check the device. It was filled with good batteries, some useful circuitry, and a series of detonators.

Blowing something up wasn't as simple as lighting a match and dropping it into a flammable liquid. That would start a fire, but a proper explosion required a more robust and fast-burning fuel source. And Titus needed something with power. A simple pipe bomb would wreak havoc if placed in proximity to delicate machinery powering the massive ship. Yet such an occurrence could be contained before becoming truly catastrophic. The ship's engineers were prepared with spare parts and replacement modules. They could swap out a damaged component rather easily. That meant that Titus needed to build something that would cause irreversible damage. It would, of course, cost Titus his life. He was prepared for that. Be it sudden or long in coming, he was prepared. He was, after all, a true believer in the cause.

He turned his street sweeper and headed back down the same avenue. His was a boring job but one that didn't require much mental energy. It left him with the time to plot and plan. At 0300, he hid the street sweeper in an alley, and from it took a small auto-mated device normally used to vacuum floors. It was one of the earliest robotic devices humans had employed. His was another generic model purchased from a retailer on Topdeck. Titus turned it on and then put his cufflink on the device. He set it off through the alley. If anyone was watching him by way of his locator, they would see him moving through the alley and assume he was picking up trash. It was another of the mundane duties assigned to him.

Instead, he took a second cufflink, one he had hacked to give him access to nearly every part of the ship. He didn't put it on or even activate it. He would do that when he was far enough from the alley that no one would make the connection between himself and the hacked hardware. He didn't fear authority. There was nothing they could do to him that would alter his focus or make him question his beliefs. But they did have the capacity to keep him from completing his mission. That was unacceptable.

When he reached the nearest bank of elevators, he activated the spare cufflink and took the elevator down to deck seventeen. It wasn't surprising that most of the passengers and even the crew were always focused on going up. The lowest decks were what most people thought of as the industrial section of the ship. It was also crowded with the most people. The tiny berths were double occupancy and offered very little in amenities. Most people preferred the upper decks, where more of the shared spaces were used for things like exercise and recreation. On deck seventeen, there were only storage and engineering spaces. All around them, packed together like sardines, were passengers. It was a lottery deck filled with people who had been selected at random. They were all single or had left their families behind on Earth. None of the berths were larger than the standard two-person, bare minimum cabin space. Everything around them was noisy, dirty, and for the most part, off-limits to anyone but ship personnel. That didn't stop Titus. He needed fuel for his device and he was determined to get it.

Stealing was one of the riskier requirements of his mission. He stopped in one of the laundry facilities. The people there were working hard and paying very little attention to anything other than the copious amounts of jumpsuits they were required to clean. It wasn't hard to find a stack of blue engineering suits. He took one and, in a storage compartment, slipped out of his orange maintenance suit and slipped into the navy blue coveralls.

No one questioned Titus or even gave him a second look. He went directly to the refueling compartment. One of the great conveniences on the *Colossus* was the surveillance system. If one could hack into it, which wasn't difficult for someone with decent computer skills, the activity around the ship could be studied. Titus chuckled at the thought of criminals in the past casing a bank before robbing it. Or watching city workers from a distance to learn their routine. He had done it all from the comfort of his berth. He knew the used fuel rods were tossed into a bin, which was then taken to a different compartment to be reloaded. The fuel was contained in tubes, which were then fed into the ship's power reactor. They were four inches in diameter and as long as his arm. The fuel was a highly combustible, long-burning fuel. On its own, it wasn't useful in explosives. But mixed with a few other simple chemicals, it became a gel that was highly unstable. Workers periodically took the empty fuel rods out in a wheeled cart. And when

Titus arrived in the compartment, the workers inside didn't even look up. The bin of empty fuel tubes was waiting and he took it.

Back in the wide open corridor, he pushed the cart, careful to stay in the light blue section of the deck. Blue was for crew use, white was pedestrian, and yellow was reserved for emergency personnel. A man with a heavy load in a navy blue jumpsuit, on the ship's crew section of the wide passageway, drew no attention. He had been gone from his post on Topdeck less than half an hour. He stopped in a maintenance compartment. There, he changed back into his orange coveralls and loaded half a dozen empty refueling tubes into a dingy, yellow mop bucket on wheels. He threw a mop in as well, then covered the tubes with cleaning towels. After stashing the refueling cart in the back of the storage closet, he set off with the mop supplies.

He took an elevator up to deck fourteen and stashed them in another janitorial closet not far from his berth. He was back up on Topdeck before anyone noticed he wasn't working. It was a simple task. He was the danger hidden in plain sight on the massive ship. And soon, he would have everything he needed to carry out his fatal plan. Hundreds of thousands of people would die, but that was a small sacrifice for the cause. And only death could stop him from carrying out his mission. So far, he wasn't even on anyone's radar. His work would soon be over and his reward would come in a place of perpetual delight.

CHAPTER
SEVEN

MEETINGS WERE the bane of Sergeant Sawyer Flint's existence. He had always hated them and being on the *Colossus* was no different. They had written an entirely new code of civil conduct for the massive colony ship, and yet, somehow no one had thought to ban meetings.

"You look like someone swapped your lunch break for a yoga session," Becky told him as he came out of his office.

They were both leaving HQ after a brief check-in the morning following her undercover date with Julius Descarte.

"Worse," he said. "Senior section leaders meeting."

"Oh, ouch, sorry, Sarge," Becky said. "No way out of it?"

"Not unless there's an active shooter somewhere on this boat."

"Can't help you there," she said, following him to the elevators.

"Where are you going?" He asked.

"Up to speak to admin," she said. "Our missing person was attempting to change jobs. Dave is tracking down the girl he was spending time with. I'm going to find out if maybe he put in for a change of domicile."

"Come with me," he said. "You can talk to the person in charge."

They got on the elevator and went up to Topdeck. From there, they took the Tube around to the Senior Officers' building, a wide, multi-story complex where the ship's administration and senior personnel lived and worked. It was built right at the front of the massive ship. The side facing the city was covered with display screens that scrolled messages throughout the day. The other side faced outer space with spectacular views.

They were met almost immediately by a tall woman with short, blonde hair. Sawyer had been expecting her and wasn't surprised that she seemed tense.

"Good morning, Commander Koll," Flint said. "You know my detective, Becky Nash."

"We've not had the pleasure," Koll said. "How is your investigation, detective?"

"Progressing," Becky said. She was an old hand at answering without giving too much information away.

"Commander Koll is the ship's executive officer," Flint said as they continued down the corridor. "She's in charge of passenger logistics."

"Including room reassignments?" Becky said.

"Don't speak to me about it," Koll said. "My staff is swamped under with requests."

"Who should I speak to about it?" Becky asked. "I need some information on our missing person."

"Why?"

"He was in the midst of a job change," Becky said. "I've got a hunch that he might have requested a cabin swap, too."

"Because?"

"His roommate is a slob," Becky explained, "who vapes synth-weed. Have you ever smelled it?"

Koll gave a single, authoritative nod.

"And," Becky continued, "we know he met a woman. They

were close. My feeling is that he's probably shacked up with her ... or someone else."

"Speak to Lieutenant Yori, office thirty-one. She can check on the information you need."

"Excellent, thank you commander," Becky said.

As Flint and Koll continued down the hallway, Becky turned back and headed for a nearby stairwell.

"I take it things aren't all roses with the ship?" Flint said.

"It's a very big ship," Koll said. "The crew I can handle, but the passengers... it's like taking a road trip with three hundred thousand children."

"The new is wearing off, I suppose," Flint said.

"And the complaining has begun in earnest. We expected some, just not so much."

"People living in close quarters, do things they're not used to... it takes some adjusting."

"We're swamped under with requests for job changes and berth reassignments. At the same time, I'm trying to keep my head above water with reports on food levels and water services. It takes five times as long to clean the water as it does to use it."

"It's a big change all around," Flint said as they approached the senior officer's lounge.

"With the ship's crew, we can just set the policy, and they're disciplined enough to deal with it. But the passengers..."

She sighed in exasperation.

"I'm sorry," Flint said. "Is there anything I can do for you?"

They were in a busy hallway. The ship's flight crews and senior administrators had passed them by many times. There was no room for an intimate moment, and it wouldn't have been proper for the executive officer to be so openly carrying on a romantic relationship with a member of the crew, but she reached out and touched his arm.

"Thanks," she said. "I'll manage. I just wish there was more time for… well, to get to know you."

"I would like that too," Flint said.

"You would? Really?"

Flint was mystified by Commander Lova Koll. She was a gorgeous woman, and yet, it seemed like she was infatuated with him. He knew he should feel the same way, and he did, to a point. But he couldn't deny the fact that his own affections were divided. There was another attractive woman on the *Colossus* who he hoped to get to know better.

"Absolutely," he said. "If you get time, even just a free hour here or there, let me know. I'll make time in my schedule."

He was used to being the busy one in any relationship. On Earth, his position as a lead investigator was always in demand. He had been married twice, and in both relationships, his job had led to trouble. It wasn't the kind of career that a person could ignore. Even when he wasn't on the job, any open cases occupied his mind. But, since joining the crew of the *Colossus*, he had much more time than he ever had. The Special Investigations Unit didn't have much in the way of cases on the colony ship. And his team was very good at their jobs. When issues had arisen, they had gotten to the bottom of things quicker than expected. Which left him time to attend meetings he really had no need to attend.

"Thank you," she said, before straightening up and adjusting her uniform.

He waited and let her go in before him. There was no regulation against the Executive Officer of the ship carrying on a romantic relationship with another member of the crew, but it was protocol to remain professional at all times. He didn't want to do anything that might make it seem like she was out of line. He pulled back his sleeve and checked his cufflink device for messages. There were none. He hadn't expected any, but still, it gave him something to do before going into the meeting. There was a tiny part of him that had hoped some crime might have occurred that would justify him leaving the meeting early.

With no more excuses, he went inside. There were two groups within the posh room. It was on the backside of the command section of the ship. Big windows that doubled as one-way display units gave sweeping views of the top deck city and its four large green spaces. Gathered at the rear of the room was a group of twelve officers. Each one was in charge of a specific area or group of workers on the ship. Officially, he was one of them, although his own responsibility was just the four other members of his tiny squad. Above him was Lieutenant Tad Janson, head of Law Enforcement personnel.

Flint saw the other end of the room, gathered near the brass espresso machine where a lowly culinary mate was making exotic drinks, were the senior officers. Captain of the ship was Walter Hastings and slightly behind him was his first officer, Commander Lova Koll. She made a point not to look up as he entered. Speaking with them was Law Enforcement Commissioner Monty Forrest, a couple of other high-ranking officials, including Everett Goddard, who was head of the ship's banking system.

Flint wandered over and joined the other junior members. Soon, the meeting started, and everyone sat down at the long table in the middle of the room. It was, for all intents and purposes, an exercise in accountability. Most of the information could be read in a report, but as each section leader gave an account of the people and resources under their charge, the Captain found at least one question to ask. He seemed keen to make each person uncomfortable. He wasn't vindictive, but that was the accountability factor. Bad news could be hidden in a written report, but face-to-face, the Captain of the ship might ask you anything.

Flint was seated next to Tad, who gave a boring report of Law Enforcement activity. When he finished, Captain Hastings looked at Sawyer.

"What about Special Investigations?"

"Yes, sir," Flint replied. "We are currently following some leads in a missing persons case."

"Foul play?"

"That's not likely in this case, sir."

"I'm more interested in the attempt on Mr. Goddard's life."

"Yes, sir, we are continuing to look into that matter, but with both of the assassins dead, there isn't much to go on."

"Someone wanted to foil the colony's success," Hastings said. "I believe that should be priority number one for your people. Have you found where the assassins hid their personal effects?"

"No, sir, we have not."

"Then find it, Sergeant Flint. I don't have to tell you how vulnerable this mission is. If we fail, it will set back extra-solar colonization … perhaps by decades."

"Yes, Captain, we will double our efforts."

Flint didn't mention that two of his officers had been wounded in the process of apprehending one of the assassins. They were lucky that neither was killed. Still, they were far from one hundred percent and the investigation was dead in the water. What Evie Norada had done with their personal effects was anyone's guess. It could be buried in compost or hidden in a nondescript container that was stashed among the millions of boxes, crates, and compartments full of supplies for the colony. They were too far from Earth to communicate with the authorities there, and the odds were high that the person or group behind the murder attempt was not on the *Colossus*.

"I suggest you do," Hastings ordered. "Janson, see that the SIU team has what it needs in terms of manpower."

"Aye, Captain," Tad Janson said. He sounded like a child playing at war with his friends.

Flint glanced at Commander Koll. If he was hoping for sympathy, he found none from her. She was focused entirely on her tablet.

The meeting proceeded and Flint pushed down his irritation. Part of him wanted to stand up and point out that it was these bureaucratic meetings that kept him from doing his job in the first place, but he knew that no good would come of it. It was odd how many things in life were like that. What a person might feel they needed to do in any given moment was almost always problematic. If he made an enemy of the Captain, it wouldn't help him do his job. It would almost certainly land him in hot water with the LEO commissioner. And if he made himself persona non grata with the senior officers on the *Colossus*, it would sink his budding relationship with Commander Koll. Flint was in no hurry to jump into a committed relationship with anyone. Two divorces had burned him on that score. But, he didn't want to close the door before he had even seen what lay on the other side, either.

Eventually, the meeting ended. Flint, grateful to be free, was hurrying for the door when Janson caught him.

"One second, Sergeant," he said, his face split into his customary wide grin. "We should plan a time to meet."

"I don't really have the time for more meetings, sir," Flint said.

Lieutenant Janson chuckled and waved a dismissive hand, as if Flint's suggestion were a joke. "I'm meeting with all the department heads. Spending a little time with them to see how we can make improvements. I just haven't gotten around to the SIU yet. But, with the Captain's order, I think now is the time. Meet me at 1500 hours in my office. We'll go over what I want to do."

"Is that really necessary?" Flint said. "I'm down a man, and Detective Bess has just come back on full duty."

"I'll have some suggestions about that," he replied with a smile. "Don't worry, Sergeant. This will be painless. I'll hang around, see how you're operating, make a few suggestions and get out of your hair."

Flint seriously doubted that. He didn't like being micromanaged, but he had worked in law enforcement long enough that there were always people who felt they had the right to tell him how to do his job. It was part and parcel of the authority he and every cop were entrusted with. Oversight was just part of the job.

"Fine," Flint said. "Your office at 1500, I'll be there."

He left. It would have been nice to have a parting word with Lova, but she had a long list of tasks from the meeting and was already coordinating with the various departments she oversaw. He didn't envy her, although at times he wished his job was as certain as most people's. There was no certainty in police work, especially at the investigatory level. People rarely made his job easy, either. He was constantly wading through lies, speculation, poor witness recall, and grim facts that few people wanted to think about. It was a tough job, but vital, and he felt a sense of fulfillment when he solved cases.

He hurried back down to the SIU offices and was pleased to find Dave and Becky waiting for him.

CHAPTER
EIGHT

"TALK TO ME," Flint ordered.

"Her name is Natalia Zatski," Dave said. "She was born in the Ukraine before immigrating to South Africa with her family when she was nine.

An image of a pretty, but sad-looking woman appeared on the big display screen. She had dark hair and dark eyes. Flint had seen the same expression on a thousand faces. It was the look of hard trauma from one's past, the specter of the ghost that won't stop haunting a person.

"She's twenty-two years old, with a degree in microbiology," Dave continued. "A lottery pick for Secundo and she works in the recycling center as a tester."

"Testing for what?"

"They do a lot in the recycling plant," Dave said. "I had to do some digging on that, no pun intended, but apparently most of the food containers are made of silica. All that trash gets fed down to the recycling center, where it's mixed with some chemical concoction that basically turns it back into soil. Natalia's job is testing the soil to see if it's got all the right vitamins and nutrients to grow stuff."

"Thanks for the school lesson, now get to the point?" Flint said.

"Guess who hasn't shown up for her shift at the recycling center in the past three days?"

"We've got another missing person?"

"We don't think they're missing," Becky replied. "Your help this morning really made a difference. There's apparently a huge backlog of requests at the logistical department. They weren't in a hurry to help until I dropped the Commander's name."

"It's all about who you know, I guess," Flint said.

"So, without going into all the boring details, we only have access to the information that's been processed," Becky continued. "When I had them look at the requests that haven't been evaluated for a decision, yet, I found three hits on our man Herzon."

"You don't say," Flint replied.

"One from the Engine Room to have him reassigned. And two from Herzon himself. He requested a new job about two weeks ago. And, three days ago, he put in for a change of location."

"To?"

"Berth six-eighteen," Dave answered. "Deck ten. It's a two-person cabin currently occupied by Sandra Milton, and…"

"Natalia Zatski?" Flint asked.

"Ding, ding, ding! We have a winner!" Dave said.

"They're shacked up?"

"Most likely," Becky said. "There's probably more to the story, but we're getting ready to head down there now and check it out."

"Do it," Flint ordered. "Let's get it cleared. The powers on high want us focused on the Goddard assassination attempt."

"Focused on what?" Dave said. "It's over. We got the guys that were plotting it."

"We got the contractors. Now, we need to focus on who was behind it," Flint said. "And the Lieutenant is planning to shadow us for a bit. They're calling it standard procedure, but we need to find what the assassins left behind."

"That could be impossible," Becky said.

"Let's hope that Jeopardy and Stu can figure it out," Flint said.

"Speaking of," Becky said. "She's getting Logan set up down in the med bay."

"His doctors cleared it?"

"I guess so."

"Have him start monitoring Norada's movements," Dave said. "When I get back, I'll focus on Manns. It'll be tedious, but we should have a month of surveillance to observe what those two were up to. My guess is she did plenty in dead zones, but that might give Jeopardy a place to start looking for their belongings."

"Good point," Flint said. "I'll make sure he's focused on Norada. Let's wrap up this Herzon case, then put our heads together to show Lieutenant Janson we're on top of things."

Becky and Dave left the office. Berth six-eighteen was in the middle of the ship. They took an elevator down to deck ten, then retrieved the electric scooters reserved for emergency workers. They might have walked the four-plus miles to the cabin if there weren't other cases that needed their attention.

"I always feel like a frat boy on these," Dave said as he pulled the scooter from the locked case by the elevator.

Becky unfolded hers. It was a simple device, easy to use and control via the long handle. She checked her sidearm to make certain it was secure.

"I don't mind it," she replied. "It's one of the few perks we have on this ship."

They set off along the blue portion of the deck, which was supposed to be reserved for fast-moving emergency personnel. Their call on berth six-eighteen wasn't exactly an emergency but time was always a factor in a missing person case. Odds were good the lovers were shacked up together, pretending time didn't matter to them. The colony's lottery committee had set a lot of parameters for the people who would make up the new settlement. Age, weight, health, and career training had all been part of the screening process. But hundreds of thousands of young, single people on a ship together was bound to result in a variety of romantic entanglements. It wasn't unusual for people to become infatuated with one another early in a relationship.

They passed hundreds of people on deck ten. Some looked at them with surprise, but LEOs on the scooters were like police cars on Earth. The novelty had quickly worn off and most people simply ignored them. They made the four-mile journey to berth six-eighteen in just over eight minutes. The cabin looked like all the rest from the outside. It was just another metal door with a number on it.

Becky pressed the call button on the door's control panel. "Colossus Law Enforcement," she said. "Open the door, please."

There was no immediate response. Becky looked at Dave, who shrugged. Becky made a second attempt.

"Natalia Zatski, Jasper Herzon, open the door or we will force entry."

Another beat, and then a voice said. "Hold on."

"That sounded like a guy," Dave said.

"Let's hope it's our guy," Becky replied.

A second later, the door opened. A man in baggy pajama pants was there, and a woman in a long tee-shirt was behind him.

"Yeah?" He said.

"Are you Jasper Herzon?" Becky asked him.

"Who's asking?"

"Detective Bannon," Dave said, showing his badge. "This is Detective Nash."

"Okay, yeah, I'm Jasper Herzon. What do you want?"

"It's a violation of ship policy not to have your cufflink on," Becky said.

"Not when you're in your cabin," he said.

"That's true," Dave cut in. "But this isn't your cabin."

"Mr. Herzon, you have missed three work shifts without permission," Becky stated. "You are legally required to attend all shifts unless you have approved time off, or illness validated by the ship's nursing system. Are you ill, sir?"

"No," he said. "But this is ridiculous. I live here, now. I moved in days ago. It's not my fault if the ship's crew can't put through a simple change of domicile request."

"We're not the morals police, sir," Dave told him. "If you want to move in here, and Ms. Zatski approves, that's your business. But if this isn't your assigned cabin, you have to wear your cufflink."

"We prefer to wear nothing at all," Natalia said with a giggle.

Becky could smell the residual odor of recreational compounds. Both Herzon and Natalia Zatski's eyes were dilated and bloodshot. There was a pile of junk food wrappers on the floor.

"You cops really have nothing better to do than hassle us?" Herzon said. "I thought we left the Gestapo crap back on Earth."

"Sorry to disappoint you, sir, but you have responsibilities to the ship and they will be enforced," Becky said.

"If you've got your cufflink, you can power it up, and we'll be on our way," Dave said.

"I don't have it," he said defiantly.

Becky sighed. "Fine, then we'll escort you to get it."

"Why?"

"That's our job," Dave said. "*Colossus* passenger policy says that no passengers are to move about the ship without their digital identification. You won't be able to use the elevators or even get into your berth if your roommate isn't there."

"Well, this isn't a good time for us," Jasper complained.

Becky wanted to tell him how little she cared, but instead, she forced a smile onto her face and said, "We can give you three minutes."

"Oh," Natalia complained. "We were just having fun."

"What if I refuse?" Jasper said.

"Then you'll be in further violation of the ship's conduct policy," Dave said. Becky wasn't sure how he could remain so patient and sound so positive, even when delivering bad news. "We would have to detain you and you'll be charged with a crime. Nobody wants that. Just come with us, pay your fines and get on with your life."

"Fines?" Jasper exclaimed. "What fines?"

"Three unexcused work absences result in a level one misdemeanor with a penalty of one day's wage and twenty-four community service hours," Dave said. "Failure to wear your digital ID carries a fine of up to a thousand credits per day. Since we've had to get involved, there will be a civil disturbance fee levied as well. Once you've got your cufflink, you'll be able to see all the charges and how to take care of them.

"Screw that," Jasper said.

Before Dave or Becky could reply, the door swished closed. Dave looked at Becky, "Was it something I said?"

She shrugged her shoulders. "I thought you made it sound like a walk in the park."

"I can't blame a guy for not liking his job. Most people don't."

"It's no excuse to be rude to us, though," Becky said. "We're just doing our jobs."

"Should we give him the three minutes?"

"I don't think we need to."

"It's not like there's a backdoor he can sneak out of."

Becky knew the passenger policy on the ship sounded overly strict. No one liked to be told what they could and couldn't do. Yet, with so many people on the ship and considering the amount of stress that many people put on the life support systems, they all had a responsibility to ensure that every job was taken care of and done well. If people just stopped showing up for the work they didn't like, the very systems they all depended on each day would fall apart. She didn't like thinking about it. A long-range colony ship was a death trap if it wasn't properly maintained. Enforcing the criminal codes that Jasper had broken wasn't really the job of the SIU squad. But, since no one had been able to find Herzon, the regular patrol officers weren't able to do their job.

"Better let him know we're coming in," Becky said. She keyed the door's intercom. "Mr. Herzon, Ms. Zatski, this is Colossus Law Enforcement. We are entering berth six-eighteen now."

She tapped a few icons on her cufflink and waved it at the controls. The door slid open. The berth appeared to be empty. It was the standard two-person room, with a pair of recessed bunks. One was open, the other had the privacy screen closed. Dave walked over and knocked on it with his knuckles.

"Stop playing games, Jasper. Let's go."

"Screw that, man. I ain't going anywhere."

There was a giggle from inside the bunk.

"Are they..." Becky asked.

"Probably," Dave said. "There are many kinds of stupid people in the world."

He used his cuff link to unlock the recessed bunk. The privacy screen slid back to reveal Jasper and Natalia. He was on his side, facing Dave and Becky. His arms and legs were braced against the walls. Behind him, Natalia clung to his back. She had her arms around his shoulders and her legs around his stomach.

"Oh, maybe we should just give up and go home?" Dave said. "How will we ever get him out of there?"

"I know a way," Becky said as she pulled her taser from the belt under her jacket.

"Screw you, pigs!" Jasper said. "You'll get the hell out of our room if you know what's good for you."

"That sounds like a threat," Dave said. "You don't want to threaten law enforcement, man. That's a whole different kind of trouble."

Jasper didn't reply. He just clenched his teeth and stared at them defiantly.

"Natalia, if I shock him and you're holding on or touching him at all, actually, you'll get some, maybe all of the charge that passes through his body."

"I'll never let go of you, baby," she whispered fiercely into Jasper's ear.

"Have it your way," Becky said.

She reached out, pressed the taser against Jasper's thigh, and triggered the stun gun with her thumb. It made a loud, crackling sound. Both Jasper and Natalia screamed in pain. Becky didn't stop the attack. She let the full eight-second discharge complete before stepping away. When she did, both Jasper and Natalia slumped down on the bed.

"Nice work, detective," Dave told Becky.

He pulled Jasper from the bunk and let him collapse onto the floor. He and Natalia weren't unconscious, but they had lost control of their arms and legs. Just holding their heads up was difficult. Dave put Jasper in restraints. Becky did the same to Natalia. They had to wait nearly half an hour before the couple could walk on their own. By that time, a pair of patrol officers had been called to the scene. Jasper and Natalia were escorted to jail by the patrol officers. Added to their failure to go to work would be the charge of resisting Law Enforcement. All that was left for Dave and Becky was to file their report for the prosecutors, then they could turn their attention to more pressing concerns.

PARTIES on the *Colossus* were a bit different from those back on Earth. Everett Goddard enjoyed being a host, especially when he could bring famous people into the sphere of his rich friends. There weren't a lot of celebrities on the *Colossus*. Famous people on Earth were desperate not to fall into obscurity. They had all opted to stay on Earth and continue doing what had brought them national or worldwide attention.

On the colony ship, there were plenty of people to gather for a party. Most of the passengers were young people just starting out in their adult lives, but there were still thousands of VIPs and wealthy business people. Everett rented the gala space inside one of the tall buildings. He hired caterers and had a trio of jazz musicians brought in to lend the party ambiance. In attendance were the future leaders of the Secundo colony. Some, like Goddard, had control over tangible things like food storage, fashion designers, and setting up the power grid. Others were leaders in a more academic sense and would influence the direction of the colony for decades: legislators, scholars, and even religious leaders. Goddard had thrown a wide net for his first party. And he had spared no expense. He loved to see everyone dressed up and mingling as he walked through the crowded party and accepted the compliments and praise of his attendees.

One such attendee was the ostensible guest of honor. Goddard hadn't framed the party that way, but everyone was aware of just how close he had come to getting killed. The tall, broad-shouldered black man named Julius Descarte was the center of attention, which seemed to suit him just fine. And for once, Goddard didn't mind sharing the spotlight.

It was, in many ways, a typical gathering. People mingled, some drank too much, others sought their next romantic partner, and still others sought connections that would help them achieve business goals. Goddard scanned the room and saw his trio of VPs. They had specific orders to make connections and glean information from people. Banking was a volatile industry. Much of it was built on trust. Goddard had to weave the illusion that he was the economic wizard who could hold everything together, not just line his own pockets.

When Descarte left the little group that had formed around him and headed for the bar, Everett Goddard moved up beside him.

"How are you enjoying the party?"

"You throw a good shindig," Julius said. "Lots of movers and shakers in this room."

"We all owe you a debt," Goddard said. "Not that someone couldn't have picked up the ball and run with it had I been killed, but I think everyone is grateful they didn't have to. It's hard to stay neutral and keep the playing field level."

"Especially when everyone's out to stab you in the back. Sorry, was that a bit too soon?"

"Too apt, maybe," Goddard said. "Speaking of… how's the hand?"

Julius held it up. There was a scar in the center where the thick needle had stabbed through it. He wiggled his fingers. "Just fine. We both got lucky."

"I did a little digging. I know you're an efficiency guy, but have you considered joining the board of directors at the bank?"

"Never thought about it, to be honest," Julius said. "If you looked at my background, you know I'm more of an operations expert."

"True, but that could come in handy," Goddard said, taking a drink and swirling it around in his tumbler. "We're going to issue physical currency on Secundo. It can't hurt to have someone who knows how to manage that sort of thing to ensure it gets distributed equitably and that we don't run into shortfalls. That's the biggest danger, in my opinion. Too much and we devalue the currency, not enough, and people start to think we're hoarding it all for ourselves."

"I'm happy to help, but don't feel obligated, Everett. I was just in the right place at the right time."

"You acted with courage and selflessness."

"Hey, had I known it was poison, I wouldn't have," he said. "It was just reflexes, really."

"You're too humble," Goddard said. "Tonight, I want you to enjoy yourself. Nothing is off limits for the guest of honor. Tomorrow, we'll talk about how you can help us navigate things on Secundo."

Everett clapped a hand on Julius's shoulder just as a woman in a tight dress joined them at the bar.

"Everett, don't monopolize Mr. Descarte," she said.

"He's all yours, Mona," Everett said.

"Good," she said, wrapping both arms around JD's forearm. "It's not every day that we get to spend time with a hero."

"I'm just a regular guy," Julius said.

"I'll be the judge of that," she said.

Everett left the pair and went to make his rounds through the party. He was pleased with how things were progressing. It was best to have people around you that you could trust. Merit was important, but loyalty was of greater value … and Julius had already proven himself to be trustworthy. All Everett needed was a little insurance to make sure that his new friend would remain focused on the right goals. Everett had already seen to it that Julius joined his little club, whether he wanted to or not.

LOGAN WASN'T EVEN CLOSE to being in shape again. His stint in the hospital had sapped his strength. Just following Jeopardy and Stu down the hallway was difficult for him. He could feel the sweat starting to roll beneath his clothing.

"I hope you don't mind," Jeopardy said, "but I brought in a few things I thought might make you a little more comfortable."

She had been given temporary guardianship of Logan, including his berth. Logan Keys would not have complained if he had been assigned a roommate. But his luck had landed him a double occupancy berth with no assigned roommate. Logan wasn't the type of person to spend much time in his quarters. He preferred to be out and about, either working or training. His berth was for sleep and showers.

Jeopardy opened the door, and Stu went right in. The police dog was right at home. Logan wasn't sure if that was good or bad. Jeopardy stepped back and let Logan go in ahead of her. And she hadn't been exaggerating. She had, in fact, changed almost everything. The austere quarters had been transformed. There was a plush rug on the floor that ran from the main entrance all the way back to the bathrooms. The sitting chairs had been covered with cushions and throw blankets. Instead of the generic overhead lighting, a pair of matching lamps had been brought in. On the small shared table was a basket with fruit.

"Wow," he said. "You did all this?"

"I wanted you to be comfortable," she said. "Too much?"

"No, not at all," Logan said.

He had been in the medical bay for almost three full weeks. The last week, he had been allowed to work, which helped, but he had grown sick of the strong chemical smells and the generic furnishings. Not to mention the constant noise and lights, even in his own tiny bay, the machines that were used to monitor his vital signs would hum and rattle at odd hours.

He settled into one of the chairs and was thankful to be off his feet. It was not his usual feelings; in fact, he had often judged those who hurried to get off their feet. But the muscles in his legs were burning, and his joints felt weak. Sitting down sent a wave of relief through his tired body.

"Let's talk food," she said, moving over to the small mini-fridge. "I've got some basics, sandwich stuff, milk, juice, berries, and some of the leafy greens you wanted."

"Great," he said. "I haven't had a smoothie in weeks."

Stu, the ever-vigilant police K-9, sat down at Logan's feet. He felt a wave of domestic bliss like he had never known before. It almost made him uncomfortable.

"I'll pay you back for all this," he said.

"No, you won't," she shot back. "It was worth every cent to get me out of that room with Alyssa."

"What was so bad about it?"

"The snoring, the sloppiness, the lack of privacy, you name it," Jeopardy said. "I don't know how, but that woman never seemed to leave. She had a job in admin, but was able to do most of it from her cabin."

"Sounds difficult," Logan said as Jeopardy began dropping things into Logan's blender.

"More than you might think," Jeopardy continued. "She complained constantly about Stu, but she was way worse than he was. And of course, they didn't get along, which didn't help. She fussed about him and never stopped talking when I was there. It was just a constant chatter, and even when she slept, she made noises."

"I probably do too," Logan said, worrying that he might dash her perception of him when she got to know him properly.

"Not like that," Jeopardy said. "Trust me, moving in here is a major relief. Thanks again."

"Are you kidding? You're doing me the favor."

She ran the blender, then poured him up a smoothie. It was packed with protein and antioxidants, yet he couldn't get one in the medical bay. He took a drink and sighed with happy contentment.

"You are spoiling me," he said.

"You're easy," Jeopardy said. "You should see what Stu has to eat."

The dog's ears perked up. He looked at Logan, then looked away and settled his head back on his paws. She settled in the other chair and tucked both of her legs up under her. The lamps filled the small berth with golden light, and Logan felt a wave of desire for Jeopardy in that moment.

"Tell me what you've been doing?" he said.

"Searching for the assassins' belongings," she said. "But we have no idea what we're looking for."

"And Stu?"

"I've taken him back to their berth a dozen times," Jeopardy explained. "I think there's more scent from me and you than from the assassins. But enough about work. Let's get you cleaned up and out of those hospital clothes."

Logan could take care of himself. He allowed Jeopardy to put a waterproof patch over the wound in his back, but insisted on getting undressed and showered on his own. Still, he wouldn't deny that it was reassuring to have her there. When he was dried off and dressed, he went out and let her remove the patch. He was a muscular man with his share of scars. Most were from his childhood, which had been difficult and often violent. The wound in his back was different. The assassin's blade had cut through his kidney and spleen, then punctured his stomach. Surgery had been required to remove the left kidney, his spleen, and to patch up his stomach. For ten days after the surgery, a drain tube had been in place. When that was removed, a double row of stitches had been put in place to help the muscles in his back heal. The wound still needed an antiseptic ointment and fresh bandages every day. The med tech had shown Jeopardy how to apply the medicines and bandages. Logan leaned against the back of his chair while she worked on him.

"There," she said, once the last bandage was taped in place. "You're all fixed up."

"Thanks."

"Do you need pain medicine?"

"No," he told her, even though he was in pain. It hurt to move, and it hurt to stay still for very long. But pain meds made him loopy and had some pretty negative side effects, which he wanted to avoid.

"How about a nap then?"

"How about we set up the computer so that I can work?" he said. He had been working, combing through the surveillance footage and building a timeline for Evie Norada's movement since coming on board the ship. "Then, we can walk down to the cafeteria and get dinner."

"I'm not sure you need to do that much on your very first day out of the med bay," Jeopardy warned.

"It's the best thing for me," he insisted. "Doing nothing is like torture to me. I like to stay busy."

"What do you think, Stu? Is he up to it?"

Stu whined, then leaned against Logan's legs.

"See, he thinks I'm fine."

"That's a matter of interpretation," Jeopardy said. "But you're the boss. I'm just here to help."

Logan knew that wasn't exactly true. She was there, in his berth, because she wanted to be. He also wanted to be there. They both wanted more than they were allowing, which had been okay. He had assumed they had plenty of time, but the attack by the assassin had changed his mind on that score. He never would have believed that someone could sneak up behind him and stab him the way Evie Norada had done. He was still having nightmares about it and it had shattered his belief in himself. Most of all, it gave him a grasp of the fact that no one was promised tomorrow.

"I am really glad that you're here, Jeopardy," he said. "I think you know how I feel about you."

She froze, then set his computer softly onto the tabletop and looked at him.

"But just in case there's any misunderstandings," he continued, "I'm crazy about you. I think about you when I wake up and when I go to sleep. When you're not around, I wonder what you're doing. When you appear, it's like someone has let air back into the room. I love you, Jeopardy."

"You… you hardly know me," she said.

"I know enough. I know you're an excellent cop. I know that Stu loves and trusts you. In my opinion, that speaks volumes about your character. I know you're smart, dedicated, resourceful and tough. Most of all, I know that I want to spend the rest of my life getting to know every tiny detail of yours."

"What drugs do they have you on?"

"None," he said. "I know we aren't supposed to fall in love with our partners, but I can't help it. If I've learned one thing on this voyage, it's that I don't want to waste another second pretending I don't love you."

He reached out with one hand and she hesitated for a second. In that instant, he felt a stab of fear. Had he misread her feelings? But then she took his hand. Her's was soft and warm. He used his other hand to help push himself up to his feet. It was almost embarrassing how difficult the simplest tasks had become. Yet he stood up and drew her close.

"You might change your mind," she said. "I'm not very good at relationships."

"Maybe you just haven't been in the right one," he said. "Besides, I don't have any expectations. I just want to be close to you."

"I want to be close to you," she said.

They kissed. It felt to Logan like it had been a long time coming. He felt an electrical current rush through every part of his body as they kissed. He forgot about everything else in that moment. Secundo, the colony, the *Colossus*, their jobs, it all fell away as he held her body next to his and kissed her. In that moment, he had everything he had ever wanted in life … and he was in no hurry to let it go.

CHAPTER
ELEVEN

WEEKS PASSED WITH NO PROGRESS. Sergeant Flint had seen hundreds of cases go cold. In some instances, nothing was worse. A missing child case that was never resolved was the absolute worst. The missing luggage that the assassins had left behind was not even close to the same feeling, but it was just as cold.

Life on the *Colossus* went on. Crime was part of that life, but consisted mostly of domestic disputes or bar fights on Topdeck. Occasionally, the SIU was called in, but it all felt like a formality. Likewise, the court system on the colony ship worked through the infractions of the ship's law. The biggest crime was unauthorized residence infractions, followed by unauthorized absence from work assignments. Almost all of which were handled by patrol officers. They did require an appearance in court and 'failure to appear warrants' were issued on an almost daily basis. When a passenger with an arrest warrant wasn't found in their domicile, the case was kicked up to SIU. Logan and Dave had become surveillance experts and used the ship's systems of cameras and geo-locators to track down the people who failed to show up to court. It was simple enough work and was easily set aside at the end of the day.

Chasing down no-shows didn't linger in a person's mind and haunt their dreams.

Commander Lova Koll had issued a ship-wide freeze on domicile and job reassignments. It was not a popular order, and many of the passengers chafed at the strict, military order on the ship. Lots of care had been taken to make the *Colossus* as comfortable as possible, but it was filled with strangers. Flint thought it might have been better to let people who wanted to be reassigned to a new berth get their wish, but he also understood the logistical headache of such requests. The jobs were a little more difficult to deal with. Most of the assignments were for general labor jobs in sectors that no one wanted to work in. But just because they were messy or unpopular didn't mean they weren't vital to the ship's well-being. Especially with so many people on board. If the plumbing system went down, even for a few hours, things on the ship would get very uncomfortable. And like it or not, they still had months of travel left to undergo.

Each morning, Flint gave out assignments. The small squad worked in eight-hour shifts when necessary, but when they had no cases to work, Flint made sure his people had downtime. Logan was already back to working out twice a day and Jeopardy trained with Stu up in the park area as often as she could. Stu had become the ship's de facto mascot. Most police dogs weren't treated like pets, but it was impossible to keep people, mostly children, from wanting to pet the muscular black dog. Fortunately, Stu's natural personality was very friendly. Jeopardy knew how to keep the animal focused on the work it was specially trained to do.

Which was why it was odd when Stu showed interest in a passenger. Flint just happened to be walking with Jeopardy when the event happened. They were talking about her own room assignment. Jeopardy had moved in with Logan to help him with his recovery. But with that recovery complete, she was worried about having to move back to the berth she had given up.

"I'll do whatever I need to," she said calmly. "What do you think?"

"I think the Commander made it clear," Flint told her. "You're stuck with Logan. But you need to inform HR."

"We have," Jeopardy said, clearly relieved that her boss didn't expect her to move back to her old cabin. "We filed the forms last week."

Flint knew that eventually it would work its way through to him. The ship's administration system was even less efficient than the Metro PD's had been. But he understood the logistics division was inundated with requests, which made the entire system jam up as the electronic forms passed from one administrator to the next. In most cases, it would have been protocol to separate Logan and Jeopardy. The law enforcement division on the ship couldn't keep officers from romantic entanglements, but it was preferable if those relationships didn't affect working conditions. Things could get frosty very quickly if partners went through a bad breakup. Flint knew that most breakups were bad, at least to one of the two people involved.

But his team were specialists and there were no other investigative divisions. He would just have to manage the fallout if Logan and Jeopardy fell apart.

"Good to hear it," he told her.

He was about to say more when Stu suddenly stopped walking. The dog's hackles went up, his tail stiffened behind him, and he dropped his head. A low, menacing growl sounded from the police dog. Flint stopped walking when Jeopardy raised a hand. Not that she needed to, Flint had seen enough police dogs in action to recognize when something was setting one off.

There were plenty of passengers in the corridor. They were on Deck thirteen, en route to look for a woman who had missed her court date. Dozens of people walked past the trio of law enforcement officers. A few glanced at Stu, some even smiled. He ignored them all, except one, a short man with very thinning brown hair and thick shoulders. He seemed oblivious as Stu fixated on him.

"Stu, *warte!*" Jeopardy said, using the German word for *wait.* "Sir, should we follow?"

"Yes," Flint said, his attention locked on the unassuming man. "Keep your distance."

"Stu, *such!*" Jeopardy said, holding his leash firmly.

They turned and set out after the passenger. Normally, the police dog walked at a casual distance in front of Jeopardy, and she held his leash in a loose grip. But since taking notice of the man, he was almost straining against the leash, which Jeopardy held tight. Flint stayed behind them. He trusted Jeopardy and Stu. There were only a few things that would trigger a police dog. Most were trained for specific tasks such as narcotics operations or counter terrorism. Stu was the rare exception who had been trained to take note of a variety of triggers. The man could be a simple chemist whose job exposed him to chemicals used to make street drugs. Or maybe he had a weapon of some kind on his person. Stu was trained to sniff out things like gunpowder or even gun oil, as well as chemicals, drugs, and other contraband. What the dog couldn't do was tell them what had set it off.

They stayed back, at least ten yards behind the man, while Flint looked him up using his cufflink. Everyone on the ship wore a similar device, which registered where they were and gave authorities pertinent information such as their name, berth and job on the ship. Flint zeroed in on his own location, then watched the running icons of the people ahead of him in the corridor until he isolated the man that Stu was locked onto.

"Titus Russel," Flint said quietly. "Berth two-eighty-one on deck fourteen. Works in janitorial services up on Topdeck."

"Has to be into something," Jeopardy said. "I've never seen Stu activate this hard before."

"Any idea what it is?"

"No," she said. "Something bad, though, has to be."

"Alright, take Stu back up to HQ," he ordered. "Get everyone in and start a deep dive on this passenger."

"What are you going to do?"

"Get a closer look at this guy."

It was clear by that point that Titus Russel was headed to the dining hall on deck thirteen, which was shared by residents on deck fourteen as well as thirteen. It was a big, common room with long rows of tables and small stool seats that reminded Flint of a high school cafeteria.

Food on the ship wasn't terrible, but it was institutional fare. Most items were reconstituted or made from freeze-dried ingredients. Bread could be baked from flour, but there were no real eggs, just powdered eggs that did nothing to help the bread rise. Most meals were filled out with pasta or rice. The vegetables were rehydrated, which made them bland. What the ship had plenty of was dry spices. Flint got in line nearly eight people behind Titus. If the unassuming man had noticed Flint, he gave no indication. For his part, Titus was perhaps the most bland person Flint had ever seen. He wore tan pants and a gray shirt. He was neither fat nor thin, his face was completely unremarkable and his hair was so short that it couldn't be considered unkempt. There were no scars that Flint could make out, no tattoos, and nothing special about the way he walked or moved. His shoulders were thick and a little hunched. Flint thought the man probably spent the majority of his days leaning forward and looking down.

Flint got a tray and was given a scoop of saucy chicken and noodles. There were tiny bits of carrot, onions, and spinach in the concoction. Next to the main dish was a flat lump of bread, along with a mound of green peas. He got a plastic cup that was filled with a grape-flavored beverage and made his way out through the tables. As he expected, Titus sat alone, and so it wasn't hard to join him.

"You mind?" Flint asked, putting on his most friendly fake persona. "I hate to eat alone."

"Sure," Titus said, barely looking up.

Flint set his tray down, then settled across from Titus. "I'm Jack."

"Bill," Titus lied.

Flint let his focus move down to the food. He had picked up several packets of Italian seasoning, and he began to flick them as he prepared to season his food. Titus had nothing on his own meal, which he ate in a steady rhythm. First, a bite of the chicken and noodle mix, then a small helping of green peas. His face showed no indication of what he thought of the meal.

"They sure know how to make food unappealing on this ship," Flint said. "I gotta doctor it up or I can't choke it down."

"Yeah," Titus agreed, but without enthusiasm.

"I'm maintenance, IT mostly," Flint said, keeping up the banter. "What about you?"

"Janitorial," Titus admitted. "I work up on Topdeck, graveyard shift."

"You don't say?"

"It's nothing special."

"At least you get a view, am I right?"

Titus nodded as he forked more of the bland food into his mouth.

"Man, I'd kill to be on Topdeck. I spend most of my days in front of a computer. It's boring and I ain't kidding."

"Do they have computer issues on the ship already?"

"My old tech instructor used to say, 'Garbage in, garbage out,' and there's plenty of people on the ship who don't know what they're doing. It's mostly fixing peripherals, you know, some fop in admin spills soda on his keyboard, that sort of thing."

"I get it," Titus said. "You wouldn't believe how much litter we pick up on Topdeck every day."

"People are the worst sometimes," Flint said. "But what are you gonna do, am I right? Can't live with 'em, can't live without 'em."

"On Secundo we can," Titus said. "On Secundo, a person could set out on their own and maybe never see another person again as long as they live."

"Yeah, I suppose," Flint said. "I never really thought of it."

"That's the best part if you ask me," Titus said. "Real solitude. A person can build their life with their own two hands and no one can tell them not to."

"Or how to, I guess," Flint said.

They talked for nearly fifteen minutes before Titus finished his meal and left. Flint got the impression that the other man felt a bit of relief that Flint didn't follow him. Instead, Flint pretended to eat and watched Titus out of the corner of his eye. When he stepped out of the dining hall, Flint pulled back his sleeve and activated his comlink via the device on his wrist.

"Bannon?"

"I'm here, Sarge," Dave replied.

"Tell me you have something?"

"No, sir, not a thing," Dave answered. "We're watching him now. He's headed back through the corridor. I've pulled up his work schedule. He's due in at 2300 hours. My guess is he's headed to his berth for the night."

"Roommate?"

"Negative, he's solo. What do you want to do?"

"Nothing yet, but keep eyes on him."

"What'd you learn from your meal with him?" Becky asked. "Anything useful?"

"He's a good liar," Flint said, getting up and returning his tray to the cleaning node. "A bit of an odd character."

"How so?" Dave asked.

"Ate his meal with no seasoning for one thing, and I mean he shoveled it in like a robot."

"It's not criminal, but it should be," Logan said.

"He gave me a fake name too," Flint continued. "Doesn't like people."

"Surprise, surprise," Becky said.

"But that could have all been smoke. He seemed focused on getting to Secundo, where, according to him, a person can go their whole life without seeing another person."

"Anti-social, with proclivities that appear to show a lack of normal sensory receptors," Dave said. "This could be a real bad guy."

"Or he could have stepped in something that smelled bad to Stu," Becky said.

"I don't think so," Jeopardy spoke up for the first time. "He's never gone off like that before. He was onto something."

"What should we do?" Dave asked. "Do we have enough for a search of his domicile?"

"Not yet," Flint said. "Dave, dig deeper into his background. Look for anything out of the ordinary. If we learned anything from the assassination attempt on Goddard's life, it's that people have hacked their way onto this ship."

"On it," Dave said.

"Logan, you up for a job reassignment?"

"Yes, sir," Logan replied.

"Go get a nap then. I'm adding you to the janitorial team on Topdeck, graveyard shift. Try to get to know Titus. See if you can get him to open up about whatever he's into. Becky, you still got eyes on this guy?"

"Yeah, he's headed home, I'm pretty sure."

"Stay on him," Flint said. "I want an alert every time his door opens."

"Got it," she responded.

"Jeopardy, I want you and Stu to do a pass by his berth once he's gone to work. Let's see if there's something in his cabin that

Stu alerts to. In the meantime, let's find the woman who missed her court date."

"On our way," Jeopardy said, as she and Stu hurried back down to meet Sergeant Flint, feeling a sense of importance at what they could do that no one else on the ship was able to replicate.

Perhaps for once, they all thought, they would be able to stop a crime before it happened.

IT WAS hours later when they returned their attention to Titus Russel and during that time, he had been productive. Paranoia was a constant for the small, unassuming bomb maker. Since his teens, he had distrusted others and suspected that they were out to get him. The stranger who ate a meal with Titus was no different. In the months he had been on board the *Colossus*, no one had shown an interest in him. He ate his meals alone. Occasionally, someone would speak to him, but no one had ever tried to have a prolonged conversation with him. The sudden attention from the man named Jack had set off all Titus' alarms.

He returned to his berth, only instead of sleeping as he had planned, he gathered up the components of his bomb. They went into a toolbox, along with all the materials he had used to make it. There was a lot of debris left over, bits of electrical devices, soldering wire, tape, plastic shavings, that had to be disposed of. Then there was the shrapnel he had collected. A bomb had incredible concussive power, but adding in bits of metal to the device doubled and even sometimes tripled the device's destructive capabilities. His bomb wasn't going to be used against people. Although he still wanted as much damage as he could muster with the device. Long hours had been spent scraping the spent fuel rods and he still had about three-quarters of the amount of fuel he felt was necessary to carry out his plan.

All of it had to be moved from his berth. And none of it could be seen as he went to and fro in the ship. There were cameras everywhere and they were watching him. Titus could feel the authorities closing in. He didn't care. His life was already forfeit. But he needed a bit more time to complete his task. Once that was done, it wouldn't matter what they did with him. Everyone on the ship was going to die. It didn't matter if he did that in his berth or in a prison cell. Not that the *Colossus* had prison cells per se. He had studied the schematics of the ship and knew they had a detention center, but that wasn't the same as a prison. Titus had been to prison. He had faced the demons in the darkness, endured their torture, and found a second chance at life among the monsters. He, too, was a monster, but of a different variety. It crossed his mind that perhaps people would never know that he, Titus Russel, had been responsible for the destruction of the *Colossus*. That was his one great regret. He was already filming short confessionals on a tablet that wasn't connected to the ship's network. He would upload it just before the bomb went off. Maybe, someday, if the wreckage of the *Colossus* was ever found, they would be able to access the ship's computer memory and find it. He took a small bit of solace in that hope.

He made several trips to different parts of the ship that day. Each time, he carried small parts of his murderous art hidden in his clothing. He was forced to do things he didn't normally do in order to seem like his trips out weren't unusual. The eyes of the ship were everywhere, and he correctly guessed that people were watching him and discussing the motivation for his every move.

Becky Nash wasn't sure what to think. She sat at her desk watching the live footage of Titus going back and forth on the ship.

Across from her, Dave Bannon was doing a deep dive into the background of Titus Russel.

"What's he doing now?" Dave asked.

"Dropping off laundry," Becky said. "This guy is the least suspicious character I've ever tailed."

"Could all be an act," Dave pointed out.

"I don't know," Becky said. "I trust Jeopardy, but there's just no telling what might have set her dog off on this guy."

"He's a janitor," Dave said. "Hard to imagine he's getting into things that would trigger the dog."

"Don't get me wrong, I think the idea of proactive policing is great. I'd much rather stop a crime than try to catch the perps after they've committed a felony. But, these types of busts never go right."

"Seems like an invasion of privacy," Dave said. "But there's too many bad guys out there hiding their nefarious deeds behind our code of civil rights."

"So, you think they shouldn't have that right? Do you really want someone pilfering through your internet search history or watching what you do behind closed doors?"

"No, but I'm a realist. The truth is, we haven't had privacy since the invention of smart tech."

"Here we go," Becky said, leaning forward on one elbow.

"It's true," Dave said. "Everyone knows it."

"There's a difference between a program that is set to catch key words in a conversation and me watching this bozo's every move," Becky said.

"I'm just saying that there are files on every person with all sorts of private information. The idea that anything we do is actually private is an illusion."

"It's not the same," Becky said.

"Okay," Dave said, raising his hands in surrender. "It's not a hill I'm willing to die on."

"So far, all I've done is watch this guy run errands. He goes out, he goes home, there's nothing suspicious about him at all."

"Maybe we're being overly concerned," Dave said. "There's nothing in his background that pops either. No arrests, no suspicious activity, not even an affiliation with anyone we would be concerned about."

"He won a spot on this ship?"

"According to the records," Dave said. "And got lucky enough to land a private berth. Otherwise, he's absolutely clean."

Dave's proclamation made the fine hair on the back of Becky's neck stand straight. She had nothing on the guy, and yet, some part of her felt suspicious of the fact that he was seemingly so innocent.

"Looks like he's going to work," Becky said with a yawn. "The only thing I can't understand about this guy is how he manages on so little sleep."

"Give me the highlights?"

"He returned to his berth after his meal with the Sarge. Then he dropped off some laundry and went home. An hour later, he stepped out and picked up some essentials on Topdeck. I can't be certain, but it looked like shampoo and maybe some shaving gel."

"And he's on camera the entire time?"

"No," Becky said. "He passed through a couple of dead zones."

Dave gave a low whistle. "So, he's either innocent or really good."

"Good at what?"

"He could be hiding something?"

"He's wearing his cufflink. We've got video of him, Dave. There's nothing suspicious about the guy."

"He's not going out of his way to find the dead zones?"

"Nope," Becky said. "I thought of that and checked the routes. They're the shortest possible to complete the task he's doing."

"Maybe the Sarge will find something."

"Maybe we're just looking for trouble where there is none."

Dave shrugged. "So? It's not like we're hurting this guy."

"But we're doing exactly what the anti-police groups say that we do," Becky pointed out.

"You don't think Stu triggering on this guy is enough to warrant a little digging?"

"Since we can't say why the dog went after him, and we've found nothing else to support the suspicion, I have to say no. I mean, we could mark him down as a person of interest, but I don't think we should be tailing him night and day."

"What about going into his berth?"

"No," Becky said. "Not this time."

"You going to voice that concern with the Sarge?"

"No," Becky said. "Not this time."

"Ha, ha," Dave pretended to chuckle. "Very funny."

Down on deck fourteen, Sergeant Flint and Jeopardy waited for word from Becky that Titus Russel had clocked into his job. It was late in the daily cycle, 2330 hours ship time. Flint was tired, but he knew that some of the best police work was done late. And there were fewer people out and about to see him go into Titus Russel's berth with the police dog.

"Are we ready?"

"Yes, sir," Jeopardy said. "How do you want to proceed?"

"We make a casual pass," he instructed. "Let's see if Stu picks something up."

They set out down the corridor. The space closest to either side where the berths were located was generally clear of traffic. Flint and Jeopardy were in civilian clothing, but of course, Stu wore his K-9 armor that was printed with police titles and warnings. Jeopardy walked with Stu close to the wall where Titus Russel's berth was located. The dog began to growl as they drew close to cabin two-eight-one on deck fourteen. Jeopardy didn't say anything until Stu stopped. He was right outside the door to Titus Russel's berth. He pawed at the door and growled.

"Stu, *fuss!*" she ordered.

The dog reluctantly continued down the passage. Flint waited as they passed three more cabins. Stu ignored them all.

"He's picking something up," Jeopardy said.

"Just at the one cabin?"

Jeopardy nodded. "Two-eighty-one," she said. "There's something in there."

Flint tapped his comlink controls. "Base, how's our subject?"

"Just starting out with a street sweeper," Becky said. "You're clear to proceed."

"Dave?"

"The report is filled out. I just added that Stu alerted outside the suspect's domicile. I'm filing it now."

"Alright, we're going in," Flint said. "Standby."

He and Jeopardy both activated video recorders that were clipped onto their shirt collars. They went back to berth two-eight-one and Flint used his cufflink's override function to open the door. It was dark inside and neat. Jeopardy let Stu go first yet kept the dog on a tight leash. He made straight for the table. Lights came on the moment they stepped inside. Flint ordered the door to remain open. Not that they wanted a lot of people making note that law enforcement personnel were searching a passenger cabin. But they weren't trying to hide the fact either. And the record would show that the door to Titus Russel's berth remained open the entire time.

Stu sniffed all around the table, and several times he rose up on his rear legs to get a better scent from the table. Then he growled and barked twice.

"He's keying on something that was on the table," Jeopardy said.

"Search the rest of the cabin," Flint ordered. "Don't open anything or touch anything the dog doesn't react to. We're on pretty thin ice here as it is."

"Roger that," Jeopardy said.

Flint felt a sense of frustration. Whatever their suspect was up to, he had been smart enough to hide it, probably because Flint had made Titus paranoid in the dining hall. But that was police work. It couldn't be avoided. They had to make every effort to get to the bottom of things with a suspect and he had dictated a report about the encounter with Titus Russel. That report had been added to the documented information they had gathered throughout the day. It would be reviewed by their superiors and, without a reason to bust Titus, it would be Flint who took the heat.

"There's nothing here," Jeopardy said. "Whatever Stu is keying on, it's gone."

"Alright, take the dog out," Flint said.

He had one last thing to do. From the wide thigh pocket on his cargo pants, Flint pulled out a tiny misting device. It was the kind used to keep eyeglass cleaner and breath freshener in. But his vial was filled with holdercine glycol. He gave the tabletop a quick misting with the chemical, then took out what appeared to be a white ribbon. It was actually a cotton strip that had been dipped in Nighgellic acid. He wiped the end of the white strip across the table top, then held up an infrared light emitter over it. The wet end of the white cotton strip turned blue.

He repeated the test two more times, recording the result, then bagging the cotton strips in an evidence bag. His job done, he left the cabin and closed the door.

"Anything?" Jeopardy asked.

"Initial result was blue," he said.

She gave a low whistle. "That's not good."

Flint was filled with a nervousness he had rarely felt in his many long years of law enforcement. Criminals were everywhere, but there were levels of danger posed by people willing to break the law. A person desperate enough to rob a business or home was rarely as dangerous as a gang member. And even though a person pushed into a corner might resort to murder, the uniform had always been a layer of protection. Most people, even those who cared nothing about the law, still hesitated to attack the police. Which meant that even though Flint had pursued bad people most of his adult life, he had rarely felt the awful sensation of being in imminent danger.

"Dave, get the spectrometer powered up," Flint ordered. "And let's get a forensic tech to the office. I want a full workup on these test strips."

It took Flint, Stu and Jeopardy fifteen minutes to reach the SIU offices. Flint was still recording everything. He put the evidence bag on a small table where a series of forensic devices were stored. The spectrometer was used to measure light frequencies and energy, which in turn could help identify materials and chemical structures. It was an automated device that spit out a lot of data that was highly technical. But the summations were clear enough for any law enforcement official to read. They also had a high-powered microscope, a chemical reaction set, as well as a magnet and energy frequency readers.

They waited another fifteen minutes for the forensic tech to arrive. Law enforcement on the *Colossus* was extremely limited. There was only one technician trained in forensic testing. His name was Gerald Walsh, and he was accompanied by a legal advocate named Clarissa Fields.

"Let's do this by the book," Flint said. "I'm recording everything. Let's get names and professional titles down before you do anything."

"I'm not sure we should be doing anything," Clarissa said. "I was on call for prosecutions tonight. I went over your initial report, and I have to say, it is very thin, Sergeant Flint."

"In this case, I can live with that," he replied.

"Maybe you can, but my job is to ensure that you aren't overstepping your bounds."

"I thought your job was to prosecute the crimes we discovered," Becky said.

"Which I cannot do if you have violated a passenger's civil rights," Clarissa insisted. "Tell me you found something significant on this search. We're on shaky ground here from a legal perspective."

"We only found trace evidence," Flint said.

"Of what?"

"I'm going to wait and let Walsh do a workup on the test strips I collected. I don't want to say or do anything that might influence the results."

Walsh went to work. He put all three of the cotton test strips through a series of tests. While one was in the spectrometer, he looked at another under the microscope, then rotated them. Once that was done, he cut tiny slivers from each strip and put them into a series of tiny vials with different chemicals. The entire process took over an hour, but when he finished, he was confident in his conclusion.

"Well?" Clarissa asked.

"It's not a slam dunk," Walsh said. "What I can say for certain is this. There were traces of combustible material on the table surface. Sergeant Flint also managed to get microscopic debris. Under high magnification, I believe there was electronic equipment of some kind being used or worked on."

"That's all?" Clarissa asked.

"There was a variety of common cleaning chemicals as well, but as far as forensic testing, the combustible material and debris were the only things of interest."

"Combustible material is what?" the advocate pressed.

"Could be anything," he said. "There wasn't enough of it to say for certain. It could be a liquid fossil fuel, say gasoline or kerosene. It could also be a synthetic, maybe Verhapin or Laxphantin."

"Don't they use combustible solvents to clean tools?" Clarissa asked.

"Sure," Walsh said. "Mineral spirits, even acetone, are used, depending on the need."

"And this suspect is a janitor, right?" Clarissa asked. "He could have put down anything on his table. For all we know, his lunch box could have gotten that material on it and been transferred to the table."

"What about the electronics?" Flint pointed out.

"What of it? Can you prove what kind of electronic device was being utilized?"

"It's not about the type of device," Walsh said. "The debris collected points to the fact that something was being constructed or deconstructed. There were slivers of copper, typically used in wiring, also traces of soldering material, and a tiny bit of tantalum, which is used in capacitors for stable voltage regulation."

"So, the suspect is tinkering with electronics," Clarissa said. "We have nothing."

"What we have," Flint said slowly, "is the ingredients for an IED."

"A what?"

"An improvised explosive device," Becky replied.

"Stu wouldn't have reacted to just random scents," Jeopardy said. "He's trained to sniff out the specific combinations of chemicals used to make bombs. And he clearly reacted to Titus Russel and again at the man's berth."

"Where we found chemical traces of agents that can't easily be explained," Flint said.

"Says you. Any third-year law student could shred what little evidence we've got."

"Hang on," Logan spoke up for the first time. "Think this through for a minute. A bomb, on a spaceship with half a million people, is not something we can afford to guess at."

"He's right," Becky said. "It wouldn't take much to cause a catastrophic event on a ship like this. Thousands could be killed."

"In the right place, a bomb might disable the ship entirely," Flint said. "We could lose power, propulsion, guidance, maybe even life support systems."

For the first time, Advocate Clarissa Fields stopped talking. Her eyes even opened wide in what Flint knew to be fear.

"We can't guess about this," he continued. "We have to know for certain."

Clarissa nodded her head.

"I've got tonight covered," Logan said. "I'll have eyes on Titus Russel the entire night."

"The rest of us should get a few hours of sleep. In the morning, we bring Mr. Russel in for questioning. Dave, you speak to his supervisor. Becky, Jeopardy, you speak with every one of his co-workers. Ms. Fields, you're with me. We'll question Titus and see what he has to say."

Logan settled in at his desk. In seconds, he had the ship's locator fixed on Titus Russel. On his secondary screen, he brought up the surveillance camera feeds on Topdeck near where the janitor was running his street sweeper.

Dave patted Logan on the shoulder. "You sure you're good?"

"All set," Logan replied.

"We'll be back at 0630," Flint said. "There's coffee already brewed in the pot next to my office."

"Thanks, Sarge," Logan said.

"I'd stay, but I need to feed Stu," Jeopardy said.

"That's fine. Get some sleep. I've got this."

"If anything changes, call us," Becky said.

"Will do," Logan assured her.

Within minutes, the SIU offices were vacated. Logan leaned back, adjusting his body in the seat. His back still hurt. It hurt when he exercised, and it hurt when he did nothing at all. The knife had damaged some nerves and the doctors speculated that they might never heal correctly. Pain was just going to be part of his life. He didn't get discouraged, not when he had so much to live for. If pain was part of the bargain, he knew he could live with it.

Two hours later, Titus Russel turned his street sweeper into an alley. There was no video coverage between the tall buildings. Logan checked the suspect's locator, saw it moving through the alley at an even rate, and decided all was well. A moment later, unseen in the SIU office, Titus Russel slipped out the back side of the alley and hurried across the city toward the nearest bank of elevators.

IT WAS A QUIET NIGHT. Titus didn't know if he had fooled anyone or not, but he couldn't afford to wait any longer. He hurried down the main avenue, which was dark at 0200 hours. The boutique shops and retail outlets had all closed down. The manufacturing spaces could have run three shifts, but opted just for two, which left that area of Topdeck deserted during the early morning hours.

In the SIU office, Logan was starting to feel antsy. Not that it was unusual for a janitor to work so long in an alley, but without being able to see the man, Logan felt that something was amiss. Still, he might have been completely fooled if not for the location indicator showing a Clint Miller making his way down a nearby street. There was nothing odd in the name, even though the location app looked like a map. It had the complete layout of Topdeck and people showed up as moving red dots. Only there were no people. The businesses were closed, and there were no domiciles on topdeck, just businesses, restaurants, offices, and entertainment venues. The board was empty, except for Titus Russel still working through the alley and, suddenly, Clint Miller was making his way across the city.

It was possible that Titus had rousted Miller out of the alley. There had been a few instances of passengers getting so drunk or high that they passed out in the alleys, usually behind the big garbage cans or next to the large heating units. But Logan's curiosity was up, and his job was boring, which was all the motivation he needed to swap the surveillance footage on his secondary screen. He wanted a look at Clint Miller. A few taps on the controls and a camera over the bank of elevators caught a great image of Clint Miller as he approached.

"Holy smokes!" Logan said.

His eyes never left the screen. He tapped the computer controls so that the locator app stayed on Clint Miller wherever he went on the ship. Then, his hand went to his cufflink and engaged the communications feature.

"What?" Flint asked, his voice thick with sleep.

"Russel is on the move," Logan said. "He's swapped cufflinks, but I've got eyes on him. He's headed down in elevator Tango One Niner."

"What?" Flint said, sounding more like himself. "Say all that again, Logan."

He did, explaining that Titus Russel was currently showing on the locator as Clint Miller.

"He must have hacked a cufflink to hide what he's doing," Flint said. "How good are you with the computer system?"

"Not as good as Bannon, but I can handle most things."

"I'll wake the others," Flint said. "You keep eyes on Russel, or Miller, or whoever the hell he is. As you can, do a surveillance search on Clint Miller. If Titus Russel is using that alias to move around the ship unseen, we need to know where he's been."

"Yes, sir," Logan said. "I can do that."

"Good man. Keep this channel open. We'll have the others join so we can keep tabs. And Logan, reach out to Prosecutor Fields. Get her into the office with you."

"Roger that. I'll ping her right now, sir."

Throughout the ship, there was a flurry of activity. In the elevator, Titus Russel was calm. He needed ten minutes to assemble the remote trigger on the device he had made. It was only seventy-five percent as powerful as he had planned to make it, but his time had run out. He got off the elevator on deck fourteen, but instead of moving toward his berth, he made his way toward a maintenance compartment in a narrow passageway that was next to a warehouse-sized space that contained one of the primary engine's exhaust components. Most of the outgassing was caught and recycled before it was vented into space. Airflow was a major component of the ship's engine. Large oxygen blowers fed the fusion reactor, but the carbon monoxide that was created needed to be removed. With a little work, that gas could be converted to carbon dioxide by adding a little oxygen to it. The CO_2 could then be pumped into the green spaces and hydroponic facilities, where the plants could turn it back into breathable oxygen.

Titus didn't care about the ship or how it worked. His only concern was finding the best way to disable it. The exhaust compartment was not the best way, but it did offer an electromagnetic shadow which hid him from the ship's location service and had no hardwired surveillance. That meant Titus could do his work without being spied on and, if worse came to worst, he would set off his device in the exhaust compartment. There was enough oxygen in the conversion equipment to propel an explosion beyond the exhaust compartment and through the ship. With direct access through the exhaust system to the main engines, perhaps even wreck the *Colossus* fusion reactor.

He reached the maintenance compartment. It was small and lined with plastic shelving that was loaded with cleaning supplies. In the back of the dim little room was a series of yellow mop buckets on wheels. One was covered in a dirty blanket. It amazed Titus that no one ever asked what it was or pointed it out to their supervisor. Had they lifted the dirty blanket and peered underneath, they would have seen a large, plastic canister. It was filled with small bits of metal, old screws, bolts, washers, and nuts. Titus had been collecting them from around the ship since he arrived. The hardware in the canister was surrounded by fuel gel that had been scraped from dozens of empty fuel rods. Had Titus been scanned with a medical device, it would have shown him to be radioactive. Perhaps, if he had waited long enough to fill the entire canister with old fuel gel, he might have fallen sick from radiation poisoning. But so far, the iodine tablets he took every day had held the effects of the unstable molecules at bay.

Titus took a pair of batteries from his pocket. He had stolen them from the street sweeper and quickly hooked them to the simple text display device he had soldered onto the detonation module. With it, he could activate the device, which was set for a fifteen-minute timer. Once he connected the magnetic cover over the battery compartment, the system's emergency circuit was completed, activating the instant detonation feature should anyone try to disarm the device. With that done, he started out with the mop bucket. It was easier than carrying the device, which had gotten heavy, and garnered less attention. People had no interest in janitors. They were insignificant to most people, at least until something wasn't cleaned to their satisfaction. Practically invisible. No one had ever stopped him, or even spoken to him, when he moved the device around the ship. At least not until the day before. Jack had spoken to him, plus even eaten a meal with him. No one had done so much, and while Titus hadn't hated having a conversation, he had been suspicious just the same. He was still suspicious.

Meanwhile, on deck eighteen, the rest of the SIU squad was gearing up. Tired, but fueled on adrenaline, they rushed to elevators, Tango One Niner.

"What's the status on Russel?" Flint asked over the comlink.

"He's off the grid," Logan responded. "Deck fourteen. I'm

sending a pin to your cufflink now that shows where he last showed up on the geolocation app."

"Damn, this guy is going for it," Becky said.

"He's smart, too," Dave added.

"Is he still in his janitorial coveralls?" Flint asked.

"Yes," Logan said.

"Stay frosty, people," Flint instructed. "We spread out. Weapons hot. We can not afford a standoff with his guy. You get the chance, you take him down."

"What if he's already planted the device?" Becky asked.

"We'll get that information from him once he's in our custody," Flint said. "Jeopardy, you and Stu have point on this. Can the dog track him without some sort of scent to begin with?"

"I think so," she said. "He picked up a danger scent when we passed him in the corridor yesterday. Odds are he'll still have that scent tonight. It might even be stronger if he has the device with him."

The device was such a horrifying thought that Flint shivered. He had expected crime on the *Colossus*, yet it had never occurred to him that someone might be willing to die to sabotage the colony ship. If Titus Russel was successful, it wasn't just a few people that might die, or even a few hundred. There were almost half a million people on the *Colossus*. Flint had felt as if he had won the most prestigious contest on planet Earth when he was picked to work the ship. But that lucky feeling had been replaced by dread. If they failed, it could cost everyone their lives.

The elevators took them down to fourteen, then they jogged to the narrow corridor where Titus had disappeared.

"Stu, *such!*" Jeopardy said.

The dog immediately started forward, straining against his leash. Flint turned to Becky and Dave.

"You two split up and try to circle around," he ordered.

"Got it," Dave replied.

"Good luck, Sarge," Becky told him.

"Good luck to all of us."

Flint followed Jeopardy down the hallway. They hadn't gone far before Stu stopped at a doorway and pawed at the floor.

"Looks like a maintenance compartment," Jeopardy said.

"Alright, stand back. I'll go through first, just in case."

It wasn't that Flint wanted to protect his officers from danger, although they couldn't take any chances with Stu. The police dog had proven himself over and over since they had come aboard the *Colossus.* Without Stu, they wouldn't have even suspected Titus Russel of being a threat. Flint had always respected K-9 units, but he felt that Stu deserved his own statue in the park.

Flint held his sidearm close to his chest. It was a small, non-lethal pistol loaded with rubber slugs that were capable of putting a big man down. Still, he would have preferred his old .45 automatic. Sweat popped out on his back with a stinging sensation, one second before he hit the door controls. There was no way to know what was waiting for them on the other side of the doorway.

The door slid open and the time for pondering his future ended. But there was no danger, no unexpected surprises. Just an empty storage room. He could see all the way to the back, which was only about ten paces. There was plenty of stuff in the compartment, but no people, and nothing that looked dangerous.

"Clear," he said, feeling slightly relieved, but still worried that their perp was missing.

"Let us get inside," Jeopardy said, surging forward with Stu.

There were times when Flint wondered how Jeopardy could hold the dog back. She was stronger than she appeared. Stu led the way into the compartment and went straight back to a rear shelf where he barked.

"Sarge, I've got a cufflink here," Jeopardy said. "How much you want to bet it belongs to Clint Miller?"

"No bet," Flint said. "Keep searching. I'm going to call this in, and I'll catch up."

"Roger that. Come on, Stu, *revier!*" She ordered the dog to search, and he hurried from the compartment and set off with his nose close to the floor.

Flint ran back to the main corridor. There weren't a lot of people out, but those who saw him gave him strange looks. He was wearing cargo pants, a plain white tee-shirt, and had his badge on a lanyard around his neck. It was probably the pistol in his hand that caught most people's attention. Patrol officers on the *Colossus* didn't carry firearms. The SIU squad kept theirs concealed most of the time. But Flint didn't have time to worry about what the other passengers thought about him.

"Logan, he ditched the cufflink. You'll have to rely on surveillance."

"Roger that," Logan responded. "But you guys are all in a dead zone. I can't make contact. Would you rather I join you on deck fourteen?"

"No, if he slips by us, you may be the only one who can track him. Call in patrol. We'll use them as runners if we have to. You're our eyes on this job, Logan. Don't leave that desk."

"I understand," Logan said. He said the words as if they were physically painful.

"Flint out."

The Law Enforcement Sergeant turned and sprinted back down the narrow hallway. Becky Nash was on the far side of the big exhaust compartment. It was several hundred meters square and created a large dead zone in the ship's network. She had just turned the corner from the main corridor and started down the long passageway when she caught sight of a janitor with a mop bucket on wheels. He was turning into the engine exhaust compartment.

"Hey! Stop!" She shouted, but the janitor either didn't hear her or pretended not to. A second after she shouted, he disappeared inside the warehouse-sized compartment.

As she ran, she saw signs printed right on the wall of the exhaust compartment. One said **Authorized Personnel Only.** That meant a person needed certain clearances via their cufflink device to get inside. She didn't know if the janitor was Titus Russel. He had been too far away to see his face clearly. But he was in an orange jumpsuit and fit the profile she was operating from. It was possible he wasn't the guy she was after. He might be a real janitor with clearance to be in the exhaust compartment. But her gut told her he was their suspect.

Becky only slowed down as she got close to the doorway. It was a standard metal door, the heavy utility kind that had a low lip around it. She had seen the janitor tilt his yellow mop bucket back so the wheels cleared the lip. As she approached the door, Jeopardy and Stu appeared at the far end of the corridor. Right behind them came Flint. They were too far away to communicate with words, she didn't want to scream at them and their comlinks didn't work in the dead space around the exhaust room. Instead, she used hand signals. Holding up one finger for a moment, she then pointed into the exhaust room.

Flint gave her a thumbs up and Becky tapped the override icon on her cufflink before waving it at the door's control panel. The thick metal door slid aside and through the opening Becky saw what looked like a knot of metal pipes. They came from a different part of the ship, fed down through the ceiling, then circled around a large tank. There were bends and wide sections of the pipes that were meant to muffle the roar from the fusion reactor, but she could still hear a deep rumble.

She glanced around the big room. It was a huge space, much of it filled with large exhaust piping. The light was from big LEDs hanging from the ceiling and there were shadows close to the machinery. A large bank of monitors were fed information from sensors in the exhaust system and controlled the oxygen conversion process. There were massive, industrial fans that rerouted the carbon dioxide back through even more pipes to a different part of the ship. Everything was labeled with black stenciled letters. There were lockers with ear muffs hanging from hooks and work benches with tall tool chests to either side. A large HVAC system was capturing the warm air from around the pipes, which were too hot to touch without safety equipment.

The entire warehouse-sized compartment was much warmer than the rest of the ship. Stepping inside was a bit like stepping out of an air-conditioned vehicle on a summer day. All of these things she took in at a single, sweeping glance, but her focus was on finding the janitor. He was nowhere in sight.

Becky started to her left, and after half a minute, Jeopardy and Stu came charging into the compartment. They went right. But before they got very far, Titus Russel appeared. His mop bucket was gone, and he held his hands up over his head.

"I surrender," he said in a calm, almost creepy voice.

Becky felt a sinking sensation in her gut as she pointed her pistol at the man. They were too late. From the way the man acted, there was nothing they could do about it.

"Find the device!" Flint yelled. "I've got the subject."

Becky nodded and set off, wondering as she went how long she had left to live.

PROBLEMS WERE common on any large vessel. Captains from time immemorial had dealt with emergencies that cropped up in the middle of the night. He was fast asleep in his bed next to a passenger of his own age, a VIP that had caught his eye. Her name was Victoria Cummings from London, a former producer and part-time writer, who had inherited a fortune and lived a very privileged life. Captain Hastings didn't wake her. He rolled out of the wide bed and left the bedroom.

His dayroom was part office, part lounge. He went immediately to the hot water dispenser and started himself a cup of tea before responding to the emergency ping on his cufflink.

"What is it?" He asked.

"Captain, the SIU squad is tracking a saboteur," Lieutenant Daniels informed him.

"What type of saboteur?"

"That is unclear, but the word bomb has come up," the lieutenant explained. "If you like, I'll patch you through to the Special Investigations team."

"Do it," he snapped.

Contrary to his gruff voice and demeanor with his crew, he had a delicate touch as he raised the fine china cup and stirred his tea. It was still steeping, the water steaming hot. He put the cup under his nose and inhaled deeply.

"This is Detective Logan with SIU," a voice said on the small speaker inside his cufflink.

"Logan, where is Sergeant Flint?"

"He's on deck fourteen, Captain," Logan replied. There was a precision to his voice that had echoes of military discipline. Hastings liked former military personnel, they understood the chain of command.

"Can you patch me through to him?"

"Negative, sir, they are in a dead zone near the engine exhaust compartment on deck fourteen."

Captain Hastings had studied the *Colossus* extensively. He was no engineer, but he understood how all the components on the massive ship worked. The exhaust system was vital to maintaining the fusion inside the engine's massive core. And, like every other system on the ship, the exhaust components were used in a variety of ways other than venting the unwanted carbon monoxide. It was not as dangerous a place as others, but there was a large oxygen tank in the exhaust compartment. If there really was a bomb in that area, the resulting disaster could be catastrophic.

"What's the status? Who are they chasing?"

"We believe that a passenger named Titus Russel has built an IED, sir."

"You believe?"

"The evidence points to that, but it is unconfirmed at this time. What I can say for certain is that the suspect has used a contraband cufflink to hide his movements."

"That's impossible," the Captain said, knowing his comment was ridiculous the moment it left his lips.

"Sir, that much is certain," Logan replied. "I got word from Sergeant Flint a few moments ago that the suspect has removed his cufflink, and I'm scanning the surveillance feeds for any sign of him."

"Without a cufflink, he won't get far," Captain Hastings said. "But if he had one contraband device, he could have another."

"As long as he stays in a dead zone, I'm blind up here, sir. I have a call in for patrol to run messages. Prosecutor Clarissa Fields is on her way here. The rest of the SIU is on deck fourteen, tracking down the suspect."

"Very good. I'll be moving to the Bridge, detective. When I get there, I'll want an update and access to your command channel."

"Roger that, sir. I'll have it ready for you."

"Outstanding. Hastings out."

He had to put on a uniform. Victoria rolled over away from the light, but didn't wake up. He left her there, trusting that she would understand that his duty was paramount. The caffeine from his tea helped. He drank it fast, which he didn't like to do, but fear was sounding in the back of his mind like a klaxon. A bomb on a spaceship wasn't just dangerous; it was the biggest threat there could be. They were already millions of miles from Earth. No help would ever reach them if they were disabled. In the cold, hard vacuum of space, even the smallest failure in their ship could be deadly to every living soul on board.

Captains had feared malfunctions for as long as spaceships had been in existence. A small issue with the wiring, a faulty component or a poor mixture in the fuel system could all be catastrophic. But a bomb was worse. A bomb had only one purpose — to kill. Why anyone would willingly build an explosive device on a spaceship was beyond comprehension. They would die along with everyone else. And Walter Hastings, captain of the first colony ship to leave the Sol system, would not be remembered as a hero if the *Colossus* failed to reach Secundo. He would be remembered as a failure, even if he had no way to stop the saboteur. It made him feel sick to his stomach, but he pushed his physical reactions away and ignored the fear that echoed in his mind.

When he reached the Bridge, which was only a few levels above his personal quarters on the Command Wing of the massive ship, he was met by a bright-eyed Commander Koll.

"We have communications established, sir," she said. "With your permission, I will go down to the SIU offices and report directly to you."

"Go, Commander. I want regular reports. Nothing is too mundane."

"Aye, Captain," Lova Koll said.

Hastings turned to Lieutenant Daniels. "Do we have an emergency alert out yet?"

"No, Captain," he said. "I've alerted the heads of all departments, but I was awaiting your order for the emergency alert."

Hastings tapped his comlink. "Detective Logan, any updates?"

"Negative, Captain. I haven't heard from anyone yet."

"And we don't know for certain that it's a bomb?"

"No, sir, not for certain."

"Very well," he said. "Take us to alert status orange, Lieutenant Daniels. And let's start considering the danger if there is a bomb on deck fourteen. We need a plan to isolate and contain any damage. Let's get LEO patrols ready to help evacuate the area."

He tried to sit down, but Captain Hastings was too nervous to sit still. His fatigue was gone from his mind, yet his arms and legs felt heavy. There was a sour, twisting sensation in his gut. He wished he could just vomit and get it over with. But there was nothing more the ship's captain could do. It was up to the people on deck fourteen. He sincerely hoped that Sergeant Sawyer Flint was the right man for the job.

BECKY FOUND IT. The bomb was still in the plastic mop bucket on wheels. It had been rolled up next to a cluster of pipes, and she could just make out the massive oxygen tank through the gaps between the exhaust pipes. As she got closer, the heat became more intense.

"Is that it?" Jeopardy shouted, as Stu, the police dog, barked in alarm.

"Has to be," Becky said.

The device was still covered with a dirty, grease-stained blanket. She reached out and pulled the blanket away. Underneath was a tall cylinder with an electronic device on one side. It was counting down from fourteen minutes.

"Oh, crap," Jeopardy said.

"Go tell Sarge," she ordered. "Get Stu out of here."

Jeopardy nodded and ran. Becky pulled out a small flashlight and looked all around the device. It wasn't connected to the exhaust system. She dropped to her knees and checked underneath it. There was nothing holding it in place. Very gently, she pulled on the bucket, which had a large black handle that controlled the drain compartment where the excess water in the mop could be squeezed out. It rolled toward her. Nothing changed. She breathed a shallow sigh of relief and started wheeling the bomb around the exhaust mechanism.

On the far side, Flint had just secured Titus Russel's hands behind his back when Jeopardy came hurrying toward him.

"Becky found it," she said. "There's a timer. Fourteen minutes."

Flint nodded. The knot in his gut was so tight he thought he might be sick, but he swallowed hard and shouted to Jeopardy.

"Go, relay all that information to Logan. If the ship's crew hasn't been notified, tell him to get on that. Then get yourself up to HQ."

"Are you sure?" She asked. "We can help."

"If that were true, I'd gladly let you," he said. "But you've done your part. Get Stu to safety and pray."

"Yes, sir!" She said.

He saw the look of relief on her face just before she dashed toward the door. And while Stu was barking, he wasn't pulling on the leash in the opposite direction from Jeopardy. Somehow, the dog knew it was time to get away.

Flint bent down, grabbed Titus Russel by the arm and yanked him to his feet. The man shouted in pain. Flint wasn't being gentle, but he didn't care if the bomber was hurt, either.

"Tell me how to stop it," he snapped, his face just inches from the shorter man's.

"You can't," Titus said.

His face was completely blank of emotion. Flint didn't know how the short little terrorist could be so calm.

"You willing to bet your life on that?"

"I already have," Titus said. "The timer is counting down. If you try to tamper with it, the emergency detonation system will be triggered. You have less than fifteen minutes until it explodes."

"Why are you doing this?"

"I have my reasons," he said.

Flint grabbed him by the throat. The smaller man's eyes bulged, and he made a gagging sound, but Flint didn't relax his grip.

"Last chance," he said. "No matter what else happens, your life, however long it lasts, will be a living hell if you don't tell me how to shut the bomb down."

"It's impossible," Titus said as Flint released his throat. "I built it so that it couldn't be stopped."

Flint punched Titus hard in the stomach. The man dropped to the floor. Flint wasn't sure he would have stopped beating him if Becky hadn't appeared. She was pushing a mop bucket with a tall IED inside.

"How do we shut it down?" Becky shouted.

"Can't," Flint said. "He made shutting it off impossible."

"Do you believe him?"

"We don't have a bomb squad," Flint said. "And if we mess with it, the bomb could detonate. We can't take that chance."

"What's it made of?" Becky asked.

Flint bent over and yanked Titus back to his feet. He was drooling, his eyes watering, and his face was red as he gasped for air to refill his lungs.

"What's your little bomb made of?" He asked.

Titus didn't reply.

"Tell me or I'll hit you again."

"Do what you must," Titus said, panting a little.

Flint drew his pistol and pressed it against Titus Russel's forehead. "Tell me what it's made of or I'll end you right now."

"Go ahead," Titus said. "We'll all be dead soon."

"This is a waste of time," Becky said. "We have to deal with this thing."

"Contain it," Flint said. "If we can't disarm it, we have to contain it."

"But we don't know how powerful it is," she argued.

"We could pile up some bags of compost around it," Flint said. "Maybe enough to neutralize the blast."

"Actually," Titus said, "compost forms methane as the organic material breaks down. And if it is treated with chemicals such as ammonium nitrate, it will increase the explosive power of the blast."

"He's right," Becky said. "Fertilizer is a controlled substance for that very reason."

"Hell, we have to do something," Flint said. "What if we put it in water, a big tank of water?"

"That would short out the electronics and set it off prematurely," Becky said. "Besides, we need all the water we've got."

Suddenly, the door to the exhaust room opened and Jeopardy led a tall black man inside. He had narrow shoulders and long limbs. He was wearing a navy-blue jumper.

"Who's this?" Flint asked.

"Supervisor Eugene Naggy," Jeopardy said. "He's in charge of the exhaust system."

"That's a bomb," the black man said, pointing at the device. The timer was down to just over ten minutes.

"It is," Flint said. "Becky, get this scum bag out of my sight."

He pushed Titus toward her.

"You sure?" She asked.

"Yes and take Jeopardy with you. No matter what happens, he has to pay."

"What about you?" She asked.

"I'm going to figure something out," he said. "Now go. Find Dave, and get to HQ. That should be far enough away if this thing blows."

He felt a wave of disgust pass through him. If the bomb detonated, it would probably kill a lot of people. And if it disabled the ship, it would kill thousands. Even if they managed to contain the blast and repair the damage, it might still keep them from ever reaching Segundo. And the weight of that responsibility was resting squarely on Flint's shoulders.

"Can we disarm it?" Naggy asked.

"No," Flint said. "We mess with it, we'll set it off."

"Man, that's bad," the black engineer said. "We need to get it off the ship."

"How do we do that?"

"Put it in an airlock."

"Where?"

"Not close enough," Naggy said.

He was clearly in problem-solving mode.

"We could move it, but there's no telling how much damage it might do. Can't get it far enough away from vital systems."

"Or people," Flint said. "There's a lot of innocent people down here."

"But we gotta do something," Naggy said, almost to himself.

He looked over at the exhaust system, then down at the timer.

"It might work," he said.

"What?"

"There's a chance," Eugene Naggy said, turning and walking toward the workbench, "that we can it get out. Won't be easy and I'll need your help."

"I don't know much about engines," Flint said, which wasn't true. In reality, he knew nothing about engines.

"Just do what I tell you, when I tell you. Ten minutes isn't long enough."

"Good, we've only got nine and a half."

"Best get started," he said. "There's a master kill switch on the far side of the machine. It's a big red lever with yellow stripes. Go pull it. Run!"

Flint was forty-five years old, but still in shape. What he wasn't accustomed to was taking orders from someone. But he turned and ran. The exhaust complex was large. Getting around it to the far side wasn't quick, even at a sprint. And the moment he started running, he could tell the air in the exhaust room wasn't as clean as he was accustomed to. Still, he ran, panting and sweating, his pistol felt like a brick, and his pants slowly started to work their way down his hips. Still, he ran, his heart pounding. There was no escape for him. If the bomb went off … when it went off, he would be killed. He didn't waste a single second pretending he wasn't terrified of dying. By the time he reached the far side of the huge exhaust mechanism, he was breathing hard and his hands were trembling.

"I don't see it!" He shouted.

But Eugene couldn't hear him and he couldn't hear the engineer. He had to find the kill switch. Their time was running out. He turned in a full circle before he saw it. It wasn't on the machine, but on a cluster of big pipes and conduits on the far wall that controlled the exhaust system. He ran to it, grabbed the red lever and pulled.

There was a safety pin in the lever that only let it move about an inch. Flint tugged hard, but couldn't budge the lever. Then he saw the safety pin. It was bent and didn't want to pull free, but Flint ripped it out in a mighty heave. Then he pulled the lever down.

A yellow flashing light began to blink on and off and an alarm sounded. Flint felt a spark of hope and sprinted back around the machine. Eugene was next to a large pipe. It was as big around as Flint was. Naggy was cutting through it with a plasma cutter. Sparks were flying around him and he didn't stop or even look up as Flint approached.

"What now?"

"Gloves," Eugene ordered. "From the workbench. Get them on. And bring back that big magnet."

Flint's lungs were burning and his knees felt weak. There was six minutes left on the timer. It didn't feel like enough. Flint considered recording a message to his friends on his cufflink, but quickly dismissed the idea. It couldn't upload to the ship's network in the dead space and, if the bomb exploded, the device would certainly be damaged beyond all repair.

He found a pair of heavy work gloves and on the wall was a round magnet. It helped that every tool was labeled. Flint jerked the magnet from the wall and hurried back.

"What's the plan?"

"When I cut through this, you're going to pull it off," Eugene said. "Use the magnet."

"What are you going to do?"

"Put the bomb inside," Eugene said. "How much time we got?"

Flint looked over his shoulder. "Four minutes, fifty-four seconds."

"Hot damn! This just might work."

He stepped back and waved for Flint to step up. The magnet clamped onto the section of pipe that Eugene was cutting. The engineer stepped forward and continued cutting, but gave Flint more instructions as he did so.

"By the door, there is an emergency switch that will seal off this room. You gotta hit it. Then grab us both an oxygen canister and come back."

"Got it," Flint said.

He ran to the door. Above the main control panel was an enclosed switch with a large label across it that said **Emergency** on it. Reaching up, he tried to open the cover, but it wouldn't budge. Fortunately, an automated voice told him what the problem was.

Unauthorized access is denied.

Flint had heard the same voice a thousand times. It came on whenever he got on the elevators or went to the crew-only sections of the ship. It even gave instructions in the dining hall. He raised his cufflink to the device and tried again. This time, it popped open easily. He reached out with a trembling hand and hit the emergency button. Another alarm sounded, and a steel panel slid down over the door. Flint bent down and opened a metal locker on the floor by the door. Inside were small, sixteen-ounce cans of pure oxygen with plastic breath masks on the top. He grabbed one and stuffed it in his pants pocket. After retrieving a second canister, he started back. But suddenly the floor seemed to tilt and sway. Flint threw out his arms to try and regain his balance, but he fell to his knees. At the same time, his nose started bleeding and both ears began to ring at the same time.

A single glance told him he had one hundred and eleven seconds left before the bomb blew up. He forced himself to his feet and lumbered back to where Eugene was cutting. His bead was no longer straight. But he was just about to finish the circle. Flint grabbed the magnet with one hand and held the oxygen canister toward the engineer with the other.

"Almost there!" Eugene said.

He finished the cut, and the section of pipe connected to the magnet fell. Flint barely managed to hang on. It weighed nearly fifty pounds, but he wrestled it back and held it like a platter.

"My man," Eugene mumbled as he took the oxygen.

Flint watched as the engineer held it to his mouth and nose and took a long, deep breath. His eyes seemed to clear. Flint followed the man's lead and put his own oxygen mask to his face. A little button on top released the air. He pressed it and breathed it in. Instantly, his mind cleared. His nose was still bleeding and his ears continued to ring, but he felt better.

Eugene Naggy was a few years younger than Flint. He was an unassuming man, but he picked up the bomb with both careful grace and surprising strength.

"She might blow when I drop it," he said. "Can't be helped."

"Do what you've got to do," Flint said, looking at the timer as it ticked down past sixty seconds.

"Soon as I let her go, I put the pipe back together. I'll give her two tacks, then you gotta turn the system back on before she blows."

He was feeding the tall, skinny bomb into the exhaust pipe.

"Good luck," Flint said.

"You too," Naggy replied. The display showed forty-two seconds when he let it go. They heard it clang into the curved side of the pipe, but it didn't explode. "That was lucky. There's a long curve before it leaves the ship. But if it blows in the pipe, we're sunk."

"Go! Go! Go!" Flint screamed.

He took another deep breath while Naggy picked up an arc welder and a rod. Flint pressed the heavy metal into the hole. It scraped and didn't want to fit at first. He was shaking all over as Eugene welded a tiny spot in the seam he had recently cut. Flint took another breath of pure oxygen. He was counting down in his mind. There were only twenty seconds left as Naggy tacked a second spot on the pipe.

"That's good, turn her on," the engineer said.

Flint turned and ran. He felt as if his heart might explode. His vision got blurry, and his legs felt as though they weighed a thousand pounds each. But he didn't stop. He circled the exhaust mechanism and ran to the far wall. The red lever was down. He grabbed it and thrust it upward. It locked into place, and the yellow light stopped blinking. There was a hum sound as the system came back online, then a piercing wail. The exhaust system had been shuttered when Flint threw the kill switch. When he turned it back on, those shutters opened and the pipe they had put the bomb in came under hard vacuum. The bomb was sucked out into space, where - two seconds later - it exploded harmlessly. Some of the shrapnel pelted the *Colossus*, but her hull was built to withstand small impacts.

But they weren't out of danger. The hard vacuum was threatening to rip the big exhaust pipe back open. Tools were pulled from their place on the big peg wall. Anything not battened down went flying toward the engineer. He was hit with a socket wrench and a broom. The mop bucket was pulled toward him, although it was too close to hurt the big man. Flint felt like an invisible hand was pushing him toward the mechanism. He fought his way around and found Eugene. The engineer had a big cut on his forehead from a bit of angle iron that had come flying toward the hole where the pipe was being repaired. But even that hadn't stopped him. Flint had several items on his belt that he always carried. He had swapped his cuffs for plastic restraints, yet his pistol, telescoping baton, and tactical knife with a spring-loaded blade were all there. Next to his weapons was a small first aid kit. He had to open it carefully to keep all the contents from flying out, as the air was sucked from the room. Getting his fingers on some gauze, he snapped the kit closed and pressed the highly absorbent material onto the gash on the black man's forehead.

"Ahhhhh, that hurts," Eugene said.

Blood would have been in his eyes if not for the goggles he wore as he was welding. And he didn't stop tacking up the seam he had cut. Flint used his other hand to press his oxygen canister to the engineer's face. He took two deep breaths, then nodded. Flint too two deep inhales of his own, then repeated the process. It took nearly ten minutes to seal the pipe shut again, and both men were soaked in sweat by the end. They dropped to their knees, panting and still sucking oxygen from the can.

"Your cut's pretty bad," Flint said.

"Yeah, heads are gonna roll next shift," Eugene said. "I'm always telling my guys to put everything where it goes. But whoever left that angle iron out is dead meat."

Flint chuckled. The crisis was averted, but it had been too close a call, and he couldn't help fearing that there might be more terrorist agents on the ship.

After applying some quick clot from his tiny kit to Eugene's gash. He made it over to the door and reversed the emergency status. They still had to wait for over an hour while the ship's computer system repressurized the compartment and did several tests to make sure it was stable.

"Hell yeah, it's stable. I'm a damn good welder. Been doing it since I was a teenager," Naggy complained.

Flint had found a larger first aid kit and wrapped the engineer's head in a long bandage.

"I'd say you were downright heroic," Flint said. "What made you come down here in the first place?"

"Captain, set alert status orange. All department heads and supervisors are supposed to report to their stations. So, here I am," Eugene Naggy said. "How'd y'all find out that nut case was trying to blow up the ship?"

"Police dog smelled the explosive chemicals on him," Flint said. "Stu's a hero, too."

Eugene shook his head. "Why the hell would someone want to blow us up? It's crazy."

"Insanity won't be an excuse," Flint said. "He knew what he was doing. Can't say why."

"I don't know how you LEOs do it. I couldn't spend every day around the worst of the worst. I respect you for doing it. I suppose we all owe you our lives."

"We owe you. My idea was to cover the bomb with compost."

"Oh, no, that would have made things worse."

"As my second in command pointed out," Flint said. "You came along at just the right time. You'll never have to buy another beer as long as I'm around."

"Well, I'll take you up on that, Sergeant. Free beer makes it all worthwhile."

They both chuckled and looked up as the safety hatch over the door opened and a group of medical technicians, engineers, and members of the ship's crew, including Commander Koll, came streaming into the exhaust compartment.

Flint got to his feet and helped Naggy up. He was immediately set on a hover gurney and scanned for injuries.

"You survived," Lova Koll said.

"Thanks to Supervisor Naggy," Flint said. "I was just his gopher on this op."

"You need rest, but it'll have to wait. Captain wants a full report."

"You here to escort me up?"

"No," she said with a frown. "I have to stay and make sure the exhaust system is fully functional."

"Will I see you soon?"

"I hope so," Lova said. "To be honest, I'm pretty shook up. I guess everyone who really knows what happened is."

"Soon, we'll all just be glad to be alive. And I, for one, plan to make the most of it. Find some time, Commander. You deserve a night off."

"With you?"

"Absolutely. We'll do whatever you want. Paint the town red. My treat."

"I look forward to it," she said, before stepping away.

Flint felt a pang of regret that he couldn't take her in his arms and kiss her. But that wouldn't have been proper. And they weren't really that close. One date did not make them lovers.

"I'm here to help you up to the command section," Becky said. "We've been summoned."

"Who?"

"The entire squad, even Stu."

"That dog is a hero," Flint said. "We came way too close to a horrible disaster."

"Buy him a Milk Bone," Becky said. "In the meantime, we have news. Titus is telling his advocate that you assaulted him."

"I suppose I did," Flint said. "But he's a terrorist."

"Not according to him," Becky said. "He's denying everything."

"It's kind of late for that."

"Prosecutor Fields isn't so sure. She says all our evidence is circumstantial."

"I doubt a jury would see it that way. He planted a bomb, after all."

"But there's no evidence he built it, or had anything to do with it other than our testimony," Becky said. "If you were hoping for a hero's welcome, you better adjust your expectations.

"THIS IS A DISASTER!" Captain Hastings snapped. "How the hell did you let this happen?"

Flint was angry, but he knew letting the Captain of the ship have a piece of his mind wouldn't help matters. After helping to save the *Colossus* from a terrorist bomb, Flint had been summoned to the senior officer's lounge. Only there was no barista serving specialty coffees. There were no pastries or confections set out on the glossy table in the middle of the big room. Everyone gathered and it was a full house of who's who on the ship, who were all tired and afraid. So, Flint kept his mouth shut.

The entire SIU was there, even Stu. His people were lined up against the floor-to-ceiling window that looked out over Topdeck City. Across from them stood the Law Enforcement Commissioner, the prosecutor assigned to the Titus Russel case, Clarissa Fields, her boss, the sitting judge for the *Colossus* Criminal Court, Renee St. Pierre, several senior officers, including Commander Lova Koll, and, of course, Captain Hastings.

Flint knew it was fear that made the captain angry. He had seen the reaction dozens of times and had even fallen prey to it a time or two himself. But knowing why the captain was angry and not letting it make Flint angry, were two very different things. He had been scared, too, Flint thought. He had put his life on the line, along with his entire unit. They had discovered the threat, followed up and stopped the act of terrorism before it had destroyed the *Colossus*. He felt they deserved a little appreciation for their efforts, but he was wrong.

"We didn't let it happen," Flint said. "My team stopped it."

"Oh, sure, you stopped it. You nearly wrecked the ship in the process. Do you have any idea what it does to a high-output fusion reactor to shut down the exhaust system?"

"Less than a bomb exploding in the exhaust compartment would, I suspect."

"Watch your tone, Sergeant," Monty Forrest, the LEO Commissioner, warned him.

"Your job is to keep this ship and her half a million souls safe, Sergeant," Captain Hastings continued, berating him. "And the truth of the matter is, you have failed to do your job."

"That's not true," Becky Nash snapped.

Even Stu growled menacingly, but Jeopardy shushed the police dog. Flint held up a hand to silence Becky. He appreciated his team's loyalty. And the truth was, they were just as much on edge after the attack as anyone else. But while he was willing to push back against the criticism of his superiors, he didn't want anyone else getting dragged down with him.

"We were lucky," Flint said. "There is no doubt about that. If not for Officer Bess and her K-9 partner, none of us would have known about the terrorist until it was too late. But once we discovered the threat, we went to work and did all we could to stop it."

"Why not arrest the suspect immediately?" Monty Forrest asked. "We could have avoided the danger altogether."

"That's not exactly true," Flint said. "We don't know how complete the bomb was by that point. And, more importantly, the legal code on the *Colossus* restricts us from arresting people without a warrant."

"You can detain suspects for as long as twenty-four hours before the arrest warrant is issued," St. Pierre pointed out.

"We didn't have enough evidence to detain Titus Russel," Flint said. "We did immediately bring in a legal advocate to help us make that decision."

"If a person is plotting a terrorist act on this ship, you arrest them immediately," Captain Hastings snarled. "I don't care what the bi-laws say."

"We can't function without order," St. Pierre said.

"Don't get sanctimonious with me. This is my ship and my word is law," Hastings said.

"So, we're living in a dictatorship now?" St. Pierre asked.

"At least, we're living," the Captain said. "Where is the man responsible for the bomb?"

"Titus Russel is in custody at the SIU offices," Flint said. He tapped a few controls on his cufflink and brought up the video feed that showed the holding cell where Titus sat. It was displayed on a big screen at the far end of the lounge. The man looked calm and completely unfazed by his surroundings.

"Actually," St. Pierre continued. "We don't know that he is responsible. The evidence is circumstantial at best. The only eyewitness to him having anything to do with the bomb is Detective Nash and even that is shaky."

"She saw him with the device," Flint argued.

"She saw him with a mop bucket. The bomb was covered. She didn't see it until later. We actually have no solid connections between Titus Russel and the bomb."

"He left his job," Flint said, "using an illegal cufflink, went down to where the bomb was hidden, retrieved it and planted it in the exhaust compartment."

"Yes, he broke several laws, but we can't prove beyond a

reasonable doubt that he built the device. The closest thing to evidence that you have is a dog's reaction."

"Stu is a trained law enforcement officer," Jeopardy said. "A specialist, in fact, with hundreds of hours of training."

"If you want to hash through this now, I'm game," St. Pierre said with a wicked grin. "What exactly did you find when you searched the suspect's domicile?"

"Trace amounts of combustible chemicals," Flint replied, "and evidence of an electronic device."

"Trace amounts? What does that mean exactly, Sergeant?"

"It means the suspect tried to clean up the evidence, but we still found some."

She chuckled. "How much?"

"Trace amounts."

"Does that mean you found a bottle or container with chemicals he shouldn't have had access to?"

"No," Flint said.

"No, in fact, you found nothing, and did a chemical test on his table top. But isn't it true that any number of things could have left that residue on the tabletop? And it isn't it also true that Titus Russel is a maintenance worker who is exposed to harsh chemicals on a daily basis?"

"He works in the janitorial division on Topdeck," Flint said. "I don't know what he is or isn't exposed to."

"But it's possible that the chemicals and debris you found in his cabin came from his job, and not some mysterious bomb you claim he built."

"If you say so."

"This isn't getting us anywhere," Captain Hastings said.

"The point I'm making is we really have very little to go on," St. Pierre said. "I can't even authorize an arrest warrant for the suspect on the flimsy evidence the SI squad managed to gather."

"They managed to stop the device from detonating on the ship,"

Lova Koll pointed out. It was the first time she had spoken since Flint arrived. And while he appreciated her support, he didn't want her to get on the captain's bad side.

"We are working within the bounds set forth in the ship's charter," Flint said. "We understand that we didn't have much evidence and that gathering it was of utmost importance. But protecting the ship superseded the normal protocols. We kept the suspect under surveillance and reacted to his criminal behavior. It was the most we could do in the circumstances."

"But that isn't good enough," Hastings said. "There are half a million people on this ship. And the reactor was fouled by the buildup of unvented carbon monoxide. To be honest, we're lucky that the reactor didn't fail due to lack of proper airflow. We'll have to shut the entire system down at some point in the very near future to make repairs."

"But no one died," Flint said. "The ship remains on course and operable."

"Don't tell me about *my* ship, Sergeant," Hastings snapped. "I will be adding to the official report on this matter. The truth is, I have serious misgivings about your unit and, in particular, your ability to run it."

"You have a right to your opinion, sir," Flint said in an icy tone.

Hastings glared at Flint for a moment, but the veteran detective stared right back.

"What are we going to do with the terrorist?" he finally asked.

"He'll be charged," Prosecutor Fields said. "We have irrefutable proof of him using two unauthorized cufflinks. Those felonies are enough to keep him in custody until the *Colossus* returns to Earth."

"It's possible that we can leverage him to find out who is really behind the attack," St. Pierre said. "Perhaps he will cooperate in exchange for custody on Secundo rather than on Earth."

Flint shook his head.

"You disagree?" Commander Koll asked.

"He was willing to die to carry out his plan," Flint said. "I doubt he's concerned about a lengthy incarceration."

"We have to know if the threat to the ship is still active," Captain Hastings said. "If there was one saboteur on the ship, there could be more."

"All the more reason to offer the suspect a deal," St. Pierre said.

"And if he won't cooperate?" Flint asked.

"Then your team will do sweeps through the entire ship," Captain Hastings said. "Random berth searches. I want a full overview of all our fuel system protocols, as well as a comprehensive inventory of all combustible chemicals on the ship. Everything will be accounted for."

The meeting continued until almost 0600. Flint was exhausted both physically and mentally. He would have gone home and had a stiff drink, but there wasn't time for anything more than a shower and a change of clothes. Then it was back to work.

Stu would be doing the lion's share of the new work and everything else was put on the back burner. For the foreseeable future, the entire SIU squad would be working sixteen-hour shifts. No one was happy, but they were used to following orders no matter how absurd they seemed. Jeopardy and Stu began a tour of the entire ship. The dog began sniffing every doorway to every berth. He went through the warehouse-sized storage compartments and the engineering spaces that were filled with equipment. Anything that piqued his interest was passed along to the rest of the team, who conducted searches.

News of the attack spread fast. Most of the ship had been completely oblivious to the fact that they had come within a hair's breadth of dying. When they found out, it rocked the morale of the entire ship. The mighty *Colossus* seemed more fragile and crowded than ever. Many passengers complained about their work duty despite the fact that failing to carry out the labor jobs only made the situation on the ship more precarious. When the passengers didn't show up for their shifts, the ship's crew were forced to pick up the slack. That meant general maintenance had to be put on hold while other tasks were carried out. But there was no way to improve the attitude of the passengers ... and the work of the SIU wasn't helping.

Flint was right about Titus Russel. He was immediately moved from the SIU offices to the main detention facility, where he was questioned at length by a team of judicial advocates. Titus remained silent. He didn't speak, not to the lawyers and not to the detention officers. He was held in solitary confinement and kept away from the short-timers who were held in detention after a bar fight or failure to show up for their work assignments. He took his meals, showers and exercise in complete silence. He didn't ask for anything or argue when told what to do. He was completely shut down and offered no help in the ship's search for danger.

Weeks passed, and the Special Investigations squad felt the effects of the relentless searching. A gloominess to their days settled in. They faced resentment from passengers whose cabins they searched. There was very little downtime. Sergeant Flint, as always, took the worst shifts and often worked doubles to give his people a little more rest, but it was an impossible task.

Meanwhile, more savvy criminals were taking advantage of the tense atmosphere on the ship. JD had become Everett Goddard's right hand. The banking mogul's three VPs were frustrated, but that only opened the door for the Ghetto King lieutenants to make their moves. Of the three high-ranking businessmen, one was swiftly becoming an alcoholic, while the other two were embracing darker vices with the women provided to them by Nova and Fever. Crank had already gained access to the ship's digital currency. While the rest of the gang distracted the banking overlords, he was quietly siphoning millions into dummy accounts controlled by JD and the brilliant hacker.

Somehow, the ship continued unabated. They were a third of

the way to their destination, and there was still plenty of food, booze and recreational drugs to keep the passengers mollified. But the dividing lines were forming. The ship's crew resented their passenger counterparts. The lottery winners resented the posh accommodations and perceived special treatment of the VIPs. Tempers flared easily and fights were common, which only made everyone hate the LEOs most of all. The patrol officers were tasked with keeping the peace, but their job was made harder by the SIU conducting random cabin searches. It felt like the *Colossus* was on the verge of a mutiny and most people felt like it was only a matter of time before things got out of hand. They were not wrong.

CHAPTER
SEVENTEEN

HOLLY BAXTER-WRIGHT DIDN'T CONSIDER herself to be a radical. She was twenty-six years old, single and an aspiring writer, who looked at the colony on Secundo as a chance to live free. Holly didn't adhere to most social norms. Before being selected in the national lottery, she had never worked a full-time job. In many ways, life on the *Colossus* favored her natural proclivities, from the communal laundry to the free meals prepared for her in the dining hall, and living quarters that she paid nothing for, all supported her less-than-avid work ethic. But eight-hour shifts as an air quality assessor seemed excessive and harsh to her. Nor did the attitude of her supervisor, Chief Petty Officer O'Neal, soothe things.

Being young and pretty, Holly was naturally popular, especially in the protest groups that had begun popping up all over the ship. They had identified and spread the identities of the SI squad. Many of the protest groups followed and harassed the officers as they carried out their daily assignments. Sometimes they blocked entire corridors. At other times, they lined up in front of the cabin doors and almost begged for Stu to take a bite out of them. Stu was too well trained and Jeopardy kept him under control, but the passenger protests grew day by day.

Holly Baxter-Wright was in one such protest near her cabin on deck sixteen when she was supposed to be collecting air samples on deck seven. The dereliction of duties would be discovered much later. She felt that her right to privacy and the need to stand against the ship's authoritarian captain were more important than collecting air samples. If it crossed her mind that hundreds of people might fall ill if the air filtration system didn't work as designed, or that she, as an air quality assessor, was the first line of defense for such a disaster, she chose to ignore the fact. Instead, she waited just outside her cabin with twenty-nine other protesters. They held signs and chanted in unison, *Leave us alone, this ship is our home!*

What no one other than Holly knew, not even her roommate, a bright young software engineer who was working in an office in one of the high-rise buildings on Topdeck at the time of the riot, was that Holly eschewed artificially manufactured THC. Back on Earth, she had acquired germinated marijuana seeds. Once on the ship, she had traded with some workers who had access to soil from the composting and fertilizing section. Over the following months, she had managed to grow her own *Cannabis Indica* in her cabin. The fact that it was against the *Colossus* charter never crossed her mind. But the senior officers and legislators who had decided what would be allowed on the colony ship sought to regulate the amount of THC in recreational drugs. Furthermore, Stu was trained to sniff out marijuana among other natural narcotics. So, as Jeopardy approached the crowd, hoping to convince them to let her do her job, the dog fixated on Holly Baxter-Wright's cabin.

"What do you want to do?" Logan asked, shouting to be heard over the crowd and Stu's barking.

"We don't have a choice," Jeopardy replied. "Open it up."

There was an angry shriek as Logan used his cufflink to override the lock on Holly's cabin door. He turned just as she charged at him. Logan, fully recovered from the stabbing, could have handled the woman. None of the SI squad were without compassion regarding their search and the effects it was having on morale. But before she reached him, Stu reacted to the threat. The dog leaped forward and clamped his powerful jaws down on Holly's arm. Shriek of outrage became a wail of pain.

"Stu, *halt! Lass es fallen!*" Jeopardy shouted.

The dog obeyed and released Holly, who staggered backward and raised her bloody arm. The sight of it was enough to whip the crowd into a frenzy. It was never identified who shouted for the protesters to attack, but someone did.

"Get them!" a voice screamed.

The protesters surged forward. Jeopardy reached for her baton, but before she could extend it, someone grabbed her.

"No, stop," she cried out. "You don't know what you're doing."

Stu came to the rescue of his handler just as he had been trained to do. The dog raced around Jeopardy and bit her attacker hard on the back of his thigh. He shouted in pain and released Jeopardy. She flicked her wrist in a downward motion, extending the telescoping, metal baton. At almost the same time, her attacker hit Stu hard on top of his head. The dog let go of the man's leg and then immediately bit his arm and began to shake him. The attacker went down to his knees and then onto his stomach as Stu pulled backward.

"Jeopardy!" Logan shouted, just as the protesters slammed into him and pushed him back into the open cabin.

The fighting in Holly Baxter-Wright's berth was furious. Logan, full of pent-up frustration and set ablaze with fear for Jeopardy's safety, let himself loose on the protesters. All the fighting skills he had developed over years of training gave him the wisdom to know where to do the most damage. He hit the closest protester in the throat, crushing the man's windpipe. Then followed that with a savage kick to the knee of another man, tearing the tendons and pushing the joint apart. Logan had to duck under a wild punch and countered with a bellow of rage as he hit the protester in the stomach, then followed with a wicked palm strike to the man's chin. The attacker's head snapped back, and he fell sideways, his entire body stiff from the sudden trauma to his nervous system.

Despite the violence, more people forced their way into the tiny cabin. And not all of them were men. Logan didn't hesitate. Every person between him and Jeopardy was a target to be eliminated, and he held nothing back.

In the passageway outside, people were moving toward Jeopardy. She knew that she was in danger. The protesters were shouting. Some were saying horrible things, calling for atrocities against her that shocked Jeopardy into action. She drew her pistol. It was an eight-shot, non-lethal semi-auto, loaded with less-than-lethal rubber rounds meant to stop a person. She knew it wouldn't kill the protesters unless she shot them in the head. But they didn't know it.

"Stop!" she screamed. "I will shoot! Stu, *warte! Zurük!*"

The black fur on Stu's back was standing on end, and he had moved up beside Jeopardy. He was barking and snarling, but he obeyed the order to *wait* and to *move back.*

It wasn't lost on Jeopardy that Logan was trapped in the cabin, fighting the protesters. And she heard his savage bellows of pure rage. She knew they had lost control and people were getting hurt, possibly dying, but she couldn't hold back the flood any longer. Too much distrust, anger, frustration and fear had built up. It was spilling out of the people around her and all she could do was try to keep herself and her partner safe.

"Stop!" she shouted again, and the crowd hesitated. "Don't do this. I don't want to hurt anyone."

"You're a narc!" someone shouted.

It was a stupid slur, and didn't mean what the person thought that it meant, but she knew law enforcement officers had somehow become the targets of a lot of hate on the *Colossus.* Which meant she was in real danger.

"Come any closer, and I'll shoot."

"Can't shoot us all," a short man with a protruding belly said. "She can't stop all of us."

"No, but I can put down a lot of people in a very short time," Jeopardy said. "And if you keep coming, my partner will not hesitate to attack you."

"We aren't afraid of you!" someone shouted.

"I'm afraid," Jeopardy replied. "I'm afraid people are getting hurt and killed. You know we're just doing our job."

"You're violating our rights!" Holly Baxter-Wright screamed. "You're invading our privacy!"

"You gave up the right to privacy for the duration of the flight on this ship," Jeopardy told them as she tapped the emergency help icon on the side of her cufflink. She could still hear the fighting in the nearby cabin as the protesters crowded closer and closer.

"That's not my call," Jeopardy continued. "I'm just doing my job, the same as all of you. It's not our fault that there was a terrorist on board. I don't blame anyone and you can't blame us. We stopped him."

"Says you!" another protester said. "I call BS."

"Yeah, there's no evidence of any bombs on this ship," Holly added. "You jackbooted thugs are using it as an excuse to violate our civil rights."

"That's not true," Holly said.

But the crowd wasn't interested in reason, or even the truth. They wanted blood. The short man with the protruding belly set them off again. He shouted, "Get her!" and jumped toward Jeopardy, only to be met in mid-leap by Stu. The police dog was trained to attack a person's arm or leg. But in the heat of the moment, with danger thick in the air like fog on a cold, winter morning, his training was overruled by his natural instincts. As his forepaws hit the man in the chest, the protester's head pulled back. It was a natural reaction. Fear made him want to move away from the dog, but his momentum wouldn't let him. And as his head craned backward, his throat was exposed. The dog bit hard and ripped savagely, tearing out the protester's throat, including the carotid artery and jugular vein. Blood sprayed out and up as the man fell; people screamed. Jeopardy didn't have time to warn them. The sight of blood pushed them over the edge.

Someone dove toward Stu, hitting the dog in the side and knocking him over. Another stepped forward like a soccer player preparing for a penalty strike. He would have kicked Stu in the head, but Jeopardy fired her weapon. The rubber bullet hit the kicker in the chest and sent him spinning to the ground. The pistol didn't sound like a firearm. It didn't have the booming report of gunpowder or explosive gel that propelled bullets in a normal weapon. Instead, the non-lethal sidearm used a plunger on a rail. It was electrically operated using magnetic force. Rail guns had been in existence a long time. Most were large weapons mounted on armored vehicles, boats and even aircraft. Her pistol made a dull ~*Thunk!*~ as it fired and did nothing to stop the crowd.

Jeopardy fired again, taking down a second, then a third man as the protesters surged forward. There were just as many women in the crowd as there were men, but they held back and let the men press their way to the front. By her fourth shot, people had realized what was happening and, at the same time, Stu had regained his feet and bit another protester who shoved out his hand as if it would stop the dog. Stu's bite ripped into the man's hand, and his powerful head shake tore through tendons and crushed the small bones. The protester wailed in pain, stepped back, but was pushed forward. He held up his bloody hand in front of his face. His pinky and ring fingers flopped sideways, held to the hand by crimson strips of flesh.

Each shot Jeopardy took put a protester down. There was no

compassion for the injured. The crowd just stepped over them and sometimes on them. Still, she aimed for the chest not the head. She was painfully aware that her pistol only held eight rounds. She had two more clips on her belt under the jacket she wore, but she had no idea if she would have the time to swap them before the mob reached her.

"She's killing people!" someone shouted.

"Kill her!" another protester responded.

"Kill the dog!" Holly Baxter-Wright screamed.

"Stu, *hier!*" Jeopardy shouted, calling the dog back to her.

He responded, but instantly began to bark, facing the other way. And it was that point in time when Jeopardy knew she was in real trouble. Stu was barking at people from behind her, and the group in front of Jeopardy were surging toward her again. She pulled out a spare clip and fired her final three shots in rapid succession. Three protesters fell, and the crowd hesitated for a second. It was just enough time for Jeopardy to press the release button on her pistol. The clip in the handle dropped to the floor. Before it hit the deck, she had the new one pressed into place.

An older man with a thick beard that was streaked with gray lunged forward and grabbed Jeopardy by the arm. She didn't bother with a bullet. Instead, she used the gun barrel as a club and bashed the older man on his forehead. He fell back as blood surged from a nasty gash across his scalp.

In the cabin, Logan was pressed back by the throng of people surging in. He had stopped the first few, but the next wave came too quickly. And even though he landed savage blows, breaking bones and even knocking people senseless, those behind them just kept pushing. He saved his pistol until he was at the bathroom door. There were at least ten assailants in the cabin with him. And nearly that many hurt or unconscious. A couple had even succumbed to the savage fighting and died, like the man whose throat was crushed by Logan's blow to his throat.

"You want me?" Logan snarled. "Come and get some."

He drew his pistol. It seemed small in his fist. Not all the protesters pressing into the cabin saw it. But a few did.

"Gun! Gun!" they shouted. But those behind them didn't stop, nor could they, as more protesters behind them pressed into the room.

Logan fired all eight rounds. Each shot found a different protester. People were screaming. Logan had just enough time to step back into the bathroom and close the flimsy door. It snapped as the lock engaged. Logan knew it wouldn't stop a determined assailant, and he felt terrible that he couldn't get out and help Jeopardy. But at that moment, he was trapped. He swapped out the clip on his pistol, then toggled on his comlink.

"Logan! What's happening down there?" Sergeant Flint said.

"Protesters," Logan said. He had to shout to be heard over the screaming coming from inside Holly Baxter-Wright's cabin and the corridor beyond. "They turned violent. It's a full-on riot. Send everyone!"

"We're on our way. Hold on. How's Jeopardy?"

"We got separated by the crowd," Logan said as the bathroom door creaked and the lock shuddered. "Hurry, Sarge. We're out of time."

CHAPTER
EIGHTEEN

BECKY DIDN'T CONSIDER herself a fighter. She could fight and even did martial arts training, but mostly because it was good cardio. When she had been on patrol, there had been plenty of foot chases and fights with suspects. Still, she had been a detective for years. A carefully planned operation was more her style. She liked to surround the bad guys with enough cops that they surrendered without a fight.

Still, to her credit, when the call for aid registered on her cuff-link, she didn't hesitate. Her shift had been over long enough for Becky to get a meal, and she was on her way to her cabin for a quick shower and a few hours of sleep before she had to be back on the clock. Instead, she sprinted to the nearest elevator. The ride up two levels took ten seconds and, when the doors opened, she knew things were bad. People were running, mostly in the direction of the riot. Becky, in plain clothes but still with her sidearm, restraints and a few other devices on her thick belt, joined the people running.

Nor was she the first law enforcement officer on the scene. Four patrolmen reached the crowded corridor before Becky. Two of them were already down. The others were pushing their way through a crowd toward what Becky could only guess was Jeopardy, Logan, and Stu. She could hear screams and the K-9 barking.

"Make way!" she said, drawing her pistol with her right hand and a small canister of pepper spray with her left. "Make way for law enforcement."

Most of the people around her turned, saw the gun and stepped back. She pushed into the crowd. A time or two in her younger days, she had gone to concerts where attendees were pressed into a crowd in front of the stage. As the music thundered and people cheered, she had had strangers pressed against her on all sides. The same feeling came back to her as she worked her way through the rioters and those who didn't let her pass got micro-bursts of pepper spray. It was a gel spray, sort of a sticky foam that would cling to the person and not flow back onto the sprayer. Those who got hit with it screamed and bellowed as if they were dying. Becky knew they weren't, but that was the result of failing to comply with her commands. It was the social contract that people made with law enforcement. She put her life on the line to stop criminals and protect the innocent. In return, the public agreed to comply with her and other law enforcement officials. Those that did not weren't breaking a law, exactly, but they were putting themselves at risk. Worse still, non-compliance put officers like Becky Nash at greater risk and, therefore, couldn't be allowed to continue to be defiant.

"No!" someone screamed ahead of her.

Becky recognized the sound of her friend's cry. It was followed immediately by the high-pitched yelp of her K-9 partner. It was the unmistakable cry of a dog in pain. Not just a single yelp, but several repeated cries. Becky pushed forward harder, knowing the danger.

She reached the edge of the crowd a few seconds later and wasn't sure what she would find. There were five men around Jeopardy, who was huddled over Stu. Becky couldn't see what had hurt the dog, but it lay on its side, a sure sign that it was seriously injured.

"No!" Jeopardy screamed again as a pair of men grabbed her and attempted to pull her off the dog.

Becky fired two shots. The men holding Jeopardy's arms fell and she, once again, tried to protect the dog. She got a kick in the ribs for her trouble. Another of Jeopardy's attackers grabbed her hair. He just happened to be near the dog's head. Stu, injured, still managed to raise his head and clamp his powerful jaws onto the man's wrist.

Becky shot again, taking down the kicker. The man with a bleeding wrist fell backward. That was when Becky saw that the fifth man had a knife. It was a small weapon, more of a kitchen tool than a tactical blade. Still, it had found flesh as blood glinted on the silver blade. Before Becky could target the man, he slashed it at the dog. Jeopardy dove between her partner and the assailant. His knife sliced through her coat and drew blood. Jeopardy screamed in pain as Becky shot the man. The two patrol officers still on their feet broke through the crowd. They didn't have guns, just batons and pepper spray. Still, enough people had been hurt that the riot was losing momentum.

"Stand down!" Becky shouted.

Most of the people coming from other parts of the ship were spectators. They might have joined in the riot had they not seen the blood of the injured and heard the screams of those who had been sprayed with the pepper gel.

"We will use deadly force to protect ourselves," Becky continued. "Return to your cabins, now!"

"Screw you, bit—" a man in a dark coat was shouting until Becky fired her pistol. The rubber bullet hit him in the center of his chest, bruised his sternum, and knocked the breath from his lungs. He fell backwards, clutching his chest and gagging for breath.

The crowd surged back but didn't dissipate. There was still lots of shouting, even some people trying to get the mob chanting again. Becky hit the icon for medical emergency, then tapped her comlink.

"Talk to me, Nash," Sergeant Flint said, huffing a little as he spoke.

Becky recognized that her boss was hustling, probably to get to where she was. "We have officers down, civilians, too. This is bad, boss, really bad."

She could see several people covered in blood and some others lying unconscious on the deck. The wide corridor no longer looked sleek and modern. It looked more like a street in a war-torn village.

"Help is on the way," Flint said. "Have you made contact with Jeopardy and Logan?"

"I'm with Jeopardy. She's injured, the dog too. No sign of Logan, though."

Jeopardy was still bent over Stu. The dog was panting. When his handler straightened up onto her knees, Becky saw that one leg was broken and twisted. There was also blood on his haunches. Jeopardy pointed to the nearby cabin door that was stuck open with bodies on the ground keeping it from closing.

"In there," she said.

"Don't move too much," Becky ordered. "That slash on your back needs stitches. Are you hurt anywhere else?"

There was bruising on her face. From the time that Jeopardy had reloaded her pistol, several aggressive protesters had rushed her from both sides of the corridor. She shot six of them and Stu took down another. But then a thick-bodied man in heavy workman's boots had stomped the dog's rear right leg. It turned and bit him between his legs. The big man had screamed in pain. Jeopardy swung her pistol toward the man, but before she could fire, a pair of protesters ran past her. One of them hit her hard as he went by, his fist smashing into her cheekbone. The punch knocked Jeopardy against the wall. She dropped her pistol in the melee and fell to her knees. For a moment, the world rocked in a blur, then she regained her senses just as a man with a knife stabbed Stu. The dog yelped in pain, and Jeopardy launched herself toward the men starting to gather around the police dog. She knocked one off his feet, then flung herself over Stu.

She was punched and kicked, as was Stu, but she did her best to protect the dog. Then Becky had arrived. Just when Jeopardy thought that the tide was turning, the man with the knife slashed at Stu, but cut Jeopardy instead. There was a line of fire down her back, and she felt like she was going to vomit. It wasn't the first time she had been beaten up. It had happened to her in boarding school and a few times since joining the police force. But in all those instances, she had held her own. The rioters on the *Colossus* had left her with more than bumps and bruises. She could feel herself starting to shake.

Becky left her friend for a moment and looked both ways. There were still a lot of spectators, but with more police in their black coveralls arriving on the scene, the rioters had moved further down the corridor. She stepped over and looked inside the one open berth. There were bodies on the floor, and in the back of the cabin stood Logan Keys.

"Are they gone?" he asked.

"For now," Becky said. "Are you hurt?"

"No, but a lot of these people need medical attention."

Becky could see that. Over two dozen people were down inside the cabin, which was a standard two-person berth. It was just like her own, only there were blankets pinned to the walls, and on the main table, there was a big, ugly-looking plant. She recognized the marijuana plant but there was no time for an inquiry.

"What happened?" Becky asked.

"Protesters out in the corridor blocking our path," Logan said as he carefully picked his way through the injured people on the floor.

Some had been shot but others had indications of being beaten. "Stu was triggered at this cabin."

"Probably from that cannabis plant someone's growing," Becky said.

"I went in, and the mob went crazy. How's Jeopardy?"

"Hurt," Becky said. "The dog, too. Medical is on their way."

She helped him step over the last few bodies and then he hurried to Jeopardy, just as Sergeant Flint pushed his way through the spectators, followed by a group of medical technicians.

"Logan," he said. "Are you hurt?"

"No, Sarge," he responded.

"Good, come with us," Flint ordered. "Medical, see to detective Bess and her K-9 partner right away. She is the highest priority."

"Got it, Sergeant," one of the medical personnel said.

Flint moved to where Becky stood waiting. He opened one side of his jacket to reveal a row of clips that fit their small, non-lethal handguns. He pulled two out of his belt and handed them to Becky.

"This isn't over," he said. "The protesters are heading to Topdeck."

"Why? This is insane!"

"Agreed, but we have to help. Logan, lead the way to the nearest elevator. We've got to get up to Topdeck city and put a stop to this madness before the ship is destroyed and we're all doomed."

CHAPTER NINETEEN

THE *COLOSSUS* WAS a long oval in shape. The city on the top deck was laid out in a cross pattern with the two widest streets leading to a park area in the center. All along the two main streets were skyscrapers. The ground floor of the huge buildings were retail, dining, and entertainment spaces. Above that were several thousand office buildings. Businesses from Earth wanted a footprint on the new planet. Executives spent their days plotting and planning for ways to carry their brand to Secundo.

To either side of the main cross streets were smaller avenues with all sorts of buildings, from warehouses to boutique shops. Hairdressers, tailors, shoe and boot manufacturers were in place to service the nearly half a million people on the *Colossus*. In addition, nightclubs and entertainment venues filled every inch of the busy streets. At the four corners of Topdeck City were green spaces. Two were wide and flat with manicured ball fields and a variety of courts for dozens of sports. The other two were botanical, with trees and flowering shrubs. They even had artificial streams that meandered down the green hills. There were walking paths and clearings where passengers picnicked during their off hours.

Just about anything a person might want could be found in

Topdeck. Almost nothing a person could get on Earth was missing. It was a clean, efficient city, the crown jewel of the mighty colony ship. Yet none of that mattered as the passengers began to riot. The pent-up frustrations and fears boiled over into destructive behavior. Not every passenger was involved, only about twenty percent. They came pouring up onto Topdeck and massed in the wide open soccer fields. Some were chanting, others were shouting for the mob to overthrow the ship's authorities. Weapons were forbidden on the ship, although there were plenty of firearms in the vast warehouses that were filled with equipment and supplies for the colony. But the mob didn't need guns. They had baseball bats, pickleball paddles, kitchen knives, and hand tools. Not every protester had a weapon or violent intent. In fact, most were just caught up in the frenzy. Most of the passengers on the ship were young people after all, with a desire to stand against something, as if it were somehow virtuous to fight the duly appointed authority on the ship.

In the city itself, hundreds of patrol officers had gathered. Their leadership was mostly administrative. They were all assigned to patrol precincts that had facilities on every even-numbered deck except for the VIP level. The upper deck precinct was located on Topdeck and serviced the city, as well as decks two and three. The Law Enforcement ranks on the *Colossus* were simplified. There were sergeants to handle the day-to-day assignments and normal personnel issues. They worked from the precincts, handling the radio traffic and dealing with the public. In many ways, it was the same on Earth, with Desk Sergeants handling most administrative tasks during any given shift. Above them were a handful of lieutenants, then the commissioner. The idea was to simplify the criminal justice system, with the hopes that crime on the colony ship would never be a major factor. If anyone had anticipated the passengers rioting, they had failed to properly prepare their patrol officers or obtain the right gear for such an event.

By the time Flint, Logan, and Becky made it to Topdeck, the protesters were on the move. They had formed up on the main road and were moving toward the center of the city. The patrol officers formed a line, three deep and shoulder to shoulder, to block their path, and the confrontation had become a standoff, with tempers building.

"Who's in charge?" Flint asked when his trio reached the patrol group.

"That would be McGinnis," one of the officers said. "He's in the command center."

"Which is where?" Becky asked.

"Topdeck precinct is two streets over, the big red building."

"He's not out here?" Flint asked.

"No need," another officer said, pointing to the security cameras on the buildings around them. "He can see everything. Orders are given via the comlink."

A hundred yards down the street, just past the big parks on the forward section of the upper deck, was a crowd of protesters. It was hard to get a count of them. They were packed in a tight mass, but it was easily several thousand people. Facing them was a group of just under a hundred patrol officers.

"This is going to get ugly fast," Logan said.

The crowd was already getting aggressive. They were waving their makeshift weapons and a few store windows had already been smashed.

"We need to calm them down," Flint agreed. He tapped a few controls into his cuff link. Then utilized his communications device to speak to the officer in charge. "I'm trying to reach Officer McGinnis," Flint said.

"This is Sergeant McGinnis. Who is on this channel? I'm dealing with a bit of a crisis here."

"Sergeant Flint, SIU. Sir, why aren't you out here? We need to de-escalate this situation."

"That's exactly what I'm attempting to do, but there is passenger unrest on every deck of this ship. Calling up personnel to overwhelm this mob isn't going to happen anytime soon. If you want to take a crack at talking them down, I won't stop you."

Flint didn't think the desk sergeant would do anything. He might be good at giving orders to others, but what was needed was real leadership.

"What have you heard from Commissioner Forrest?"

"Not a damn thing," McGinnis complained. "Senior leadership are conducting a meeting, for all the good that's going to do us."

"What are you officers armed with?"

"Tear gas, pepper spray, and batons," the desk sergeant said. "If it comes to it, we'll crack heads."

Flint didn't think a hundred police officers with batons was going to stop a crowd over a thousand people strong. The crowd also had weapons, and the patrol officers had no armor or even shields. It would devolve quickly into a melee, just as it had on deck sixteen. While Flint hadn't gotten into everything that happened there, he knew a lot of people had been hurt. Some were even killed in the fighting. He was grateful none of his officers were dead, although he also understood that there would be a reckoning. When the finger-pointing started, it would be the SIU that took the brunt of the blame, despite the fact that they were just following orders.

Flint turned to Becky and Logan. He had already given them the extra ammunition he had brought along. But sixteen rounds of non-lethal ammunition wouldn't be but a drop in the bucket against the crowd of protesters.

"I've got to turn them back," Flint said. "If it turns into a fight, it will be a blood bath."

"Do what you think is best," Becky said.

"Yeah, we'll cover you, Sarge," Logan replied.

At that moment, Dave Bannon came running toward them from deeper in the city.

"Wait!" he shouted. "I'm here."

"Took you long enough," Becky said.

"I was asleep," he said, panting as he joined his fellow SI squad members. "What did I miss?"

"We've got an unruly mob that could destroy the ship," Flint said. "You armed?"

"Yes, sir," Dave said.

"Good. Stay with Becky and Logan. No matter what happens, we look after one another. Nothing is worth your lives."

"That goes for you, too, boss," Becky said.

He nodded, but Flint knew he was walking into a lion's den. He slipped through the rows of patrol officers and made a show of removing his pistol from his belt and handing it to Becky.

"If things go south," he whispered. "Get the others out of here. I'm counting on you."

"We won't leave without you."

"Yes, you will," Flint said. "We meet back at SIU headquarters. Tell the others and stay cool. Keep a close eye on Logan."

"Roger that," Becky said. "Good luck."

Flint turned and walked toward the crowd of protesters. They were shouting, even screaming. He didn't understand how they had gone from frustrated individuals to an outraged mob on the verge of committing violence. But he didn't have to understand anything. He wasn't there to study them or record the history of the *Colossus*. His job was seeing that no one got hurt and that no property was destroyed. Of course, property had already been destroyed. There was broken glass on either side of the mob. Some of the stores had been looted. Flint guessed that some of the protesters had even gone up to the offices above and were probably threatening people or destroying property. But the fringe element could be mopped up later, once he had de-escalated the large group of protesters.

"Please, please, give me just a minute of your attention," he shouted, raising both hands.

The mob didn't fall silent, but they did quiet down a little.

"My name is Sawyer Flint. I'm a sergeant in the Special Investigations Unit."

"You're a pig!" someone screamed.

"Kill the cops!" someone else shouted.

One man, young with what looked like blood on his face, rushed toward Flint with a baseball bat. He had on a flannel shirt with the sleeves ripped off. There were tattoos on his arms, and his hair was buzzed down to short little bristles that seemed to stick straight out.

Flint didn't move. There were still thirty yards of distance between himself and the crowd. The man ran halfway, brandishing the bat.

"Bash his skull!" someone urged.

But the man with the bat stopped and stared at Flint, who stared right back.

"I'm not here to fight," Flint said. "I don't want that. Too many people have been hurt already."

A woman stepped forward. It was Holly Baxter-Wright, although Flint didn't know that at the time. She had a police baton, the narrow, telescoping kind that Flint's people carried. He felt a sinking sensation at the sight of it.

"You can't treat us like cattle," she said. "We have rights and we won't let them be trampled by fascists like you."

"I'm not a fascist," Flint said. "I'm a law enforcement officer doing my job and looking forward to colonizing a new world, just like you."

"Your people have been conducting illegal searches and profiling passengers for weeks!"

"We have, that's true," Flint said. "There was an incident that could have been catastrophic, but we managed to stop it. Still, there might be other people on the ship who will stop at nothing to sabotage the colony on Secundo. What we've been doing has been in search of them."

"Oh, nice story, but we're not buying it," Holly said, pointing her baton at Flint. "You can't just make up some fake news and expect us to go along. We're not sheep, man. We're not stupid."

"No, you aren't," Flint said. "You're passengers on this ship, which is our shelter and our haven while we make our way to Secundo. Please, just think about that for a moment. I know you're angry and I don't blame you. Really, I do not blame you for being mad about the situation. But you have to understand that the safety of the ship is the highest priority. We aren't searching your domiciles for anything other than evidence of sabotage or plans to harm the ship."

"What gives you the right!" someone in the crowd screamed.

"You're not our overlords!" another voice bellowed.

"No, I'm just a cop. But I was one of the people who stopped the terrorist."

"What was his name?" Holly demanded.

Flint knew it was improper to talk about an ongoing investigation with the public. And that whatever he said, the defense would use against them in court. But he also felt like the passengers had a right to know. The thoughts flashed through his mind like lightning and, just as quickly, he decided to tell the protesters the truth.

"His name is Titus Russel," Flint said in a calm, almost quiet tone. The mob fell silent as he told the story. "Our K-9 officer smelled the bomb making chemicals on him. It's a bit of a miracle, really. They passed in the corridor and our dog reacted."

"So what?" Holly responded. "It could have been anything. He could have had drugs or maybe he worked in food service and smelled like meat."

"That's true," Flint said. "All we knew at that moment was that something had triggered the K-9. So I followed him to the dining hall and sat by him. During that meal, he lied to me about his identity."

"Maybe you weren't his type!" someone shouted, which garnered a wave of laughter.

"It wasn't enough to bring him in, but it was enough to keep tabs on him. When he left his assigned job in the middle of the night, using an illegal cufflink with a separate identity, we closed in. And it was a good thing we did, because he placed a bomb in the engine exhaust compartment on deck fourteen."

"You have proof of this?"

"I have eyewitness testimony," Flint said. "That space is a dead zone, so no surveillance footage was taken, but several of us saw him with the device. We arrested him then, but the bomb had already been activated. Myself and one of the crew supervisors found a way to get it off the ship before it detonated. Now, I know you all heard about the disturbance that night. It was the talk of the entire ship. And I don't blame those of you who feel it wasn't legit. We haven't been as forthcoming about the incident because we didn't want to frighten people. Nor did we want to taint Titus Russel's prosecution, but that's what really happened."

"Liar!" someone shouted.

"He's making it up," another person bellowed.

Before Flint could respond, a voice came over the ship's loud-speakers.

"This is Captain Walter Hastings. I repeat, this is your captain, Walter Hastings. I'm ordering everyone who is not a member of the ship's crew back to your assigned berth. This is not optional. As per the charter of the *Colossus*, in this time of emergency, I'm ordering all passengers to their assigned domiciles to await further orders from me. You have one half hour to comply. Anyone found not in their berth after that will be taken into custody and charged with mutiny. Let me be absolutely clear. Anyone convicted of seditious charges will not be allowed to join the colony on Secundo. All convicted felons will return with the ship to the Sol system, where they will be turned over to the authorities for the remainder of their conviction. This is your captain speaking. Return to your berth until further orders are issued."

There was a moment of silence, then someone from the mob shouted, "They can't arrest us all!"

From that one defiant outburst, a chorus of outrage erupted. Flint's opportunity to stop the protest was failing. But, when the man with the bat charged forward again, he saw one last option. He raised a hand behind him to keep the other members of his squad from putting the attacker down. Then he bent his knees a little.

The tattooed man with the bat raised his weapon high with both hands. Flint stood ready, waiting. The man closed the distance between them quickly. Everyone was watching. Flint was unarmed or, at least, appeared to be. He looked almost bored as the younger man with the bat rushed him. At the last moment, just as the attacker started to swing the bat down onto Flint's head, the savvy LEO slid to the side. But he didn't just let the attack go by, instead as he slid out of the bat's trajectory, he pivoted on one foot and used his legs to generate power into a punch that he launched into the side of his attacker's jaw.

The man with the bat lost his grip and stiffened before folding over at the waist and crashing to the deck. His baseball bat went flying across the road, clattering as it fell. Flint straightened and looked back at the mob, which had fallen silent.

"I don't agree with the captain's order," Flint said. "But he has the right to issue it. We are all here under his authority for the duration of the voyage. I know you can all understand that. We must comply."

There were a few more shouts of defiance, a few more calls for violence, but the wind had gone out of the protesters' sails at the sight of one of their own being defeated so easily. Fear was starting to replace their outrage and Flint understood that. He was counting on it.

"No one wants to miss the opportunity to go to Secundo," he said. "Please, please, return to your cabins. I'm going right now to speak to the Captain. I will insist that we release all the evidence about the terrorist's thwarted plan so that you can understand why we've been searching the ship so thoroughly. Please, return to your cabins. We can work all this out."

Relief hit Flint like a physical blow as the mob started to turn away. Most of the protesters were just along for the ride. They had been caught up in the excitement, but the threat of not getting to colonize a new world, of having to go back to Earth, it was just too much to ask. They moved away from the city center and toward the elevators.

"Oh, man, you pulled it off," Logan said. "I didn't think it was possible."

Beck knelt down by the man who had attacked Flint with the bat. "Looks like his jaw is broken."

"He's lucky that's all that's broken," Dave said. "Should we cuff him, Sarge?"

"No," Flint said. "Let's alert medical services."

"That was a hell of a punch, boss," Logan said.

Flint sagged a little. He suddenly felt on the verge of exhaustion. There was nothing more tiring than danger. He hadn't realized how tense he had been facing the mob, but he suddenly felt like standing up was a major chore.

"Logan, stay with this guy and make sure he gets to medical. Then check on Jeopardy. I want an update as soon as you have one."

"Roger that," Logan said.

"What about us?" Becky asked.

"Start going through the video surveillance on fourteen. We're not out of the woods yet. There were a lot of people hurt in that dust-up."

"We'll get it," Dave said.

"I'm going to see the Captain," Flint told them. "But I'll need proof that our people were justified in the use of force. Send me what you get as soon as you can. And Becky, that includes a report. Just dictate what you saw and what you did. I need the concise version, but don't exclude the messy parts."

"Yes, sir," she said.

"And someone check in with Sergeant McGinnis," Flint added. "Let him know that there could still be protesters in some of the office buildings."

CHAPTER
TWENTY

THE CRISIS WASN'T OVER. Riots had broken out on other decks. There were too many protesters for the limited patrol officers to corral. Flint was waiting to meet with Captain Hastings when another ship-wide announcement was made.

"Passengers and crew of the colony ship *Colossus*, this is your captain speaking. I am reminding you of the curfew I have ordered. You have eighteen minutes to return to your cabin before you are charged with mutiny. I will give law enforcement the charge to search our surveillance system and bring charges against those who refuse my order. We are working to protect the *Colossus* and all passengers from harm. Do not think that we will not enforce the rule of law on this ship. Myself, and the crew, stand ready to do whatever is necessary to quell the unrest and restore order. You must return to your berth within the next seventeen minutes, or be prepared to face criminal charges. That is all."

Flint wasn't sure that threatening the already frustrated and stressed-out passenger was the right move, but it wasn't his decision to make. He was waiting in the lounge when Captain Hastings came striding in. Commander Koll and Commissioner Forrest were in his wake. Flint could see the anger and stress on the captain's face. His skin was red across his cheeks and dark, almost purple under his eyes.

"What the hell is going on!" Hastings demanded. "We have passengers killed, Sergeant. You better have a damn good explanation or your entire unit will be held criminally liable."

"Sir, we've been carrying out your orders," Flint said. "And my officers were attacked by a large crowd of protesters. They were acting in self-defense."

"The med bay is almost at capacity," the captain continued. "And my sources say your people started this fiasco."

"Sir, I know my people. They're good police."

"Law Enforcement Officers," Forrest interjected. "We are no longer calling ourselves police."

Flint carried on without acknowledging the commissioner's criticism. "They didn't start the violence, I'd bet my career on that fact."

"You are, Sergeant," the Captain said.

"We'll have the surveillance footage any minute now," Flint said. "And you'll see exactly what happened."

"My people have it," Commander Koll said. "With your permission, captain."

"Go ahead, commander. I want to see what we're dealing with."

On the big display, a double image came up. It was divided in the middle of the tall screen, with one view on top, the other on bottom of the display. They showed surveillance footage of deck sixteen from two different angles, but cued up to the same exact time. Flint hadn't seen the video, and he could feel the muscles in his shoulders and neck tensing up.

"There's the crowd of protesters," Koll said. "It looks like they're blocking the passageway again."

"Idiots," Captain Hastings muttered.

Flint wasn't sure what to think of the captain's outburst. He agreed that the passengers were out of line, but he also felt their orders were on the verge of draconian. It would not have been possible to do random searches back on Earth, in other nations, maybe, but not the United States. They all had to adapt to life on the *Colossus,* which wasn't a free nation, but rather an enclosed environment that was fragile in many ways. The entire ship was ultimately under the Captain's control, and the passengers protesting in the name of tyranny and authoritarianism weren't off the mark. Yet Flint knew that the Captain's power was absolutely necessary when the operation and functionality of the ship was the only thing keeping the people on board alive. They had passed the point of no return, and no help would ever be able to reach them in time to save them if something went wrong. It was the unique nature of traveling on a spaceship between star systems.

"What's happening here, Sergeant?" Koll asked.

"The K-9 officer was triggered by something in that cabin," Flint said.

"What types of things might trigger the dog?" Forrest asked. "Bombs?"

"The K-9s are trained to react to certain scents, such as powerful chemical agents that are known to be used in bomb making. That's what our K-9 reacted to with the terrorist Titus Russel. But it's also trained to react to illegal drugs and cadavers. It's how we found the body of the girl who had been stuffed into the cooling mechanism a few months ago."

"We need sound," Captain Hastings said as the crowd reacted to Logan opening Holly Baxter-Wright's cabin.

Things happened quickly at that point, but there was no denying that the crowd rushed the law enforcement officers. The reactions of Jeopardy and Stu would be debated for weeks.

"The dog drew first blood," Captain Hastings said.

"In response to the danger to its handler," Flint spoke up.

"We can't see what happened in the cabin," Monty Forrest said.

"It's obvious a lot of people are pressing in on that officer," Lova Koll replied.

"Detective Logan Keys," Flint said. "He was forced to defend himself, and that's where the majority of deaths occurred."

"He used a weapon?" Captain Hastings assumed.

"No, sir," Flint replied. "He didn't draw his sidearm until he was forced into the bathroom."

"The SIU has non-lethal weapons," Monty said.

"Detective Keys was forced to put down his attackers as quickly as possible," Flint said. "He didn't set out to harm anyone. It was self-defense."

They continued watching the riot, including when Jeopardy and Stu were wounded, and detective Nash's response.

"It's a bloodbath," Captain Hastings said. "I can't imagine a more catastrophic outcome. What are the casualty numbers, Commander?"

Lova Koll looked at her data tablet. "Fifty-three passengers were injured, and four more were killed. Law Enforcement Officer Jeopardy Bess and her K-9 partner were also wounded in the fighting."

"Four dead," Hastings said as he leaned against the back of one of the posh sitting chairs. "How serious were the passengers injured?"

"Most were just bruised from the less-than-lethal rounds fired at them. But we have seven with open wounds from dog bites and six more with fractures and dislocations. None of the injured are listed as critical other than Officer Bess."

"This is an unmitigated disaster," the captain snapped. "How the hell did you let this happen?"

"Sir," Commander Koll responded. "I don't think we can lay the blame for this at one division's feet. The lottery system was compromised back on Earth. And our passengers simply aren't used to naval discipline."

"We were trying to do what you told us," Flint said, after

glancing at the report that Becky had just sent to his cufflink. "Today's incident was set off when our K-9 officer reacted to a passenger growing a cannabis indica plant in her berth."

"A riot… over a plant?" Captain Hastings said with contempt. "Is that really our best, people?"

"Sir, if you want the truth, the riot was caused by you," Sergeant Flint declared.

"Sergeant!" Commissioner Forrest thundered. "You are way out of line."

"I'm not sure that's exactly what it sounded like," Commander Koll said, trying her best to take the heat out of the moment.

"It's true," Flint insisted. "You have every right to demand anything you think is necessary to keep this ship safe. But the passengers are chaffing under your naval discipline. They didn't join the Navy; they signed up to be colonists on a new world. And one of the biggest reasons so many people want to go to Secundo is so that they can have privacy. They want to do things their own way and build the kind of life they envision. You sending us to do surprise searches all over the ship has cost us a lot of goodwill and made the entire ship tense."

"If they don't have anything to hide, they shouldn't be concerned," the captain said as he stepped closer to Flint.

"Alright, then you won't mind if we go and search your cabin, sir?" He was making a point, but he had no idea if it would land. It might cost him his job. In all likelihood, he would end up spending the rest of the voyage working in the sewage treatment facility, but he was tired of the way Hastings was running things. "We'll go through every drawer and locker, just to be certain there's nothing that isn't supposed to be on the ship."

The captain's face turned red, but he didn't respond at first. When he did, his voice was barely a whisper.

"You know I'm not a threat," he said.

"But you know there are things in your personal space that no one has a right to dig into," Flint pressed on. "That's why people are worried. And frankly, sir, your order of charging passengers with sedition is the wrong move. We should release all the information we have about Titus Russel. People need to know what really happened."

"You can't do that," Judge St. Pierre declared. "It would taint the jury pool and give the terrorist grounds for a new trial."

"Who cares?" Flint said. "He isn't going anywhere. No one on this ship is going to fight for his freedom. If they feel we were unjust and want to give him a new trial back on Earth, that's fine. But people are frightened, and there are a lot of voices pushing the conspiracy theory that the entire attack was fabricated so that the ship's crew could violate the passengers' civil rights."

"That's absurd," Commissioner Forrest snapped.

"I've already told the passengers all they need to know about that incident," Captain Hastings said. "Anything more and we risk frightening everyone unnecessarily."

"You've told them," Flint said. "Now we need to show them. We need them to be confident that everything we're doing is to keep them safe."

"You'll never convince everyone," Commander Koll said. "Even with the video from the ship's cameras that showed the object being jettisoned and exploding. Some people will say we doctored the footage."

"Some will," Flint agreed, "but most won't. We need to show the passengers we aren't tyrants. Give them the evidence and they'll understand why we're searching cabins."

"I'll consider it," Hastings said. His response surprised Flint and everyone else in the room. "But for now, I want the violence dealt with. I want people calm and orderly."

"We'll see to that, Captain, sir," Law Enforcement Commissioner Monty Forrest said.

The meeting went on for several hours, but once everyone's

tempers were calm, they were able to make sense of things. Reports came in from every deck. The damage was done, in the tall office buildings on Topdeck, down to the dining facility on deck eighteen. The schools and law enforcement centers throughout the ship took the most damage, but no fires were started. Graffiti and physical damage, such as that done to the drink dispensers, which seemed to be the easiest targets, were recorded for the ship's official log. Miraculously, only six people died in the riots, four from physical confrontations with law enforcement officers, and two were crushed when the mobs panicked after the captain's call for order.

Flint left the meeting without having lost his job, although Commissioner Forrest was still angry with him for speaking to the captain as he had. There was plenty of mop-up work to do, but the SIU wouldn't be involved. With Stu wounded by the rioters and his people having done most of the searches, it was agreed that they would stand down, at least for a while.

Flint went immediately to the medical facility. By that point, most of the rioters with minor injuries had been treated and released. They were escorted back to the cabins by patrol officers ostensibly to keep them from being detained for being out of their berths after the captain's curfew. But it was really to ensure they caused no more trouble on their way home. Surprisingly enough, the *Colossus* had a small hospital wing. It was mostly due to the health screening that took place before passengers and crew were allowed on the ship. There were half a million people on the colony vessel, but they were mostly all young, healthy people. The need for a large medical facility had been rejected in favor of more storage space on the enormous ship.

Logan was still in the medical bay and saw Flint coming. He met his boss and led him to Jeopardy's room.

"How is she?"

"Resting now," Logan said. "The bastards hurt her, Sarge. She needed over a hundred stitches in her back."

"Any organs damaged?"

"No, thank God. She's pretty bruised up, though."

"What about Stu?"

"That's what she asked as soon as she woke up," Logan said. "A team of vets took him. There are no animal facilities on board, but there is a training station in the university's veterinary medicine department. They took Stu down there."

"When she wakes up, tell her I stopped by," Flint said. "You stay with her, Logan. I'll go check on the dog. Keep your comlink on."

"Roger that, Sarge."

It took a while to find the right place in the ship's sprawling academic facility. The *Colossus* had professors and experts in agriculture and land management. One quarter of the ship's passengers were either getting degrees or were scheduled for special training at some point during the voyage. There was a big vocational department as well, with training on everything from mechanics to metallurgy. There was even a gunsmithing class and an entire wing on mining technology. Eventually, Flint found the small veterinary department. The university had four professors of veterinary medicine, all with plans to start a school on Secundo. They had nearly a hundred students on the *Colossus*. Most had already started their vet training before getting selected for the Secundo colony. Most of the students had gathered in one of the auditoriums and were watching the professors complete the surgery on Stu via live streaming to a large video display.

Flint waited outside the surgical theater, which was actually a simulation room where the students could practice with VR and holographic training programs. The colony would be raising a large number of domesticated animals and perhaps identifying others once they were on Secundo. Flint didn't have to wait long before one of the professors came out and spoke to him.

"They're finishing up now," the man said as he pulled off his paper surgical gown. "The operation was a success."

"What did he need?" Flint asked.

"His hind leg was broken. You don't see compound fractures in animals all that often. And the stab wound cut into his colon. We had to surgically repair it. He'll lose some weight not eating for a while, and he'll need around-the-clock care."

"We can give it to him."

"Actually, while that would be the normal treatment plan, I'd like to suggest that you leave the dog here with us. We don't have any animals other than the calves, piglets, poultry, and lambs down in the ark. That's what we call the storage section where the live animals are kept. Those are all in good shape, so I'd like to see to the dog's post-surgical care and recovery. It would be a great learning experience for the students."

"Stu's a police dog," Flint said. "Highly trained and valuable."

"We're all animal lovers here, Sergeant," the professor said. "We'll take good care of your dog."

"His handler's in the hospital. I'll let her know Stu's in good hands. Just remember, he isn't a pet."

"Yes, thank you," the professor said. "I'll make a special note of it and we'll document his recovery. If your officer would like to view that log, you can give her the department's computer information. It will all be on the university servers."

"Thank you," Flint said.

He shook the professor's hand and made his way back to SIU HQ. Becky was there. She looked frazzled and tired, which Flint understood. He couldn't remember how long it had been since he last slept. His life had become literally filled with work since taking down Titus Russel. It was the same for his people and he sent Becky to her cabin with a promise that she would not return for at least ten hours.

In his own office, he took the time to transmit a fast message to Logan, who refused to leave the medical facility. Under different circumstances, he might have needed to, although with their orders to stand down and the rest of the ship confined to quarters, there was no reason to deny him. Flint sat in his seat and leaned back. He propped his feet on the corner of his desk and closed his eyes. He was asleep in seconds and stayed that way until the call came in an hour later.

CRANK DIDN'T MIND BEING CONFINED to his cabin. He had his official cufflink on and pinging with the ship's surveillance system to show him in his berth. But what he did in the privacy of his domicile was for his eyes alone. Life on the ship had become boring in a sense. The gang was busy insinuating themselves into the lives of the bankers. It wasn't so much a long con as it was an attempt to compromise each of the men so that no one would ever question JD's possession of so much money.

Crank had already checked his computer program that was quietly redirecting a tiny fraction of the processing fees collected by the bank into a separate account. The bank called their fees the cost of doing business, but it was a shake down no different than what a gang might do back on Earth. Crank wasn't a fool. He knew money was essential for a civilization and that no one could be expected to do work for no pay. The bank had a right to collect fees, and yet, in his mind, Crank could see no difference between the bankers and a gang. They were selective about who they allowed into their ranks and used their power to get what they wanted from people. Most people needed what the bank had — money. To buy a house or a vehicle, to go to school or start a business, people needed money.

The bank would loan people money, but not their own. Oh no, they took money from a thousand customers and loaned it to someone. The bank then collected fees and interest on that loan, but shared none of it with the people who had put their money in the bank for safekeeping.

It was like most things in life, which was sanitized in reputation, but in actual practice was no different than the operation of organized crime. Crank had to hand it to JD, the leader of the Ghetto Kings, had seen the truth first. The voyage to Secundo was making it possible for JD and his small crew to create a legitimate operation that was as profitable as any felonious caper. But it wasn't just about the money; the gang needed to be accepted by the system. Otherwise, the enforcement arm of civil society, the most powerful gang in the world, would take their money and condemn them as criminals. Law enforcement was, in fact, exactly like a street gang. From sporting their own colors to the rules they operated by, they were a gang. Only they had been legitimized so that their use of power was accepted by society at large, even when they broke their own rules and harmed innocents.

But Crank had no ambitions to become a leader in the world, new or old. And he wasn't involved in the con job with the banking executives. Instead, he filled his time watching people on the ship. He had tapped into the *Colossus'* surveillance feed on day one, but it had taken him weeks to narrow things down and learn to quickly navigate the thousands of streams of video being recorded by the ship's law enforcement division. It had become his obsession. Even before the captain's curfew, Crank was spending every hour of the day and night in his berth, but watching events all over the ship. Not only that, he was quietly fomenting the protests by sending clips of the SIU squad going into passenger cabins to people anonymously. It was a failure of law enforcement that they didn't have a cyber division on board. They had been much too optimistic about the passengers, believing that they would get through the two-year voyage with just crowd control and a handful of detectives. Crank was quietly gathering a war chest of information, some above board, some incriminating. He had video evidence of people cheating on their partners, stealing from the ship, stealing from their employers and seeking out illicit goods. Crank was not a student of human nature, but he knew that everyone was susceptible to vice. Different people were tempted by different things, but they were all drawn to something dark. His grandmother had called it the total depravity of man, although Crank saw it as entertainment and opportunity.

It hadn't been hard to recruit several members of the janitorial staff. Crank had built his own pin-sized cameras and used housecleaning to place them in various cabins. They were shortwave devices, essentially a battery, a lens and a microscopic processing chip. The casing served as the transmitter and could send a signal up to twenty feet away. Fortunately for Crank, the *Colossus* had a wireless system hub in every cabin. In less than a day, he had built a back door system for his own spy cameras. In his personal cabin, hidden in one of his lockers, he had a rack of liquid-cooled servers and large-capacity solid-state storage drives on which he saved all the juicy video evidence of his secret spying system.

JD's cabin had been the first to get bugged. And then his lieutenants. Crank reviewed their footage regularly to ensure that he would not get blindsided. The second leading cause of death for a gang member after getting killed by a rival was getting killed by a member of one's own gang. Betrayal was part of the life, but Crank was careful. He worked diligently, often spending eighteen hours a day monitoring his spy systems to ensure he wouldn't get caught off guard if JD or members of his crew decided they didn't want Crank around anymore.

After a few months of work, Crank had eyes and ears all over the ship. But his obsession was watching the detectives in the SI squad. He had a total of four cameras in their headquarters, including one in the sergeant's office. JD's interest in Becky Nash had triggered a secret infatuation on the hacker's part. It was his own vice, one of many, actually. Crank was not physically attractive. He was skinny, with watery eyes, acne, and a bald patch on the back of his head that was growing by the day. He had never been popular with women. Just being around them often made him so self-conscious that he made a fool of himself. Yet his proximity to JD gave him a modicum of power within the gang, and even the neighborhood they had ruled back on Earth. What he really wanted more than anything was to have the beautiful women who flocked to his boss look at Crank the same way they saw JD. And to that end, he had become infatuated with more than one of JD's paramours. Becky Nash was just the latest in that vice that plagued the hacker.

Even though little had come of the relationship as the detective had been overwhelmed by work and had almost no time for JD, the spark remained. Crank's boss looked in on Becky occasionally, while Crank watched her obsessively. He had been watching when she was sent back to her cabin after the curfew and he was still watching her; his tiny camera had a decent view of her bunk, which she kept open since her roommate had moved out. Becky Nash had no idea that Crank was behind that. As his obsession with her had grown, he had searched the ship's database and discovered that Becky's roommate had put in for a change of domicile with the logistics division. It was a low priority; in fact, there was no notation on the file that even showed that it had been seen by the ship's crew. The logistics division was flooded with tens of thousands of requests, from change of domicile to work transfer requests. And like every bureaucracy, there was a hierarchy of priorities when it came to the logistical requests. So, it was a simple matter for Crank to approve the request and ensure that Becky Nash had a private berth.

He was watching her sleep when her cufflink pinged with a

comlink chime. Becky groaned and sighed, but then she reached out and took the cufflink from the charging station on a shelf recessed in the wall of her bunk. She tapped the icon to activate the comlink without opening her eyes. Crank was impressed, but then, he was impressed by everything Becky did. His only regret was not getting a camera into her bathroom. That would have been too revealing a request to make to the janitorial staff he had recruited. They thought the little cameras were simply listening devices, and Crank made it worth their while to install them where he wanted them. But there was no need for a listening device in a bathroom, so making that request would have given too much information away. Crank was a firm believer in the power of information. He used it to boost his importance with JD nearly every day.

Becky Nash wasn't the type of person to move about her cabin undressed. She utilized the small bathroom for that and Crank had contemplated breaking into her cabin and installing a way to see her in the bathroom. Yet the truth was, he was too big a coward to do it himself. It was easier to hide in his berth and manipulate others into doing his dirty work.

"Yeah," Becky said, her voice thick with sleep.

"Sorry to wake you," her boss said. "We've got a missing kid."

"What?"

"Deck four, the Arlington family. Their fourteen-year-old didn't make it back to their cabin before curfew. They made requests to law enforcement, but the kid hasn't been picked up."

"Boy or girl?"

"Boy," Flint said. "On the autism spectrum. I'm going to do the interview now. I'll need you to join me."

"Yeah, sure," Becky said, rubbing her face with one hand. "On my way."

"Thanks," Flint said.

Their communication ended and Becky sat up on the edge of her small bunk. She needed sleep. There were bags under her eyes and it was obvious that just standing up was difficult for her. She staggered over to the drink dispenser and put a pod of highly caffeinated coffee into the pot. After starting the brewing process, she went into the bathroom.

Crank muttered under his breath while he waited and then did a quick information search on a separate computer for the Arlingtons. A picture of the family came up. A mom, dad, teenage daughter and son. The father was a mechanical engineer with eighteen years designing automated farming equipment for the Lexico Corporation. The mother was a doctor. They had been highly recruited for the colony despite the fact that their fourteen-year-old son, Oliver, was on the autism spectrum. He was highly intelligent, like his parents, but functionally mute and socially delayed. His twin sister was the opposite. She was involved in a wide variety of extra-curricular activities. He looked younger than his fourteen years and she looked older.

When Becky came out of the bathroom, her hair was wet, but she was dressed for work in clean clothes. She preferred bluejeans and sweatshirts that didn't flatter her. She poured her coffee into a travel mug with a lid, then took a sip. For a moment, she savored the hot liquid, which clearly helped pep her up slightly. With the first caffeine pumping through her system, she strapped on her belt. It was a wide, leather belt that held her pistol, cuffs, a canister of pepper spray and a telescoping baton. She added a small flashlight and stuck some gum into her pants pocket. Then she hurried out the door. Crank wondered where she got the energy and dreamed of when he could get her all to himself.

TWENTY-TWO

BECKY NASH HAD no idea she was being watched. Sergeant Flint had sent the Arlingtons' cabin number to her cufflink. She took the first set of elevators, went up to Topside, then took the Tube around to the far side of the ship. Over the weeks of living on the ship, she had grown used to the process of getting around. In many ways, it wasn't all that different from living in a megacity on Earth. There were times when she felt she was in one of the enormous hotels in Las Vegas, the kind a person could spend two weeks in and never need to leave the facility. But being in the parks on Topdeck helped. It gave the massive ship a sense of atmosphere. It wasn't like being outside on Earth, but it was enough of an escape from the massive ship that she didn't feel claustrophobic.

Still, when she imagined being married and having a family on the ship, she thought it would be much harder. At night, she dreamed of having a house of her own, with a small lawn and maybe a garden in the back. On Earth, everything was grown on massive, corporate-owned farms, but there were a few older women in her building who had little herb gardens hooked onto their exterior windows. She could get whatever herbs she wanted from a grocery delivery, but there was something exciting about growing something herself. It was organic and natural. Becky fantasized about having her hands in dark, rich soil, not compost that was manufactured, but natural dirt where she could grow things on her own terms.

She had planned to take a few online classes about agriculture on the voyage, but the SIU had been so slammed with work she hadn't had time. It was partly why she wondered if she would continue in law enforcement on the new world. She would be needed, but maybe could find another vocation that didn't put her in contact with the worst of the worst on a daily basis.

By the time she reached the Arlington's cabin, it took a strong act of will to pull herself out of the fantasy in her mind. There was still over a year to go on their voyage and if Becky knew anything about police work, it was that it required one's complete focus. Anything less put herself and her peers in danger.

The door to the cabin was open, and a pair of patrol officers were stationed outside. Becky showed them her badge.

"We know who you are," an officer with the name Stankowski printed on the front of his coveralls said. "You saved the day with that riot down on sixteen."

"How's the dog?" the other officer asked.

"He'll make it," Becky said, glancing into the cabin. "The vets are keeping him at the university for now. Any progress on finding the missing kid?"

"Not that we've heard," Stankowski said. "Sergeant Flint is inside with the family."

Becky nodded to the patrolmen and stepped into the cabin. It was twice the size of hers, with a small kitchen in the back. The children shared a bedroom and a bathroom; the parents had their own. There was just enough room in the shared space for an arrangement of comfortable-looking furniture, with a round dining table and four chairs near the mini-kitchen. Becky could smell coffee and wondered who had the peace of mind to brew it, given the circumstances.

Flint met her just inside the door. Becky could see the mother, her face grim, but there were no tears. She appeared to Becky like a woman accustomed to dealing with bad news. The father was not as stoic. His hair was askew and his eyes were red. Between them was the daughter. Becky knew she was the missing boy's twin. It made her a bit sad to see a fourteen-year-old with a fully developed body, which the girl was showing off in a tight shirt and yoga pants.

"The boy's name is Truman," Flint said. "He was at the computer lab. His parents say he likes to spend time there, but when the riots started, the kids were all sent home."

"Someone searched the school?"

"Yes," Flint said.

"Any chance this kid is with his buddies somewhere?"

"Doubtful," Flint said. "According to everyone I've talked to, he doesn't have friends."

Becky felt another pang of sadness. At a glance, she could see that of the two children, the sister got what most people considered to be the good genes. The boy might be smart, but it was hard to beat popular and pretty. The mother got up and walked to meet them.

"Detective Nash, this is Doctor Fiona Arlington," Flint said. "I've got a pretty good grasp on things, but Detective Nash probably has questions."

"Sure," the mother said. "However, we can help."

"We've checked his cufflink?" Becky asked Flint.

"It's turned off," he said.

"Is that normal for your son?" Becky asked.

"He tolerates wearing it," Mrs. Arlington said. "Truman doesn't like electronic devices on his body. Back on Earth, he didn't want a phone or even a tablet."

"But he likes computers."

"Very much," the mother explained. "He likes rigid structure and rules that can be counted on. A computer operating system is his playground. Truman is on the autism spectrum. He's highly intelligent, but struggles with sensory overload and social inter-actions."

"He doesn't speak," Flint said.

"That's correct. His vocal capacity is the same as yours and mine, but he prefers written communication. He hasn't said more than a dozen words to me his entire life, but I get long emails from him nearly every day."

"He doesn't have a lot of friends?"

The mother shook her head. "He struggles to make them without talking. Most kids his age don't have the patience to look past his struggles."

"What about enemies? Any of the kids at school bullying him?"

The mother turned and looked at her daughter. "Tabitha, does your brother have enemies?"

The girl on the sofa wasn't crying, but she looked scared. There was something about her that made Becky think the girl was hiding something. Had she been a suspect in a crime, she would have taken her to the station and interrogated her. Tabitha shook her head.

"Some of the kids teased him at first, but they never touched him. I wouldn't have allowed that. I think they got used to him."

"He likes to help," the mother interjected. "If Truman sees a person struggling academically, he'll reach out to help them, usually via email or text."

"And he does all that from his computer?" Becky asked.

"Yes," the mother said. "Either the computer lab at the school or his own computer."

"Have we checked it?"

"Can't," Flint said. "It's password-protected, and no one knows the password."

"Okay, but if he is sending messages on the ship, it will have to go through the mainframe. We should be able to access it. Is Bannon in the office?"

"Should be by now," Flint said. "I called him right after you."

Becky tapped the icon on her cufflink that activated the communication system. Dave answered immediately.

"I'm here," he said. "What do you need?"

"The missing boy communicates via messages and emails. We can't get into his computer, but you can access his messages on the mainframe, right?"

"Most of 'em," Dave said. "If he deleted them, the ship's servers will overwrite that data after a set period of time."

"We're most interested in who he was talking to recently," Becky told him. "See what you can find."

"On it," Dave said.

Becky turned to Dr. Fiona Arlington again. "If he had heard the warning from Captain Hastings, would that have gotten through to him?"

"Yes," the mother said, her voice cracking as she answered. "He… he's a strong proponent of command structure. It's one of the reasons we agreed to come on the voyage. He loves rank and military command systems. He wouldn't have disobeyed the ship's captain if he could help it."

"You said he's smart. Maybe he was too far away from home to get back within the time frame. Are there places he likes to go? Topdeck maybe?"

"He doesn't like crowds," she admitted. "It's why we mainly eat here at home. He hasn't ever been up top. There's just too many people."

"What does he do when he's not comfortable in a situation?"

"He shuts down."

"Does he ever lash out or get violent?"

"No, never. He's incredibly kind."

Becky sighed. Finding a boy like the one she was describing should have been easy. Her gut told her there was more to the situation than they were being told. Not that it seemed like the mother was holding out. But the daughter maybe was.

"Could I get Tabitha to show me around their room?" Becky asked.

"Of course," the mother said.

The daughter looked less certain. She stood up, and Becky was surprised to find that a fourteen-year-old was as tall as she was. Tabitha had naturally blonde hair that was thick and hung a little past her shoulders in curls and waves. She wore almost no makeup, but had the flawless skin of youth. The girl led the way into the bedroom. There wasn't a lot to it. One wall had double recessed bunks, not unlike the ones in Becky's cabin. On the opposite wall were four standard lockers and on one side of them was a vanity with lights and all the accoutrements of a beauty regimen. On the other side of the locker was a desk with a computer on it. There were no posters or toys in the room. Becky noticed that one bed was neatly made up and the other was messy.

"Let me guess," Becky said.

"Yeah, it drives him crazy," Tabitha said. "That's probably why I don't make it."

"Do you get along?"

The girl in a grown woman's body shrugged. "We're different, so it's kinda hard sometimes."

Becky turned and faced the girl. "Did you hurt him?"

"No," the girl responded quickly and with more than a little outrage at the very idea of it. "I wouldn't hurt him. I won't let anyone else hurt him either."

"So, what aren't you telling me?"

"What? Nothing."

"Tabitha, I've been doing this a long time. And in my line of work, you get used to people lying to you. I can spot someone not coming clean a mile away. Why don't you tell me what's on your mind, and we'll keep it between us."

For a moment, the girl tried defiance, but it didn't hold up. Becky guessed that with good parents and the ease of being the best-looking person in almost any room, Tabitha didn't need to lie very often. She certainly didn't seem comfortable with conflict. After her moment of rebellion, she sighed and nodded.

"Fine, but you have to swear you didn't hear this from me," she said.

"What?" Becky asked.

"My mother would flip out," she said.

"Over what?"

Tabitha breathed a deep breath, then shook her head. "Truman had a friend."

"At school?"

"No, online. He liked to get onto the forums where he could talk via text. I think it made him feel normal. The people online didn't know he was… different."

"And he met someone?"

"I know he was messaging someone, usually at night. I heard him laughing. That's rare, I mean, really, really rare."

"Do you know who it was?"

She shook her head again. "I never asked, you know. I mean, we've all heard the warnings and the cautionary tales about trusting people online. It's my mother's biggest fear, and I should have told her, but he seemed so happy. I didn't want to ruin it. Besides, I didn't think he could get into trouble on the ship."

Becky felt a sinking sensation. She tapped her cufflink again and wondered what horrors lay ahead to be discovered in their search for the missing boy.

DAVE BANNON WAS TIRED, but he drank a cup of coffee before even reaching the office and, as soon as he was there, he brewed an entire pot. Then he settled into his desk. There was comfort in his space. The *Colossus* had equipped him with a state-of-the-art computer and a trio of displays. He booted up the computer and opened three separate apps on the three screens. One showed the surveillance video from the hallway outside the Arlington's berth. There were three patrolmen loitering in the hallway, waiting for orders. He couldn't see into the cabin, but he knew Sergeant Flint and Becky Nash were inside.

Becky was an excellent cop and a good partner. He had wondered about their compatibility at first. She was pretty, with dark skin and prominent cheekbones. Her hair was kept in long, thin braids, which were usually pulled back into a ponytail or neatly arranged on top of her head. He had thought at first that she might be a drama queen. But, it turned out, she was a workaholic just like he was. But they had different skill sets. Becky knew her way around a computer, but Dave was far more adept with technology. And Sergeant Flint knew Dave well enough to play to his strengths. Besides, Becky had a way of getting people to let their guard down. So, while she worked with people, he worked on the computer.

After Becky called him the first time, he logged into the ship's mainframe and started a search for Truman Arlington's messages. There were plenty to his schoolmates and parents, but nothing that seemed out of the ordinary. But then Becky reached out to him again.

"Dave?"

"Shoot," he said, his comlink synced to a small speaker on his desk that allowed him to continue working his computer controls while having a conversation.

"Our missing kid was having online conversations with someone."

"I've got lots of messages here, partner. Any idea what I'm looking for? A name, maybe."

There was some talk in the background, but then Becky said, "It was someone he met on a forum."

That was a good lead. Dave knew that people on the chat forums didn't use their regular names. They might use a portion of it, or a nickname, or something completely out in left field. He felt his chest tighten a bit at the prospect of trying to find out what the missing boy's handle was.

"He would have spoken to this person last night," she said.

"Alright, but the only messages under his name in the system last night were an email to his mother and a report to his history teacher."

"Anything out of place in the communication with the teacher?"

"Negative," Dave replied. "It's very pedestrian."

"Then we need to look somewhere else," Becky said.

"People use handles on the forums," Dave said. "Any idea what this kid might use?"

There was another pause, and some talking in the background, then Becky replied, "Try *Homo Veritas*."

Dave chuckled. He knew just enough Latin to get the connection. Homo for man, veritas was Latin for truth. Their subject's name was Truman, and after a quick search, a host of messages and emails for a user with the handle Homo Veritas came up.

"Bingo," Dave said. "Looks like he was chatting with someone by the name of *E Z Scroller*."

"Who comes up with these names?" Becky said.

"The virtual world is whatever you make of it," Dave said. "Let me scan through a few of these and see if I can make a connection to a real person on the ship."

"Copy that. I'll update Sergeant Flint."

Dave glanced at the screen that showed the hallway. He recognized Logan's long stride.

"Logan's at your location," Dave added.

"Thanks," Becky said. "I'll leave this channel open."

He did the same while he scanned a few of the messages. There was a lot of discussion about computer science. Most of it, Dave didn't understand, but he didn't need to have a grasp on every subject the two talked about. He was more interested in a few specific things. A few minutes later, Dave felt confident he had what he was looking for. And, as if his boss could read his mind, Sergeant Flint joined the comlink channel with Dave and Becky.

"Bannon, what have you got?"

"Lots of praise for the kid's computer IQ," Dave said. "No leads on who EZ Scroller is, but they are laying it on thick."

"What about a meet-up?"

"Yeah, there's talk of that, too," Dave said. "But no specific place is mentioned. The person our subject was talking to was encouraging Truman to meet them, but it doesn't say where. I'll have to keep digging for that."

"Is there the usual grooming behavior? Any request for photos or that sort of talk?"

"Actually, no," Dave said. "The suspect was stroking the boy's ego, but it's not the usual stuff. There's no talk of looks or acceptance, just a lot of praise for intellect."

"Keep digging. We need a name and a location," Flint said, before almost whispering, "time isn't on our side."

Dave Bannon wasn't a computer expert or a hacker. He didn't have programs for digging a person's identity out of cyberspace. But he understood that every person's IP address was linked to their physical location. There was no way to hide if you were jacked into the colony ship's network. So, he began there, searching the various locations where the elusive EZ Scroller messaged from.

As expected, the suspect moved from one place to another. The dining hall on deck seven, the recreation facility on deck seventeen, and several places in between. The suspect, trying to avoid revealing their true identity, never worked from their cabin, or any cabin for that matter. But Dave understood that the criminal's behavior was a mistake. There was no place to log into the ship's network that didn't have surveillance. Most of the places were busy with dozens, sometimes even hundreds of people in the same place. But he could pull up the video footage from the dining hall on deck seven, and the recreation facility on deck seventeen, and all the places in between. In each message's metadata was the time and date in which is was sent. So, with a little cyber sleuthing, Dave located the individual and then used the ship's geo- location info to discover his identity.

"His name is Norman Scarsdale," Dave told the group, which had been updated to include Logan. "He's a computer technician who works in the ship's communications department."

"You're sure?" Flint asked.

"Absolutely," Dave replied. "I tracked him down using IP data, then I had to follow him on surveillance. The guy was smart enough to shut his cufflink off when he was messaging, but there's no hiding from the eye in the sky."

"You sound like a super villain, bro," Logan said.

Dave leaned back in his chair and put his hands behind his head. "You're all just jealous of my detective skills."

"Where's his berth?" Flint insisted.

"He's got a private cabin on Deck nine. I can meet you there, but that's not where he's got the boy."

"What makes you say that?" Becky asked.

"Because the clues he left don't add up to a cabin," Dave said. "They were meeting at a secret place. I'll have to do some digging into the messages to figure it out."

"You do that. We'll search his berth," Flint said. "And Dave, good work."

"Thanks, boss. Not bad on two hours' sleep, huh?"

TWENTY-FOUR

LOGAN WAS DIVIDED. He wanted to be with Jeopardy. During the riot, his worst fears had been realized. She wasn't killed, but she had been hurt. When it happened, he hadn't been able to get to her. That's what really bothered him. He had failed. It didn't matter that fighting his way through the crowd was impossible. He couldn't have done it with a machine gun or even a flamethrower. He had been trapped in a confined space and there were simply too many people between him and Jeopardy when the fighting took place.

He had watched the surveillance footage. It shouldn't surprise him or anyone else that Jeopardy had saved Stu, or that Stu had fought like a savage to protect her. And yet, when it was all said and done, they had both nearly been killed. They would have been killed if not for Becky Nash showing up when she did with patrol officers in tow.

He had stayed in the hospital with her until she woke up. When she did, she was groggy from the pain meds. Seeing him, she asked if he was okay. He couldn't be sure if that was what she cared about most or if she was just being polite because he was there. But she had asked about him and that felt good. He knew the number of people who really cared about him was small. In their time together, since his own stint in the hospital, their relationship had grown. Still, he worried that he was merely a convenience for Jeopardy. Life on the *Colossus* had a way of making everything feel forced and temporary.

Once he assured her he was okay, she asked about Stu. There was no doubt that her concern for her K-9 partner was genuine. She was worried about his surgery and Logan promised to give her an update as soon as they knew more. But she had ordered him out of her room and out of the medical bay.

"Go… work…" she said in a weak voice.

"I want to stay with you."

"Can't… do anything…" she said. "I'll… just… sleep…"

And just like that, she faded into unconsciousness. Logan knew the power of the drugs that were used to stop the pain. They had made him feel like he didn't need to move for hours. The drugs cut through the pain and made him sleepy. Sometimes, they made him feel tingly all over or like an electric current was flowing through him. But mostly, they made him feel nothing at all and there was something very appealing in the nothingness. It was more than just a good feeling. It actually made him forget about all the normal things that usually crowded his mind and made him feel worried. Without that, a person could just float on the feel-good chemicals and maybe even just float away.

He didn't want to leave, but he knew his team needed him. They were all exhausted. It had been a long, long shift. Logan had fought hard and even killed a few passengers. That, he knew, would come back to haunt him. So, knowing that his time with the team was probably short, he reached out to Sergeant Flint, who told him about the missing boy.

Logan Keys was not a natural detective like Becky Nash. Plus, he didn't have computer skills like Dave Bannon. His gifts were more physical in nature. But he knew how to work cases and he could be tireless when the need arose. So, he pushed his fatigue away. It wasn't much different than running after a workout, going another round in the boxing ring. He simply told himself to do it and ignored what he felt. Pain was just a signal from his body to his brain, after all. At least that had been what he thought before he was stabbed. The knife wound had shown him what real pain was, the kind that didn't go away with an act of the will, the kind that left you weak and shaking in its terrible grip.

He moved up to the Arlington berth, and after checking in with Sergeant Flint, he paid his respects to Dr. Fiona Arlington. She worked in the medical center. Her speciality was general care, which meant dealing with people after surgery. He had argued with her a few times in his efforts to leave the medical facility early. She had been kind, but firm.

After meeting the family, he joined the SI squad on their way to the suspect's cabin on deck nine.

"What do you think?" Flint said as they waited for the elevator. "We gonna find this kid in the guy's cabin?"

"Doubtful," Becky said.

They knew they still had to search it. Norman Scarsdale's cufflink showed him in his residence, but the SI squad didn't expect him to actually be there. Nor did they need to discuss why the suspect would have lured Truman Arlington away. They had seen the horrors of pedophilia back on Earth. No matter how civilized and advanced they became as a people, there were still problems with lunatics who derived some type of pleasure from doing evil.

Logan was not a saint, but he was certain there was a devil and a host of demonic beings that were very much at work on Earth. It had been a little disheartening to discover that man's worst behavior had followed them to the *Colossus*. Their first missing person case had been of a teenage girl. They eventually found her body stuffed into the cooling system in one of the many engine compartments on the ship. She was frozen solid, as was the tiny embryo she had discovered just hours before her death. When Logan saw that, he knew nothing would change on the second planet mankind called home. It would buy them time, but the same faults and evils would follow them there. He would be needed to stand against the tide of darkness even on a brand new world.

"Let's do this by the book," Flint said as they rode down to deck nine. "I want body cams on when we go inside."

"Copy that," Logan said.

The unspoken reality was that the deaths during the riot were going to cost them. Not just the SIU, but law enforcement across the ship. Everything they did would be questioned. Decisions made in a split second that were often the difference between life and death for the officers involved would be judged more harshly because he had killed people. And Logan felt each death. Killing hadn't been his intention, despite the fact that it was almost certainly the intention of the people trying to reach him. He had reacted to the danger just the way he was trained. He put people down as quickly and as ruthlessly as possible. There would be idiots who tried to argue that Logan should have let the mob kill him rather than take the life of the people caught up in a violent frenzy. He knew that was idiocy and that those people who were rushing to hurt him would have continued on, hurting others once they were through with him. In fact, it could also be argued that, having killed Logan, their bloodlust would have only increased.

They took a moment in the corridor outside Norman Scarsdale's berth and drew their weapons. Flint looked at Becky and gave her the signal to unlock the door. Then he pointed at Logan and signaled for the younger man to follow his Sergeant into the home.

Everything happened fast. Becky overrode the lock on the door using the law enforcement commands on her cufflink. The door swished open and Sergeant Flint charged in. They all knew that in kidnapping cases, the faster they worked, the greater the odds of finding the missing person alive. But there wasn't much to see in the little cabin. It was only slightly larger than Logan's own and smelled of dirty laundry.

"Main room clear," Flint called out as he headed toward the bathroom. Logan knew that would be clear, too. He and Becky began searching.

There was a computer on the table in the main section of the small cabin. Despite having a private room, there were two recessed bunks. One was where Norman Scarsdale slept, the other was loaded with drawings and photos. Logan gave them a glance, then looked away. Most were technical in nature, schematics of the mainframe computer and various hardwired programs.

"Bathroom's clear," Flint said. "Search everything."

"We've got pictures and photos," Becky said. "It's not child pornography, but this guy's obviously got a screw loose."

"The computer is password protected," Logan said. "But take a look at this."

He held up a notebook. It had several pages of questions and answers scribbled in the spaces between.

"Looks like he's trying to hack the ship's surveillance system," Flint said.

"Is that possible?" Becky asked with a shudder."

"With computers, anything is possible," Flint said. "So, we have a guy with serious problems looking for a way to tap into the video feed from all over the ship."

"What for?" Logan said. "Is this a fetish or…"

No one wanted to admit that there could be another terrorist or assassin on the *Colossus*.

"Do you guys get the feeling that we were never supposed to reach Secundo?" Becky asked.

"It makes you wonder," Flint said. He tapped on his comlink. "Dave, we've got evidence here that Scarsdale was trying to hack into the ship's computer system."

"Makes sense from my end," Bannon replied. "Most of his

messaging is about computer stuff. It's not a manifesto, but there's enough chatter about the need to watch for more terrorist activity that I think we might be dealing with a vigilante."

"Not a terrorist?" Becky asked.

"You'll have to ask when you find him," Dave said. "This could all be a smoke screen. It's pretty hard to tell. But what he was after were ways to access the ship's higher systems remotely."

"He wanted Truman Arlington to help him do it?" Becky asked.

"Again, hard to say for certain, but it seems like Truman is the only person who was willing. And from what I've read, it wasn't about a noble cause for the kid. He was convinced he was helping Scarsdale to make the systems stronger."

"Playing to Truman's weakness," Becky said.

"But we're no closer to finding him," Logan said. "There's nothing here that gives us a clue."

SERGEANT FLINT KNEW that there were only so many places on the ship where a person might hack into the mainframe without attracting attention. But he was no computer expert. He could fill out a form and file a report, but when it came to most things electronic, he was a bit behind the times.

"What now?" Becky Nash asked.

"All we can do is look for them," Flint said. "It's possible they're working together."

"It's also possible that Scarsdale didn't realize the kid was mute," Logan pointed out. "That meet-up could have turned ugly."

"All the more reason to start looking," Flint said. "I'll send a report to the patrol officers to be on the lookout for Truman Arlington and Norman Scarsdale. I want the two of you to head up to the computer control section. My gut tells me that if they want to hack into the mainframe the probably need an access point."

"They can't do it remotely?" Becky asked.

"I suppose we should ask someone who knows," Flint said. "Get started. I'll have Dave coordinate from HQ. Once I get the BOLO to the rest of our people, I'm going back up to sit with the family. If you hear something or find anything at all, let me know."

"Will do," Becky said.

Logan nodded and the two of them hurried off. Flint took his time walking back to their offices. It was a good way to think. He had always been a pacer, but on the big ship, he could walk the corridors while his mind ran laps in his brain. And it helped that the passageways were empty. There was only the lightest foot traffic after the captain's mandatory curfew. Of course, there were essential services and work that had to be done. The passengers and crew in those areas were already being put back into service.

As Flint walked, his mind worked back through the facts. Police work was often a cerebral exercise. That wasn't the way it played out on television, but in reality, cops needed to be smarter than the criminals. The Arlington boy was communicating with Norman Scarsdale. The older man seemed to be in control, but it helped to consider all the possibilities when contemplating a crime. One couldn't simply assume to understand the criminal mind. Flint wasn't even sure he was chasing a criminal. It seemed more likely that Scarsdale and Truman Arlington saw themselves as vigilante heroes working behind the scenes to save the *Colossus*. Just as there were conspiracy theorists who promulgated the lie that there had been no bomb and it wasn't a terrorist plot, there were others who insisted that the ship's crew were in on the misdeed. It was surely being quietly spread around that the very people in power over the ship didn't want it to ever reach its destination. And even though they were passengers, Flint knew that there were some people on the *Colossus* who didn't believe Secundo existed or that the ship they were traveling on could reach speeds fast enough to carry them between star systems.

So, what if Scarsdale didn't lure Truman away to harm the boy, but so that they could work together? That made sense to Flint, not just because of what they had found in Scarsdale's berth, but because of Truman's mental limitations, and also because of the timing. It probably wasn't a coincidence that the pair had run away to carry out whatever plan they were hatching right when the ship's captain was exercising his most tyrannical control over the ship. Flint didn't think Captain Hastings was a tyrant any more than he thought the protesters were evil. They were both victims of their station on the ship. The passengers felt overwhelmed, frustrated and afraid because they had no real say in how things were done on the *Colossus*. Captain Hastings was a man used to giving commands and being obeyed. Having a ship full of unruly passengers was not something he had ever experienced before.

Flint was liking his theory, but doing his best to keep an open mind, when he reached SIU headquarters. He was just opening the door when he heard Dave shout, "Got you!"

"Got who?" Flint said.

"Oh, hey, Sarge, take a look at this," Dave Bannon said. "I've been going through the messages, but I set the ship's computer to search for Norman Scarsdale at the same time."

"We found his cufflink," Flint said. "He isn't wearing it."

"Right, but the ship also has facial recognition and behavioral trait identifiers," Dave said. "We know who we're looking for, so the ship just checked every person who passed in front of a surveillance camera."

"And?"

"And I found him," Dave said. "He's on deck eleven. He stepped out of a dead area for just a minute, but that was long enough. Probably didn't think he was in range of the nearest cameras, but we caught him."

"Where on eleven?" Flint asked as he tapped the transmit button on his cufflink so that he could speak to Becky and Logan.

"Port side, stern section delta," Dave said. "There's a big power substation down there that supplies electricity to the server farm."

"Good work," Flint said. "Becky, Logan, do you read me?"

"Loud and clear," Becky responded.

"The computer just spotted Norman Scarsdale on deck eleven," Flint said.

"We're on our way," Becky said.

"Keep me informed. I'll be there as soon as I get the BOLO sent out."

"I can do that for you, boss," Dave said.

"I've got it," Flint ordered. "You keep reading the messages. We have to know what they were up to."

Dave settled back at his desk as Flint went into his own office. Sending a ship-wide alert to be on the lookout or BOLO was simple enough. He was nearly finished when a knock at his door interrupted him. Flint looked up and saw the cheerful face of Lieutenant Tad Janson. Suddenly, Flint felt anything but cheerful.

"You're in, that's good," Janson declared. "I was afraid we might have to wait for you to return."

"We?" Flint said, standing up.

A woman with a stern face stepped in behind Janson. She had on a patrol officer jumpsuit complete with a thick belt and baton, but on her shoulders were the insignia of a sergeant.

"Yes," Janson said. "Sergeant Flint, meet Sergeant Moya Guavanna."

"It's a pleasure, I'm sure," Flint said. "Lieutenant, I'm sorry, but I'm pretty busy. We've got a missing teenager."

"Oh yes, I'm aware," Janson said. "But the Commissioner is a bit worried. He wasn't too happy with the way things were being handled with the SIU. There may need to be some changes."

Flint straightened. He felt as though he had been punched in the gut, even though he had already come to grips with the fact that he might be reassigned or relieved of duty altogether. But it seems he wasn't as prepared for that possibility as he thought.

"Sergeant Guavanna has experience that could be useful,"

Janson said. "She's been added to your team. I think it's best if she shadows you for now."

Flint rubbed his chin and tried to calm his boiling rage. He knew that in every crisis, someone had to be sacrificed so that the people actually responsible for the carnage could maintain their position and avoid any blame. He should have known he was the scapegoat for the protests. He was the head of the SIU, which was at the heart of the unrest on the ship as they searched for any other possible terrorists. But he had been so busy actually doing his job that it never crossed his mind. It didn't matter that the orders to carry out the searches on passenger cabins had come from his superiors. They could still point to him and say the way he carried out their orders was the real problem.

Janson didn't seem to notice the look of stony rage on Flint's face or perhaps he just didn't care. "There will be a few other additions, I'm sure. We're compiling candidates now," Janson continued. "But don't worry, they'll all be solid. Okay, well, that's all for now. I'll let the two of you get acquainted."

Flint didn't say a word as Lieutenant Janson, head of LEO personnel, left his small office. Sergeant Moya Guavanna stood in the doorway staring at him. When Flint had collected himself, he spoke to her.

"You have experience investigating?" he asked.

"Si, I was an inspector in Madrid before being selected for the colony," she said with a thick accent.

"Alright," Flint said. "I'm sending out a BOLO, then heading down to deck eleven, where the suspect we're after was spotted. You can tag along, if you like."

She didn't say anything, but gave a tiny nod to acknowledge that she had heard him. Flint sat down, finished creating the announcement and then sent it out to every member of law enforcement on the ship.

"That's done," he said. "Let's get moving."

"Si," Guavanna said. "You lead, I follow."

If only that were true, Flint thought. He took a deep breath and blew it out, trying to release his stress with it. But it was a futile gesture. The truth was he loved his job and couldn't imagine giving it up. It took all his mental fortitude to push down the tsunami of emotions racing through his mind. But he did it because there was a child to find and, until that job was done, nothing else mattered.

TWENTY-SIX

WHILE THE SIU searched for the missing teen, another crime was taking place. JD and his lieutenants had brought along a harem of sorts, nearly sixty women all told. They were all from the same neighborhood back on Earth, although diverse in their ethnicity and, according to the ship's records, they hailed from all over the United States. They each had simple jobs on the ship and shared cabins. It was all arranged by Crank, who had hacked into the lottery system back on Earth and then the *Colossus* computer system, the very first day he had been brought on board. The women understood that they had traded all their rights for passage on the Secundo. When the GKs called on them, for any reason, they had no choice but to respond.

Slash was the lieutenant in charge of the women. He dropped by unannounced and kept tabs on them. When it was necessary to pimp them out, he was the guy doing it. The gang wasn't pushing prostitution on the ship the way they had back on Earth, but it was still a valuable commodity that was used to help further their interests. Several of the women had been used to get the banking VPs into precarious positions and even to record the men in ways they would never want others to know.

One of the women was named Felicia Rojas. It was inevitable that the women would eventually fall prey to the temptation to have a relationship outside of the gang. Slash was just surprised it hadn't happened sooner, but he had been expecting it. What he hadn't expected was that Felicia Rojas would fall for a man like Mike Banister.

They met on the job. Felicia's on-board vocation involved cleaning and refilling the drink dispensers within a set area of the ship. The dispensers were linked to the ship's water supply and used a variety of powders and syrups to make the various drinks. Twice a week, each machine was put through a cleaning cycle, then flushed with clean water, to make sure it was sanitary for the hundreds of people who would use the device each day. Mike Banister was part of the ship's maintenance division. His specialty was looking after small appliances in the culinary sections. And so, when one of the drink dispensers stopped working correctly, Mike met Felicia and made repairs to the device. There was instant attraction between the two of them. Felicia didn't have a lot of freedom to move around the ship. She was supposed to stay on the same deck as her cabin when she wasn't working. The gang wanted her available at all times. But when Mike asked her on a date, she took a chance.

All the girls knew the rules. They were property of the Ghetto Kings, a designation which came with some perks. They were provided for, not just on the *Colossus* but back in the old neighborhood too. They were protected as well. To harm one of the GK girls was a direct attack on the gang, which would be met with immediate and harsh retribution. In the hierarchy of life on the street, the GK girls were above the prospects and in many ways equal to the street thugs. In exchange for such provision, protection and social standing, they did whatever they were told with whoever they were told to do it. Some were prostituted out, others were kept for the more powerful members of the gang. Of the fifty-eight women the GKs had brought on board, twenty-seven of them were reserved for JD. They had no other duties other than to satisfy the gang leader's every desire. Sometimes that meant cooking or cleaning, but more often their role was more physical in nature.

Of the thirty-one other girls, anything was possible. They were called on by the four lieutenants often and for various reasons. When they weren't needed, they could do what they wanted within certain limits. Foremost among their boundaries was engaging in relationships with men outside the gang. Felicia knew the rule, but after weeks filled with nothing but work and sitting around in her cabin waiting for a call she never wanted to get, Felicia decided to take a chance.

Had Mike Banister been a player, their dalliance might have slipped under the radar. But Mike wasn't looking for a hookup and had no designs on simply seducing Felicia. In fact, right from the outset, Mike Banister felt a deep connection with her and wanted to know everything about her. Their date on Topdeck went well and led to more meetings closer to their cabins. It helped that they were both living on the same level of the ship. Soon, they were having every meal together in the dining hall, and Felicia was slipping out of her cabin almost daily to stay with Mike.

At first, the other girls kept quiet and even covered for Felicia with Slash. They all expected the relationship to burn out fast. But it didn't. After a few weeks, Mike was certain he had found his soul mate after Felicia came clean to Mike about everything involving her life with the GKs and how she ended up on the *Colossus*. And so it was, despite the captain's curfew, that Slash went to the cabin shared by Felicia and another GK girl named Mona Siddiq.

"Where's Felicia?" Slash asked.

"Not here," Mona said.

"I can see that," Slash said. "She supposed to be. You gonna tell me where she is or do I need to convince you?"

Mona shook her head. There were times when partying with

Slash was all fun and games, but every woman who met him knew he was dangerous. While Mona might have tried to cover for her roommate under different circumstances, she could feel the threat radiating from Slash like heat from the sun. She liked Felicia, but she wasn't willing to take a beating for her. Besides, Mona knew that Slash would get the information he wanted, either way.

"She's with her boo," Mona said.

"Her what?" Slash shouted.

He had rushed at Mona, who was already pressed against the wall. There was no escape from the violent man. She turned away and Slash was so close to her that she felt his hot breath on her cheek.

"She been seeing a guy named Mike," Mona said. "She's with him."

"Where?" Slash asked.

"Four-oh-nine," Mona said. "Down by the laundry."

"This deck?"

Mona nodded, still not looking at the man. She felt him step away.

"How long?"

"A few weeks."

"And you didn't tell me?"

"I didn't think it would last this long," Mona said.

The violence she knew was coming was quick. He grabbed her throat in one hand and in doing bounced her head against the wall. It hurt and her entire body tensed up. When he spoke, he was so close his lips brushed against her ear.

"You lyin' to me, Mona, I'm gonna make you regret it."

"I ain't," she said, already crying.

Slash slapped her backside. It wasn't a playful gesture. The blow was powerful, lifting her off her feet for a second and sending her sprawling into the table. But she expected more. She expected to find him on top of her, his weight pressing her down and making it hard to breathe. Instead, he walked out. Mona collapsed to the floor, crying and trembling all over. She knew things would be worse for Felicia.

Slash didn't wear his cufflink. That was back at his cabin. He wore a counterfeit device that showed him as crewman Antonio Jones of systems control. It gave him access to most of the spaces on the ship, save for the command center. While he wasn't actually on the ship's crew, if he had been questioned - perhaps by a patrol officer - it would have shown that he had an essential function and, therefore, the right to be out during the curfew.

But no one stopped him or questioned him. He passed two pairs of patrol officers at different times during his trek toward cabin four-oh-nine, but he didn't fit the BOLO they were on the lookout for. Slash arrived at the room he was seeking and pressed the button on the controls that alerted the people inside that someone was at the door.

The people inside were Mike, Felicia, and Morris Wiley. They were gathered at the little table in the cabin, playing cards. When the chime sounded, Mike got up. He went to the door and answered it calmly.

"Help you?" He asked.

"I'm here for Felicia," Slash said. "Be back for you, later."

Mike and Felicia had already discussed the issue. She knew what was coming. She had tried to convince Mike that he should let her go. Mike, already in love with her, wouldn't hear it. He was not a pushover. Mike Banister was twenty-five years old and had been a starter on his college football team until his knee buckled the wrong way and ended his athletic career. It had cost him his scholarship as well, but Mike didn't mind. He had no dreams of going pro. He had only tolerated school for the chance to play ball. It took a year to rehab his knee and, during that time, he got a vocational degree and landed a good job with full benefits and a salary that was more than most college grads earned. He also continued to work out. His six-foot-four-inch frame filled the door of the cabin. He had a barrel-shaped chest and thick legs. Slash, on the other hand, was five feet nine inches tall. He weighed one hundred and sixty pounds, though it was all wiry muscle. Speed was his advantage in a fight and he had no qualms about using whatever he needed to get the job done.

"She don't belong to you," Mike said. "Not anymore. You got a problem with that, you deal with me."

Slash did have a problem, but he needed to get out of the corridor where the surveillance cameras were recording his every move.

"Alright, but I need to speak to her," Slash said. "Let me in, I'll have my say, then I'll be gone."

If Mike had a sense that Slash was lying to him, the temptation to break the gang's hold over Felicia was too good to pass up. Besides, he would be with her and able to protect her. So, Mike did the one thing he never should have done. He stepped backward and let Slash into his berth.

Slash came in and closed the door behind him. Things inside berth four-oh-nine on deck fifteen went from bad to worse more swiftly than anyone thought possible.

DAVE BANNON HEARD everything that went down with Sergeant Flint and Lieutenant Janson. He was bothered and a little frightened by it. Dave had known Sawyer Flint a long time. They had worked cases together on Earth, and getting asked to join the SIU on the *Colossus* was a huge compliment that had literally changed his life. On Earth, he could have retired after twenty years and taken a private security job or gone the full thirty with the East Coast Metro PD and then piddled with a hobby or two. It would have been a fine life, but the chance to join the colony on Secundo opened up a host of opportunities that were completely out of reach on Earth.

And the truth was, since coming aboard the *Colossus*, Dave had bonded with the squad. He didn't make friends very easily, yet the job was a bond he counted on. There were plenty of recreational distractions on the colony ship, and lots of pretty people too, but real friends were hard to come by and Dave was certain that Jeopardy, Logan, and Becky would be his friends for life. Dave felt the same way about Sergeant Flint. It angered him that the brass would step in and replace the SIU's senior person. It also frightened him to think that other members of their team might get transferred or removed from duty. He was the only person in the squad who hadn't been directly involved in the riot. It wasn't lost on Dave that people had died. There would need to be consequences, but Dave was also convinced that the fault for what had happened lay squarely on the shoulders of the protesters.

While Flint finished up the BOLO, Dave sent a private message to Becky. He was keenly aware that everything he said or wrote could be accessed just the way he was accessing the messages between Truman Arlington and Norman Scarsdale. So, he kept his message neutral enough that it wouldn't get him in trouble down the road.

Heads up, he typed on his cufflink, *Sarge has a new shadow, per orders from LT Janson.*

They didn't often send text messages to one another. Dave chose to do it that way in order to quietly transmit the information, but also because he assumed that Becky would realize the need to keep their thoughts about the situation private.

A few seconds later, there was an acknowledgement that she had seen the message, but no direct reply. Dave was fine with that. The smaller the paper trail, the better in his mind.

"Dave," Flint said as he left his office. "Anything new?"

"No, sir," Dave replied. "They haven't come out of the dead space on deck eleven."

"We're heading down there," Flint said. "This is Sergeant Guavanna. She'll be working with us for a while."

"It's a pleasure," Dave said.

"Detective Dave Bannon has been running the computer side of things," Flint told his new shadow. "Let's add her to the group comlink channel."

"Right away," Dave said.

The woman said nothing. Dave wondered why she was so openly hostile and guessed she had worked Internal Affairs back on Earth. He would take a look at her personnel file later, but first, there was a child to find.

Dave didn't like missing person cases. In his opinion, they carried too much pressure. A robbery could sometimes result in recovering missing goods, but despite the mental anguish, most of the time, the victims could rely on insurance to cover the loss. But a missing person couldn't be replaced. And while it could be argued that a kidnap victim was better off than a straight-up murder, as far as the police were concerned, a murder was much easier to deal with. In his career, Dave had worked several dozen missing persons cases. Half were elderly people who were usually disoriented and lost due to declining mental acuity. Most of the others were children. Domestic kidnapping was a problem back on Earth. But there were a few cases, some of children, some of young women, that were like scars on his psyche. He recalled working around the clock in the hopes of finding the victim, only to be hours, and sometimes minutes, too late. Others were clearly victims of terrible crimes, but there wasn't enough evidence to track the person responsible down. Those missing persons remained missing, their families never getting closure, the open wound festering day after day. Those types of cases took a toll on everyone involved.

As Dave scanned the communications between Truman and Scarsdale, two things were apparent. The first was that Truman was probably a savant in computer engineering. The technical information was way over Dave's head, and from the messaging, he guessed it was over Scarsdale's, too. The other thing that was becoming clear was that Scarsdale had convinced Truman that only the two of them could save the ship. There were clear signs of grooming and gaslighting, but not in the usual way. Scarsdale wasn't a deviant who planned to abuse Truman. He was a conspiracy believer who seemed to be acting from delusions of grandeur.

Dave was just about to report his findings to Sergeant Flint via the comlink when a strange woman walked into the SIU office. She was short, thin, with silky black hair cut in a bob, and she carried a briefcase-sized object with hardened plastic on the outside. Her outfit was the standard jumpsuit most people wore. Her's was baggy on her slender frame, and navy blue with stripes on the shoulders. She seemed a little surprised to see him.

"Can I help you?" Dave asked.

"This is the SIU?"

"Yes, I'm Detective Bannon."

"Oh, good," the woman said, sounding relieved but still looking around as if she were searching for something.

"And you are?"

"Chief Bright, CC division."

"Is there some problem down in Computer Control?"

"I was told to expect some," she said, setting down her case on the desk opposite from Dave's. "Someone's hacking the ship's systems, I think."

"That desk is taken," Dave said, knowing Becky rarely used it, but still not wanting to give ground to the stranger, especially after what Lieutenant Janson had done to Sergeant Flint.

"It's only temporary," the woman said. She was still looking around as if she were thinking about what she might change in the SIU bullpen.

"Why are you here? We're in the middle of a case."

"That's right. I'm here to help you."

"I don't think we need any help."

"I was told you didn't have a computer specialist."

"We don't, but I know my way around the system."

"You work on it, but I built it," the woman said. "I prefer to be called Edge, but we can stick with protocol if you prefer it."

"Edge is fine. I'm Dave."

"It's a pleasure, Dave. Tell me what you've found."

"We've got a missing teenager. He's autistic and maybe a savant."

"Right, I know about Homo Veritas. I take it he wasn't kidnapped by some pervert?"

"No," Dave said, his mind still spinning. "I've been reading their messages. A man named Norman Scarsdale has been asking all sorts of questions about the ship's computer system."

"Never heard of him."

"He's using the handle EZ Scroller."

She laughed. It was a bright, happy sound, and despite himself, Dave couldn't help but smile.

"That's hilarious," she said. "EZ Scroller, what a buffoon."

"He seems pretty intent," Dave said. "They want to piggyback on the ship's surveillance system."

"Impossible," Edge said. "We're monitoring the system at all times. If there were hackers, we would know it."

"There are," Dave said. "The assassins who tried to kill Everett Goddard hacked their way onto the ship. We also know the terrorist Titus Russel hacked several cufflinks."

"Right, but they didn't infiltrate the ship's operating system, which is what a person would have to do to get access to the restricted programs like surveillance. Anyone with a computer and access to the information network could slip into the logistic files and make a few changes. That entire division is overworked and understaffed."

"If they can get into logistics, what's to stop them from getting into life support or the navigation system?"

"Me," Edge said as she opened her case. Inside was a portable computer. She pulled out a power cable and plugged it in.

"You're cyber security?"

"I'm a jack of all trades, really," Edge said. "I have a PhD in computer engineering, with an emphasis on operating systems. The *Colossus* is a closed system, sort of like a wheel. The mainframe is the central hub and the spokes are the different divisions within the Computer Controls. Sure, there are people up on the Bridge *flying*," she used air quotes when she said it, "the ship. But let's be real. The computer is doing the heavy lifting. It computes ten thousand variables every second so that when the pilot moves the controls, this enormous ship actually does what he wants. I mean, think about the size of this vessel. It's just too big for a person to mentally understand how the mass is affected by gravitational forces.

"And then there's the systems within the ship that everyone is counting on to stay alive. From clean water to breathable air, even the artificial gravity that is essential to the passengers and crew, it's all controlled by the computer."

"Which you control?"

"I don't control it, I nurture it," Edge said.

"It's not alive," Dave argued.

"It's a living system, the way that the U.S. Constitution is a living document. No, it isn't organic or sentient, but it's constantly changing. My job is sort of like a gardener. I prune it, fertilize it and direct its growth so that it can be as fruitful as possible for the half a million people who are depending on it every hour of every day."

"Man, that's some ego," Dave said.

"You scoff because you don't understand it," She insisted. "That's okay, most people don't. You take it for granted, like so many other things in your life."

"I don't need a sermon, lady. My job is to find a missing kid."

"And my job is to ensure that whatever that kid is doing doesn't kill us all," she said. "And I could use a cup of coffee."

Dave had already brewed a pot. He didn't want to admit it, and he certainly didn't want to get her any, but there was no way around it.

"We don't have lattes here," he said.

"Good, I like drip coffee. I'll take mine black."

"It's pretty strong," Dave warned her."

"The stronger the better," she said as she connected a hardline into the computer interface on Becky's desk.

Dave walked over and poured her a cup of coffee. When he handed it to her, she stopped typing for a second, took a sip, then nodded. "Approved."

Dave wanted to tell her he didn't need her approval, but she was already back to work. Her fingers flew over the keyboard and, despite himself, he felt a sliver of admiration for her. She certainly took no guff and didn't let anyone intimidate her.

"How you brew coffee is important," she said without looking up. "It says a lot about a person. You made this?"

"Yeah," Dave said. "We've been working pretty much non-stop. I'm operating on just a couple hours of sleep."

"Oh, wow, I'm sorry," Edge said. "Feel free to catch a quick nap. I'll wake you if you're needed."

He felt his resentment building up again, yet decided to ignore her. He activated his comlink and transmitted to Sergeant Flint.

"Sir, I have an update for you."

"Go," Flint said.

Dave glanced at Edge, who didn't look up from her computer screen. He moved slightly so he could see what she was doing. The entire screen was filled with computer code. Dave could operate programs, but he didn't write code and he certainly couldn't read it.

"Sir, the overwhelming majority of the messages make it clear that Scarsdale was grooming Truman to hack into the ship's mainframe."

"Actually, that would be the operating system," Edge said. "The mainframe is the hardware. You would have to get into the central computer control center, which is highly restricted."

"Who's that?" Flint demanded.

"Sir, a computer specialist is here in the office. Chief Bright is trying to help us."

"Good," Flint said, which Dave hadn't expected and didn't agree with. "We're sweeping the dead space on deck eleven. Not much luck though."

"They wouldn't go there," Edge said. "Not if they want to hack surveillance."

"The servers are there," Dave reminded her.

"True, and a big shadow zone where the electromagnetic frequency would keep them from wireless access to the system," she responded.

"Maybe they jacked in."

"There isn't a good place to do that down on eleven," she said. "If it were me, I would search the systems control area on Topdeck. They've got six floors of the Armstrong building. It's essential work, but only about half of the available consoles are being used at any one time. Homo Veritas could be hiding in plain sight."

"Sir, did you hear all that?" Dave asked.

"I did. Is the surveillance system still scanning for our people?"

"It is."

"Would it catch them where the computer specialist suggested?"

"On the way to and from that area, it would," Edge said. "But there isn't any surveillance in the system control area. It's limited to the ship's crew."

"Get up there and check it out, Bannon. Keep me posted," Flint ordered.

"Copy that, Sarge," Dave said. "I'm adding Chief Bright to the comlink channel. If you need computer help, she'll have to do it."

He tried to give her a smug look but she didn't glance up from her computer screen. Dave stood waiting for a second, then, feeling deflated, left the SIU headquarters and the enigmatic woman behind.

CHAPTER
TWENTY-EIGHT

MAYBE MIKE BANISTER expected the punch, or maybe he didn't; no one ever got the chance to ask him. Slash got his name because he hit hard and fast and moved away before his opponent could retaliate, which was what he did to Mike Banister. The smaller man lashed out, driving his right hand in an open palm strike with his entire body. It reminded Felicia of a snake striking a victim. And just like a snake, Slash had a pointed metal spike fixed to a thin sheath under his wrist. When he pulled his hand back, the spike extended, turning what would have been a simple palm strike to the chin into a devastating wound to his throat. The metal spike penetrated through the soft flesh, past the muscle, and straight into Mike Banister's windpipe. He staggered back, choking on his own blood.

Felicia leaped to her feet only to be struck down by a wicked backhand from Slash. She screamed and hit the deck as Slash turned back to the man who dared to take from him. That was how the gangster saw things. To him, Felicia was property. It didn't matter that she was a person who could make decisions about what she wanted and didn't want. Or that she had fallen in love with a man outside the gang. To Slash, Mike Banister was stealing, and there was only one way to deal with such an outrage.

As Mike leaned forward, trying to clear his throat, Slash struck again using the same spike and open hand. His palm hit the larger man's forehead, but the spike pierced through his eyelid and punctured his eyeball. Mike Banister's scream was more of a desperate gurgle. At his feet, Felicia was bleeding from a cut on her cheek. One of her eyes was already swelling shut. Still, she found the strength to grab Slash by the leg. He looked down and cursed her. Lifting his free leg to stomp down on the wayward whore, he was caught completely off guard when Mike's roommate, Morris Wiley, snatched up a metal water container, the kind used for keeping one's beverage cold, and swung it at Slash's head. The metal container connected with force and split the skin on Slash's forehead right above his brow. The skin gaped open as the Slash fell backward and blood gushed into his eye.

Mike Banister was on his knees, one hand on his wounded eye, the other covering the wound in his throat. Felicia crawled to him. "Baby," she said, barely getting the word out around her sobs. "Oh, baby."

Slash hit the floor, rolled instantly to his knees, and shook his head. Blood spattered across the deck.

"Now, you done it," he snarled, looking up at the trio with his face full of gore. "Now I'ma kill you all."

"Call for help, Felicia," Morris said.

He was a heavy machinery mechanic, shorter even than Slash, and with small, almost delicate hands which could reach deep into the big mechanisms he worked on. He stepped over Felicia just as Slash got back to his feet. If the blow from the metal container had hurt Slash, he didn't show it. Growing up on the streets, to show weakness was to invite death. The gangster's head felt like a giant bell and the hammer was falling with every beat of his heart. But all

Slash could think of was murder. To him, killing was as easy as breathing.

Morris and Slash brawled in the narrow space between where the other two lay on the floor and the door to the cabin. It was no boxing match, and there was no strategy other than to beat the other person down. Both men landed blows. They hit one another with closed fists as the blood flew between them. Slash landed a hard shot straight into Morris' nose, which crushed the cartilage and sent blood pouring from both nostrils. Morris countered with a punch to Slash's wounded eye. There was so much blood on the gangster's face from the gash that he never saw the blow. It landed hard, turning the killer's head, but he immediately bounced back. Most of their shots missed. Punches glanced off shoulders and grazed the side of each man's head. A few hit the chest, but it was an uppercut from Morris that landed squarely. The punch was so hard it broke several of the small bones in the mechanic's hand and caused Slash to bite through his tongue. He staggered back, and Morris moved in for the kill, but Slash swiped at him with his hand pulled back. The spike stabbed into the side of Morris' face and ripped through his upper lip, gouging the gums and knocking several teeth loose.

It was Morris' turn to stagger back, and he tripped over Felicia. Anything can happen in a fight. Luck, good or bad, always plays a part. Morris fell backward, unable to slow himself before his head struck the side of the metal table that was part of the furniture built into the small cabin. The impact knocked him unconscious and fractured his skull. Internal bleeding immediately began to put pressure on his brain, and within half a minute, the inside of his head grew so tight that the vessels supplying blood and oxygen to his most vital organ were pinched off.

Slash moved forward, reaching for Felicia, but Mike launched himself toward the gangster. Under different circumstances, and with medical help, he would have survived the initial wounds he suffered. But the big man drove himself straight into Slash, tacking him just as he had been taught playing football. They went crashing into the door, which pinned Slash down, but didn't stop him from extending his spike and stabbing through the bigger man's ear. The weapon fit easily through the auditory opening, punctured his eardrum and tore through the inner ear before lodging deep in Mike's brain. He spasmed all over, his large body shaking hard while simultaneously heaving up the contents of his stomach and soiling himself as his bowels released.

Slash shoved the big man's body, already dead, off him just in time to have Felicia leap on him. She had found the metal container. It was a tall cylinder with a plastic flip-top cap. It held twenty-four ounces of fluid inside the metal, double-walled insulation. There was a rubber ring around the bottom, but it did nothing to soften the blows that Felicia rained down on his head. The metal was a little stronger than the bone of Slash's skull. Felicia hit him over and over, using all her strength, fueled by rage. The skin broke, blood flew first, then bone and, eventually, gray matter. It spattered the walls and the door.

When she pulled back in exhaustion from her efforts, the other three occupants of cabin four-oh-nine were dead. Felicia fell onto her back. She knew she needed help, but all she could do was breathe deep, ragged breaths between the sobs that would not stop. From a young age, she had been discouraged from dreaming. Hope was hard in the hood and she had stopped expecting much of life. Meeting Mike Banister had been like learning to breathe again. Her deeply held beliefs about what her life would be, had given way to a future she could scarcely imagine. Love had found her. It had revived her wounded heart and eased the pain of past memories of which she was deeply ashamed. On Earth, she had done what was necessary, no matter how vile, to survive. On the *Colossus*, she had found love and acceptance. Joy had flooded the dark corners of her mind and lifted her out of the mire of fear she had been trapped in.

But it had all been taken from her in an instant. The pain of her loss, not just the man she had grown to love, but the future she had begun to hope for, was too terrible to accept. The crushing weight of her misery, along with the pain of her injury and the exhaustion from killing Slash, swept her away to unconsciousness before she could even call for help.

TWENTY-NINE

FINDING lost things was part of the job. It was a bit like looking for one's keys, only with more pressure on the results, and oftentimes more danger to the searcher. Becky Nash was a searcher by nature. She could never let a mystery go unsolved and helping people was something she enjoyed. Her job brought her endless opportunities to feel like she was making a difference in the world. Unfortunately, she was no longer in the world, but on a colony ship hurtling between star systems and things were different in space.

As they moved down the corridor toward the server compartment on deck eleven, her cufflink buzzed. She glanced at the message and tapped the acknowledgement icon just before they crossed into the dead space, and no more messages could get through. She felt a rising tide of frustration. It really wasn't much different than the protesting passengers felt. If they took policing away from her, she didn't know if she could go on. She loved her job, but in the end, she had no control over it.

"You okay?" Logan said. "You kind of stiffened up back there when you got that message."

"Yeah, I'm okay," Becky lied. "But you should know, the brass is probably going to replace Sergeant Flint."

"What?"

"They've already got someone shadowing him. Better prepare for the worst. We'll probably all be scrubbing toilets before long."

"Damn, it's over the riots, huh? It's my fault. I'll tell them that."

"It's not your fault," Becky said. "You couldn't just let them kill you. We did our job, you, me, Jeopardy, even Stu. But that doesn't matter now. It's all about the optics, you know. Doesn't matter that the protesters attacked you or that they trapped you in a cabin and were trying to kill you."

Logan shook his head. "I'm sorry, though."

"Don't be. I probably would have resigned in protest if they pinned it all on Sergeant Flint anyway. Who knows, in fifteen months we'll be free on a new world with no more rules."

"There's always rules," Logan said.

"I guess you're right. But we can't worry about it now," she said as they approached a side corridor that went around the back of the server compartment. "We've got a kid to find."

"Let's do it," Logan said. "Might as well go out on top."

Becky feared they might not ever find the boy and the mystery of it might haunt her for the rest of her life. But all she could do was try her best. That wasn't nothing.

"You go right, I'll go left," Becky said.

"Got it," Logan said.

They were in the dead zone, and both of them drew their weapons. It didn't matter what they thought of Norman Scarsdale or his motives for luring a teenage boy away from his family. It was a crime and criminals had to be dealt with in a decisive fashion. What a law enforcement officer could never do was to drop their guard around a suspect and allow that person to put them in danger. Becky would search for Truman and his abductor because that was who she was, but she would do it carefully and armed for battle.

Deck eleven, like all the other decks below the highest level, was made up of compartments. Long rows of cabins were built around larger spaces that contained the machines that powered the ship and made it livable. Even larger spaces were packed with vital equipment, food, supplies for the colonies and the stored belongings of the passengers. Each floor was like a maze, and the ship's many mechanisms, from the computer servers to the various components of the power system, created electromagnetic fields that interfered with the ship's wireless information network. That network was the life force of most of the ship's many support systems, including the vital surveillance program.

Becky went quickly down the corridor. It was not one of the wider main thoroughfares and was just about deserted. She checked every compartment along the way. Any people she met, she gave close scrutiny before waving them on with her free hand. There was no checking in with her partner or supervisor. As long as she was in the dead zone near the server hub, she was on her own.

She hadn't known what to expect when she found the suspect. In most cases, they either froze in fear or fought her. What Becky found was just a door that wouldn't open. Using her law enforcement override, she could hear the locking mechanism disengaging, but the door didn't open. She holstered her pistol and pushed on the door. Like most hatches in the ship, it was a thin, metal door that slid on a track into the wall when open. She couldn't push it in or pull it out, but she leaned into it, trying to slide it open. It moved a few inches, but when she stopped pushing, it snapped closed.

Frustration was setting in. Could Truman Arlington be on the other side of the door? It was possible. It was also possible that while she fought with the door that didn't want to open, Norman Scarsdale could be doing any sort of nefarious thing to the autistic teen.

"Hey!" Logan called as he jogged toward her up the long hallway. "You find something?"

While she had been wrestling with the door, he had circled around to her side of the compartment they had split up to search.

"Maybe," Becky said. "This door won't open. It could be broken."

"Or our suspect could have it jammed," he said as he reached her. "Let me try."

"Wait," Becky said. "I can get it open an inch or so. When I do, get your fingers in the gap and see if we can pull it open."

Logan nodded, and Becky turned back to the door. She could feel the sweat popping out on her back as she pushed against the door. Suddenly, her coat seemed like too much clothing. The *Colossus* was a cool vessel, which was understandable considering how cold space was. Her coat was both a garment to keep her warm and useful in concealing her weapons.

"Got it," Logan said. He leaned back and heaved. The door opened nearly eighteen inches. "Hang on," he said as he pivoted around and stuck himself in the gap. When he pushed from that position, the door slowly opened all the way.

Becky drew her pistol and ducked in under his arm. The compartment wasn't very large. There were rows of server racks and fat wads of thick cables that ran up into the ceiling. The computer servers looked like black boxes with just a few golden yellow lights on the front. Each was the size of a briefcase. They were mounted with the wide side horizontal so that several could be stacked on top of one another. Between them were thin, metal tubes that zigged and zagged, pumping a compressed chemical that was far below freezing. In the ceiling between the cable hubs were large fans. Some blew down and others sucked the excess air upward. It made the room much colder than the corridor outside.

"Chilly," Logan said, moving up beside her and drawing his pistol. A cloud of condensation puffed from his mouth like smoke when he talked.

Becky held up two fingers and motioned for him to go left. She moved right. The compartment was full of racks that were loaded with servers. She felt the power even in the cold room. Fortunately, she didn't have to go far. Normal Scarsdale was sitting on the floor in the back corner.

"Norman, get your hands up," Becky ordered. "You make any sudden movements and you're a dead man."

It was not a legitimate threat. She had no means to kill him, but he didn't know her pistol was non-lethal. He slowly raised his hands. It was her first good look at the man and she felt she could tell a lot about a person that way. Looking at photos was different; they were a moment in time, often posed to bring out what the photographer or the subject wanted people to think when they saw it. But seeing a person face-to-face left nothing out.

Norman Scarsdale was pale, with short hair and fingernails that were too long. His clothes were dirty and looked as though he hadn't changed them in weeks. He had raised his hands but he rubbed his face against one sleeve and then the other. She noticed dandruff flakes on his shoulders and red marks on his neck from where he had been scratching himself. She had seen similar indications in homeless people. No one on the *Colossus* was homeless. And Normal Scarsdale was smart enough to use a computer and find a naive victim in the online chatrooms.

"You're too late," he said.

"Logan, I've got Scarsdale," she called out.

"Copy, on my way," he replied.

"Your fascist regime is crumbling," Scarsdale said. "The truth will be told."

Logan came from the back side of the compartment, sidling between two server racks with a set of plastic hand restraints ready.

"What is this loon talking about?" he asked.

"Beats me," Becky said. She was getting serious vibes that Norman Scarsdale had suffered a mental break with reality. Back on

Earth, they would call in a mental health professional, but with Scarsdale being their only link to a missing teen, he was probably staring at a very uncomfortable interrogation.

"You're agents of an authoritarian dictatorship," Scarsdale said. "I can't believe they've got even their stormtroopers duped. Open your eyes!"

"How 'bout you just shut your mouth," Logan said, pushing Scarsdale against the wall. "You got anything on that might hurt me?"

"Just a free mind," he said.

"Good one," Becky said. "If you're so convinced this is all just a trick to make you someone's slave, why'd you come?"

"I had to," Scarsdale said as Logan patted him down. "I was destined to be the shoe thrown into the machine."

"The what?" Logan asked.

"He's referring to sabotage," Becky said. "A long time ago, workers would throw their wooden shoes called *sabots* into the machinery during the industrial revolution as a form of protest during labor disputes. I'm pretty sure that it isn't true, though."

"Wooden shoes sound pretty hard on the feet," Logan said as he pulled Scarsdale's hands behind his back and tightened the plastic restraints around his wrists.

"Where's Truman Arlington?" Becky asked.

"I don't know anyone by that name," Scarsdale said.

"The boy. The fourteen-year-old you lured away from his family."

"I did no such thing," Scarsdale said.

"So, what are you doing in here?" Logan asked.

"Nothing," he said in an almost petulant tone. "I have to get out from under the tyrant's thumb to make my plans."

"Plans for what?" Becky asked.

"Revolution," Norman Scarsdale declared. "We're going to change things. We're going to make things right."

"Who's we?" Detective Nash asked.

Norman shut his mouth and frowned. His lips pressed hard together until they were white.

"Let's get him out of here."

They escorted their prisoner out of the server room and back toward the main corridor. When they reached it, they found Sergeant Flint and his new shadow, Sergeant Moya Guavenna, moving quickly toward them.

"You found him?" Flint called out.

"Scarsdale, but not the kid," Becky said.

Flint walked right up to Scarsdale and took hold of the collar of the smaller man's coat. "Where's Truman?"

"I don't know anyone by that name," Norman insisted.

"Try Homo Veritas," Flint said. "You know anyone by that name?"

Norman's lips pressed together again.

"You can tell me now and pray he's not hurt when we find him," Flint said. "You're looking at a lot of trouble, Scarsdale. There's no getting out of it now. Cooperate and maybe you'll buy some good favor with the judge."

"Maybe you'll get to serve out your sentence on Secundo," Becky added.

Norman laughed. "You really think we'll ever reach Secundo? You are the blind leading the blind. But not me. I know the truth."

"What's the truth?" Flint asked.

"This is all just an experiment," Scarsdale said. "We were tricked into giving up our liberty. There is no planet. There will be no colony. Sooner or later, the powers — I mean the real powers, not you, you're just pawns — will pull the plug and we'll all be dead."

"Neat," Flint said. "I'll take this numbskull back to HQ and alert the Commissioner. You two keep searching for the kid."

"Yeah," Becky said. "He has to be around here somewhere."

She did her best to stay positive, but in the back of her mind, she feared something terrible had happened to Truman. Her confidence that they would ever find him was dwindling. It seemed like no matter how hard they tried, evil triumphed on the *Colossus*. All she and her fellow law enforcement officers could do was clean up the mess that was left behind.

CHAPTER
THIRTY

WHEN DAVE REACHED the Armstrong building, the rest of the SI squad had Scarsdale in custody. He rode the elevator up to the fifth floor with a feeling that he was on a wild goose chase. When the elevator door opened, he found himself in a vestibule that was lined with snack machines and beverage dispensers. There were several small groups of people clustered together, some getting refreshments, others just talking. Coffee seemed to be the beverage option of choice, while adding creamer and sugar took on an art form with the software engineers.

"Hi," Dave said. "I'm Detective Bannon, SIU. I'm looking for this boy. Have you seen him?"

He held up his cufflink for people to see the photo displayed on it. The people in the break room shook their heads and went back to their own conversations. It seemed that missing teens wasn't interesting enough for the IT crowd.

Dave toggled on his comlink. "Edge, are you sure about this?"

"Absolutely," she replied.

"I just met some of the workers. They showed no interest."

"Exactly," Edge said. "That's why it's the perfect place to hide the missing boy."

Sergeant Flint broke into their conversation. "I'm not sure I'd say this guy has the brains for that kind of reasoning. Scarsdale is having trouble with his grip on reality."

"Just go in and search the cubicles," Edge urged. "It's worth a shot."

"On my way," Dave said.

Every level on the ship was a giant maze, but the computer control rooms in the Armstrong building were no better. Dave spent nearly twenty minutes meandering through the desks and looking at the workers. Most of them didn't even look up at him, and none asked who he was or what he was doing in the restricted space.

It was faster to take the stairs up to the sixth floor, which he did. It was identical to the fifth down to the groups of people in the area beside the elevators. Dave asked them if they had seen Truman, but no one had. He took his time searching the entire work area. He could see how a person could effectively hide among all the workers. Each cubicle had a desk with a computer, but it was the tall sides of each cubicle that gave the worker a sense of privacy. Dave didn't mind intruding. A few people told him to beat it, even though most never even looked up from what they were doing.

The urge to give up was strong, but Dave believed in being thorough. Good police work often came down to doing the grunt work that didn't seem important. It was where breaks were made and connections established. It wasn't glamorous; it was vital. And so, he pressed on to the seventh floor, found no help with the workers in the break area and searched the work stations.

Truman Arlington was in a tan jumpsuit just like all the other crew members. It was too big and the hat he wore with the bill pulled down over his face may have thrown off the ship's feature recognition, but it set off alarm bells for Dave Bannon. As a patrolman, he had learned to spot the ways in which a person tried to hide their face. Hoodies, hats and even wigs were often employed, yet it wasn't just the headwear. The real clue was in how they wore things. Truman's hat was pulled low, and he leaned forward with his chest against the edge of the desk, and his rear stuck out at an angle most adults never used. His hands were delicate but agile as they moved over the keys. Dave moved past him, then called in the find.

"Sergeant Flint, I think I found him," Dave said. "Should I move in?"

"Yes," Flint said. "Is he hurt?"

"No, sir, I don't think so."

Dave went back to the cubicle. He stood there for a second or two until Truman stopped typing.

"Hey there, Truman," Dave said. "You okay?

The boy's shoulders pinched together slightly when Dave said his name, but he nodded.

"You've got a lot of people worried. We need to take you home. Is that okay?"

Truman shook his head and then reached out and tapped the edge of the display. Dave wasn't sure exactly what he was seeing. Like Chief Brighton back at SIU headquarters, Truman's monitor showed lines of code. But he had one line highlighted and he seemed concerned.

"Okay, let's see what you're working on."

Dave leaned forward. He couldn't understand it, although Edge came to his rescue.

"Officer Bannon," she said. "What console is Truman at?"

Dave glanced around and saw a small number in white on the corner of the computer's monitor. He read it off to her.

"I think it's seven-two-two," he said.

"Alright… give me a second… Got it. I'm screen mirroring his computer… that's…" she laughed nervously. "That's not right. He's in the OS code."

"I have no idea what that means," Dave admitted.

"It means…" he could hear her typing. "Oh, no, that's… that's impossible."

"We have the boy, and we have control of his computer station," Flint said. "I'll alert the family. Dave, can you escort him down to his parents?"

"Yes, of course," Dave said. He knelt down and turned Truman's chair so that the teenager was facing him. He looked young for his age and a bit frightened with his hat pulled so low. He didn't meet Dave's gaze and the detective didn't force it. "Hey, Truman, the best computer engineer on the ship is taking over for you. She found what you were showing us. That was good work."

Dave didn't know if the highlight was something he had done or something he had found. The computer skills were beyond him, but his people skills were good enough to recognize that the teenager wanted it found. Truman nodded and rocked back and forth in his seat a little.

"It's time to get you home. Your parents are pretty worried," Dave said. "Can I take you back down to them?"

Another nod and Truman stood up. Dave activated his comlink. "Truman and I are on our way back to his berth," Dave said.

"Excellent work, Detective. When you're through with the family, head down and try to find Becky and Logan. They're in a dead area on deck eleven. I'll send the coordinates."

"Copy that," Dave said, careful not to make any sudden movements or make Truman feel crowded. He was no expert in dealing with autism, but he knew to be careful.

When they got back to his cabin, they found his parents in the corridor waiting for him. They ran to meet him. Only his mother dared hug the teenager. He stiffened but didn't resist. He also didn't hug her back, which Dave noticed. Truman's father was crying and the family thanked him repeatedly.

"It really wasn't me," he admitted. "Someone else made the call;

I just did the legwork. I'm guessing we'll need to question Truman soon, but for now, he can stay where he belongs."

"Is he in trouble, officer?" Mr. Arlington asked.

"That, I don't know," Dave said. "He might be. Like I said, we'll be in touch."

He shook hands with Mr. Arlington and hurried out to find Becky and Logan, but by that time, they had come back into radio contact, and Sergeant Flint ordered them all back to HQ.

"THIS IS A DUPLICATE ORDER," said Chief Bright, whose given name was Lavonne.

"I don't know what that means," Sergeant Flint said. It had become something of a mantra as Edge explained what Truman had found.

"It's a command that creates a mirror image of everything that comes after," she said. "That mirror image gives someone control over the system. Someone who is not us. Someone not even in our section of the ship, most likely."

"I thought they had to be connected to hack in," Dave said.

"So did I," she said. "I never imagined this. It's really quite brilliant. They must have created it before coming on board. I wrote the operating system on Earth in what was supposed to be a secure lab. Obviously not. With this in place, a person could jack into any station, in any cabin or compartment of the ship and build out the duplicate. The only restraint would be the need for a powerful workstation. Not something anyone has clearance for on the *Colossus*.

"Can I just say this is insane?" Becky complained. "I mean, really, how many crises do we have to face on this voyage?"

"Are you people always so emotional?" Moya asked Flint.

The Sergeant thought that Becky might leap over her desk and throttle the Spaniard, but Becky managed to keep her composure.

"It's not emotion," Flint said. "It's passion for the job."

"So, what kind of danger are we looking at?" Logan asked. "Is someone sabotaging the ship?"

"Actually, no," Edge said calmly. "I'm now into their side of the operating system. Everything they've done is recorded, stroke for stroke. There's no evidence that they're writing anything in the command systems. In fact, the only systems on our side they've hacked are the logistics/personnel module and the surveillance network. They changed room assignments and job assignments for about sixty-five people."

"So, it's an organized group," Flint said. "Can you put it up on the display screen?"

"Let me help," Dave said.

"Alright, here's what I have so far," Edge said. "Five passengers have been given special treatment. The others have been modified, but not by much. They're all still working and participating in their responsibilities."

"We'll need to know who they are," Flint said. "Right now, I'm more concerned with what they're doing."

"That was my concern, too," Edge said. "So, I did a run through the entire system. The only other hack was in the banking system. They're siphoning money from the transaction fees."

"They're stealing money?" Becky asked.

"A lot of it," Edge said. "And since the system is blockchain, we can follow the money. It's going to a holding account. It's not visible unless you dig for it, but it's there. They've racked up millions so far."

"Where's it going from there?" Flint asked.

"It's not," Edge said. "The perpetrators aren't stupid. They're stealing yet keeping it all together. I'm not a finance person, but my guess is they'll let it build up all the way to Secundo, then leave the ship as billionaires."

"Won't it just be discovered then?" Dave asked.

"You would have to ask the banking people," Edge said.

"Let's not do that," Flint replied. "It's time to dig in, people. We need to know who's involved in this heist and what they're plotting. If they have sixty people on the ship, it's not just a crime of desperation. They're organized, smart and resourceful. We have to make sure we get ahead of them before they find out we're even aware that they exist."

Moya pulled Sergeant Flint aside. "It's time we push this up the chain of command," she insisted.

"They will want answers, not theories," Flint said.

"If what they've found is real, how we proceed is not our call to make."

"It's not?" Flint asked. "We're the Special Investigations Unit, Sergeant. Our job is to dig into these matters and find answers, not just point out problems and wait for someone to tell us what to do about it."

"It's that kind of cavalier attitude that got you into trouble," she said, her accent making her sound harsh. "I would expect no less from an American, but then, perhaps you are not the best candidate for this job."

Flint felt the heat rising in his face. He preferred to keep his emotions private, but Sergeant Guavanna questioning him and passing judgment on his motivations without even knowing him was hard to take.

"If you want to inform the brass, go right ahead," he said in a quiet voice. "I suppose that's what you're here for anyway."

She frowned, although she didn't argue. Criminals all claimed to hate rats and snitches, but when push came to shove, most succumbed to the temptation to lessen their discomfort by revealing all they knew about other criminals. The old saying that misery loves company was proved true in police stations every single day. Flint knew the police were just as passionate in their hatred for whistleblowers and officers who carried complaints up the chain of command. Still, in every class of new recruits, there were people who felt it was their duty to report on their fellow officers. Most were recruited into the Internal Affairs Division. Not that Flint supported dirty cops, but he wasn't the type who believed his way was the only right way. He had learned too much from officers who did things in a completely different fashion.

Still, he knew of cops who were more interested in gaining favor with their superiors than in police work. They were usually quick to run to the boss with any information or even rumors about their fellow cops, no matter the damage. He was getting those vibes from Moya Guavanna.

"You sure we shouldn't alert the bank execs?" Becky asked Flint. "It's their money that's being stolen."

"If they don't already know about it, then a few more days won't hurt," Flint said. "And if the thieves are sophisticated enough to hack into the computer system, then they've probably got eyes and ears on the banking people. I would."

"You've got a point," Becky said.

She returned to her desk and helped the others looking into the hack. It was a bit like trying to unravel a wad of delicate thread. They could see that a wrong color had been tangled up, but getting it straightened out again wasn't easy. It took work, with each detail needing to be checked and rechecked. It was a little surprising to have an outsider leading the charge, but Chief Bright was smart. More importantly, having developed the operating system, she understood it better than any of the people in the SIU.

Moya stepped into his office and actually closed the door before reaching out to their superiors. He found it to be almost infuriating to have her in his space, even though he knew there was nothing he could do about it. She was Commissioner Forrest's pick to spy on him and nothing would be denied to her. He could boss her around and be mean, but it wouldn't help his cause. So, while he felt attacked and betrayed by his superiors, his duty was to the passengers and crew of the *Colossus*. There was still a crime being committed against them and it was his job to put an end to it. As long as he had the badge, that was exactly what he planned to do.

"YOU LOOK CONCERNED," JD said, sliding onto the edge of Everett Goddard's desk.

"I am," the bank president said with a shake of his head. "Captain Hastings just informed me that someone has hacked into the ship's computer system."

JD raised his eyebrows as if he were surprised. It was a gesture he had noticed people make. On the streets, a captain never showed surprise or emotion. He had to maintain the illusion that he was always ahead of everyone else. But in learning to insinuate himself with Everett Goddard, he was doing his best to play the part of a businessman.

He had intended to provide something for Goddard that would incriminate him. His lieutenants had already done that with the banking VPs. Crank had all the evidence they would need to keep those men silent and willing to agree to anything the Ghetto Kings wanted. But Everett was a harder nut to crack. What do you provide for the man who's been rich all his life? He already had any and every thing he desired. In a way, his wealth insulated him. But JD wasn't giving up. He had simply changed tactics. If he couldn't catch the financial wizard in a compromising situation, he would become his closest friend. He found that a person could be just as influential as a trusted counselor ... as he could be with blackmail.

"That sounds bad," JD said. "I thought the system was hack-proof."

"That's what we were told," Everett said. "Just another empty promise. Of course, the bank is the target. They've already stolen millions. How that slipped past us I cannot imagine."

JD knew. His lieutenants had threatened Goddard's underlings, therefore they turned a blind eye to the theft. Besides, it wasn't their money that was being stolen. It was the bank's money, just a tiny bit of the constant stream of income that was flowing into the organization.

"When things are working, people rarely consider the possibility that something might be wrong," JD said.

"Of course, you're right. But we'll have to do a full audit. Everything is blockchain, so we'll follow the trail. I should have insisted on bringing along cyber security experts, but I was promised the ship's IT people could handle it."

"Hey, brother, don't beat yourself up over it," JD said. It turned his stomach to call the rich white man his brother, but if there was one thing all the money in the world couldn't buy, it was genuine friendship. JD was playing the part of a wealthy man who was impressed by Goddard's financial acumen, but not jealous of it. Nor was he the type that needed Goddard to pay for everything. JD was rich. Crank had worked his computer magic and moved digital funds from all over the world into JD's account on the *Colossus*. But the gang needed more than money; they needed influence and control. Which was exactly why JD was playing Everett Godard, even to the point of pretending they were as close as brothers.

"It infuriates me," he said. "People like you and me give up so much in service to others, only to have lowlifes always looking to take what we've earned."

JD didn't think Everett Goddard, who had been born rich, had earned anything at all. And it chafed to be called a lowlife, when he could see no difference between himself and the rich fools on the *Colossus* who were just playing games all the time. Relationships, business deals, affairs, purchasing rare items just to show them off. It was all a big illusion. The elites were just people and no better than the Ghetto Kings.

"You'll get it back," JD said. "To me, that's always been the difference between us and everyone else."

"How's that?" Everett asked.

"We have the means to get what was taken back from those who took it," he said.

The bank president gave an appreciative nod at that idea.

"Look, if you need me, I'm here for you," JD told him.

"No, no, of course not. The police, I mean, the law enforcement division, are onto the thieves. They'll handle it."

"Good," JD lied. "I've got a few things to do before the party tonight."

"You'll make it, right? An old friend is preparing dinner. She's an excellent chef."

"Wouldn't miss it," JD assured him with a pat on the banker's shoulder.

He stood up, straightened his suit jacket and then walked out. JD had become a regular in the banking offices. Everyone knew him by his false identity, Julius Descarte. He was the man who had saved Everett Goddard's life. That had not been part of the plan, but it had worked to JD's advantage. He had been chummy with Everett long enough to know that the man was private and had a natural distrust for people he didn't know. Getting close to him any other way would have been more difficult than he planned. Yet everything had worked out. In fact, JD had begun to think that he could have what he wanted without his lackeys. The GK lieutenants he had brought along on the voyage were his closest allies, although JD never let his guard down around them. He might pretend to, but his paranoia was high and he secretly questioned every move they made. Crank was the only member of his crew that he really trusted and then only because the pitifully awkward hacker owed his entire life to JD.

Yet, despite everything that he had done for his crew, they had failed him. The plot to steal a fortune on the way to their new home had been discovered. But JD didn't need that money. He already had several hundred million at his disposal as Julius Descarte. It had been his players who needed to steal more. Not because they didn't have small fortunes in their false names, but because that was all they knew. JD could get what he wanted without them and that was becoming the best option.

He didn't rush to his cabin. There was no need for desperation. Crank hadn't alerted him to the danger, which meant the police weren't far enough along to tie anything to him. Crank was the only link, and, despite their years of close association, JD felt no kinship or affection for the hacker. He changed out of his expensive suit and into a simple tracksuit. He packed a duffel bag so that he looked like anyone who might be headed to work out at one of the ship's many training facilities. He removed his cufflink and put it on the charging station. Then he strapped on a different cufflink, one with an alias he had yet to use. With the cufflink in place, but not yet activated, he left his cabin and went back up to Topdeck. He activated the counterfeit cufflink on the Tube platform, then took the zero-gravity train around to the far side of the ship.

A few minutes later, he was outside Crank's door. JD glanced down at the improvised weapon in his open gym bag. It was a simple device, just a metal tube, barely larger in diameter than a drinking straw. Attached to one end was a small canister of compressed air. Loaded into the tube was a slug made of soft metal. He could hold and fire the weapon with one hand. It was a one-shot device that was only effective at close range, but it would serve his purpose with Crank just fine.

The door opened and the hacker stood just inside looking more and more like a destitute beggar than a rich gangster. The smell of body odor was strong in the cabin.

"What up, dog?" JD said. "Let me in."

"Sure," Crank said, stepping back.

The small cabin was dirty, with trash piling up and dirty clothing littered on the floor. None of the lights were on except a tiny desk lamp near his bank of computer monitors.

"What's up?" The hacker asked.

"Got news, yo. Got news. You need a honey to clean this crib up, dog."

"Yeah," Crank said.

JD would have normally ordered it to happen. He would periodically send a few GK girls to look after the pitifully awkward hacker who could work wonders on the computer but couldn't pick up his own clothes off the floor. But there was no need for that now, not with what JD had planned.

"What have you got going?" JD asked.

Crank shrugged and went back to his desk. "Same ole, same ole," he said.

"Yeah?" JD told Crank as he walked into the dark cabin and the door shut behind him. "I think I found a way to make it all work out just like we planned."

"Had to be something that dude was into," Crank said, referring to Everett Goddard.

"You know it," JD told him as he withdrew the tube.

In the dark, and standing behind Crank, the hacker had no idea what his boss was doing. JD held the device in a casual way, looking over Crank's shoulder. On the monitors were several video feeds from various surveillance cameras around the ship, but none from the secret cameras that Crank had installed. Those he kept hidden.

"How's our money?"

"Growing. We should have several billion by the time we reach Secundo."

"Enough to set us all up for life," JD said.

"Exactly," the hacker said, fully convinced that he was giving his superior what he wanted.

In reality, both men were lying. Both had secret ambitions and neither was trustworthy. Crank had secretly recorded JD and had incriminating evidence that he was the mastermind behind the stolen funds. That information was on an unsecured drive that was plugged into his old school laptop computer, which Crank used as a cover for the powerful machine he had built.

Behind him, JD felt no guilt or remorse at what he was preparing to do. Crank, like every person in JD's life, served a purpose. When they failed to serve that purpose, or he no longer needed that service, they could be dispatched. He had no sense of value in anyone's life but his own.

"You do good work, Crank," JD said as he raised the device and pointed it at the back of the hacker's head.

It fired with a *~Thoomp!~* sound that wasn't very loud. The bullet smashed into the back of Crank's head, splitting the skin open and smashing through his skull. It expanded as it ripped through the soft tissue of his brain, then hit the front of his skull hard enough that his right eye popped free and dangled down his face. The bullet didn't hit the eye and had lost sufficient force to break through the front of his skull. Instead, it broke apart and bounced back through his brain matter.

Crank slumped forward, his head, sans one eye, bounced onto the controls for his computer. JD stepped back and turned on the light above the small kitchen sink. He inspected the front of his outfit. The tracksuit was crimson in color and any blood spatter blended in. He would need to dispose of the clothing, but until he could, nothing would attract undue attention.

JD found the plug for the sink and began running water into it.

From his duffel bag, he retrieved a small vial of hydrochloric acid that he had smuggled onto the ship inside a container of shaving cream. He opened the vial and poured it slowly into the water. That done, he turned back to the desk and retrieved the old laptop. He ripped out the connections, including the unsecured flash drive. It was a simple mistake, but one that would come back to haunt him.

JD slid the computer into the water, which was made highly corrosive by the hydrochloric acid. It began to bubble and, convinced that he had destroyed any evidence linking him to the hacker, JD left. Eventually, he would need to do the same with his lieutenants, but he wanted to space their deaths out so as not to attract attention. He had a small kit with several poisons and drugs that would end a life without drawing the attention of the authorities. His plan was well underway and soon he would be free to fully assume his new life. It was all he had wanted since the opportunity to join the voyage to Secundo had arisen. All that was left to do was seize his place in the new world, which he intended to do forcefully. He had escaped the neighborhood and risen above the ghetto he had been born into. Soon, he would take his place with the aristocracy on a new planet. He would establish his legacy on the blood of lesser men, but hadn't that been the way of great leaders throughout history? He thought so and the irony of it made him smile.

"WE'VE GOT A CALL," Flint said, stepping out of his office. "How's the search going?"

"We're close," Becky said.

"Edge is a genius," Logan said.

"The person who hacked us built some defenses, but they're coming down," Edge said. "I should have something solid in a couple of hours."

"Until then, let's head down to sixteen," Flint said. "Becky, Logan, with me. Dave, you stay and help Edge."

Dave responded with thumbs up.

"What's the call?" Becky asked.

"Patrol responded to a report of a dark liquid at the base of a door," Flint said. "There's no response from inside the berth. The fluid looks like blood."

"Did they open it up?" Logan asked.

"No, I told them to wait on us," Flint said, looking over at Moya Guavanna as he spoke. "We're the investigative unit for the entire ship, after all."

Moya didn't respond and Becky felt a pang of sadness for her boss. It was mixed with trepidation. She hadn't killed anyone in the riot, but she had been involved. In her opinion, any incident of violence against a member of law enforcement has the very likely outcome of someone getting killed. She certainly didn't blame Logan. Having been at the scene and seeing what was taking place, she felt completely justified in the use of force against the protesters. Even though she doubted other civilians felt the same way. The police were supposed to protect and serve, not kill. That power was reserved for judges and juries. Still, it angered her to see Sergeant Flint being flanked by the stern-faced outsider.

They made their way to cabin four-two-two on deck sixteen without incident. When they arrived, a small area had been cordoned off with tall, lightweight panels that were meant to keep the civilians passing by from seeing the carnage. There were three patrol officers outside the cordoned area. They waved the rubber-necking passersby on down the corridor.

Becky followed Sergeants Flint and Guavanna into the area. Logan stayed by the narrow opening so that he didn't crowd the others in the tiny space. A patrol officer was standing by the door controls. There was blood in the track of the door, and a little had spilled over into a puddle just outside.

"Any updates?" Flint asked the patrolman.

"No, sir, we identified the blood, brought in the security barriers and waited for you. I will say this, the amount of blood seems to be slowly increasing."

"Good work," Flint said. "Join the others outside the barrier, please."

With a few taps on his cufflink, Sergeant Flint overrode the door's lock. It slid open, and the body that was propped against it thumped onto the deck.

"*¡Dios mío en el cielo!*" Moya said.

"Four bodies," Becky said. She had discovered early in her career that it was easier to deal with human carnage by taking a clinical approach.

"Let's check for vitals," Flint said.

He and Becky moved forward. For the first time since being assigned to him, Moya didn't try to stay beside him. She waited outside the cabin with her hand in a fist, which she placed over her mouth.

"You okay, Sergeant?" Logan asked her.

She gave a curt nod, but it was wholly unconvincing.

"Unresponsive," Becky said. "Logan, we're going to need medical down here."

"On it," he responded, typing the emergency call into his cufflink.

"No pulse here either," Flint said.

Becky moved to the next body. It was a female. She was breathing, but unconscious.

"She's alive," Becky said.

"Looks to be the only one," Flint said, standing up. He pointed at the table. There were playing cards on the surface.

"You think their game turned violent?" He asked.

"It's possible," Becky said. "I don't see any money, though."

Money on the ship was digital, but when people gambled, they used plastic chips or some other item to substitute for currency. She had seen potato chips, dry beans, even candy being used. But there was no sign that the people playing cards were doing so for money.

"Let's check identities. The patrol officers should know whose cabin this is."

The start of any crime investigation was the gathering of information. Sometimes it was evidence, and other times it was more basic, such as identities and ownership. If a body was found in a vehicle, the police needed to identify the victim and the owner of the vehicle. If they weren't the same, it was important to start connecting the two.

"I've got a Michael Banister, a Morris Wiley, and the guy in the crew uniform is coming up as Pedro Scott."

"Pedro?" Logan asked.

"Yeah, that's what's on his cufflink," Becky said.

The patrolman in charge had already checked the ship's records to discover who was assigned to berth four-two-two on deck sixteen.

"Wiley and Banister are assigned to that cabin," he said.

"Surprise, surprise," Logan remarked. "Pedro is out of place."

"In more ways than one," Becky said. "Our female victim is registered as Felicia Rojas."

"Sending it all up to HQ," Logan said. "Dave is running checks."

"Med team is here," the patrolman outside the cordoned area said.

The next half hour was instructive. Felicia came to. She was concussed and clearly grieving. Becky questioned her, but she refused to talk and the medical technicians weren't helpful. Still, Becky got the feeling in her gut that Felicia was like a thousand other girls she had met on the streets.

"She's a culinary worker," Logan said. "Lives on this deck. Her job was servicing the beverage dispensers in a given area. Your two roommates were in mechanical. Wiley was a big machine mechanic, and Banister was a small appliance tech."

"Small appliance, as in beverage dispensers?"

"That would be the case," Logan said with a grin. "Probably the most likely connection."

"So, Rojas and Banister meet on the job. They start seeing each other."

"Which doesn't make our man Pedro too happy," Logan said.

"Three homicides as a result of a lovers' quarrel?" Becky wondered. "That seems extreme."

"I don't know," Logan countered. "Pedro shows up to confront Felicia. Her man, Banister, steps in, and the rest is history. Seen it a thousand times."

"So have I, but what I don't get is the shiv and the false uniform."

"Maybe Pedro is a bad guy," Logan said.

"There aren't supposed to be gang bangers on this ship."

"Not supposed to be, and not, are two different things," Logan said.

Dave was still in the SIU offices with Edge, but he spoke up via their comlink. "Hey, guys, I traced your man Pedro back to a berth on deck eight. It belongs to a specialist named Malcolm Bennet. There's no record of a Pedro Scott on the ship's list of berths, but he is listed as a maintenance supervisor."

"A crewman with no berth?" Becky asked.

"Yeah, it set off our alarm bells up here. Edge ran Malcom's info. Get this, he's one of the five men involved in the OS hack that doesn't have an assigned job on the ship."

"Get out of here," Becky said.

"We're still sorting out a lot of stuff with the hack, but that much is clear."

Becky looked at Logan.

"This could break it all open," he said.

"But she won't talk to us," Becky said.

"Leave that to me," he said. "There's an empty bed in Jeopardy's room."

"Is she up for that?"

"Wounded, drugged, confined to a bed and she'll still get it done," Logan said. "She'll be mad if we don't let her do it."

"Fine by me," Becky said. "But don't tell Flint until she gets us something."

"You think he'll object?"

"Not him, his shadow," Becky said. "No sense letting her sabotage this investigation."

Logan nodded. Most cops were protective of their own. They stood shoulder to shoulder against the bad guys, but when Internal

Affairs got involved, they would circle the wagons. There was a natural distrust of the people willing to investigate the officers putting their lives on the line every single day. They would all admit that it was needed. Every good cop hated dirty cops. But they hated IA almost as much.

While Logan took care of managing Felicia Rojas' placement in the medical bay, and Sergeant Flint continued to work the crime scene, Becky made her way up to deck eight. By the time she reached Malcolm Bennet's berth, Dave had confirmed via facial recognition that Pedro was Malcolm.

"It's a private room, no surprise there," Dave said. "Be careful, though."

"Will do," Becky said as she buzzed the alert button on the door's controls. There was no answer from inside. She rang again, but when no one answered, she unlocked the door and went inside. The cabin was spacious, one of the two-bedroom berths normally occupied by small families. It had the small sitting area near the entertainment console, a round table, and a mini-kitchen. There were also two bedrooms, one primary, the other with a pair of bunks.

As she stepped inside, she knew instantly that she wasn't alone.

"Law enforcement," she said in a loud voice as she drew her sidearm. Becky held it against her chest with her index finger straight across the trigger guard. "Come out with your hands where I can see them."

Two women in slinky nightgowns emerged from the room with two bunks. They each had a blanket around their shoulders and frightened expressions. Neither wore their cufflinks.

"Over here," Becky said, waving to the small sofa with her pistol. "Have a seat. You have anything that might hurt me?"

The women did as they were told and shook their heads. Becky patted them down, then stood across from them.

"Names?" She demanded.

The women glanced at each other and shook their heads.

"Look, I know a few things. One is that this isn't your berth, which means that during the curfew, you aren't supposed to be here. Two, you're without your cufflinks, which is against the ship's bylaws. I can take you both in for that alone. And three, Malcolm, or Pedro, or whatever his name really is, can't hurt you. He's dead. Someone bashed his brains out down on deck sixteen. So, you can talk to me here and tell me what I want to know, or I'll run you in and let you work your way through the legal system."

The girls looked at one another again, then the shorter of the two said, "Slash."

"What?" Becky said.

"Slash was his name."

"Slash? Who's he affiliated with?"

"GK's," the taller girl said.

"Ghetto Kings, East Coast," the shorter girl said.

Becky felt as if she had been slapped in the face. Throughout her entire career, she had dealt with gangs. Three-quarters of all the violence in the East Coast Megalopolis involved street gangs, but she had thought that the criminal elements had been left behind when the *Colossus* left the Sol system for Secundo.

"Is he the shot caller?" Becky asked.

The girls wouldn't answer, which was a clear sign that Pedro wasn't at the top of the GK hierarchy.

"And you're his girls?" Becky continued to question them.

"We service the crew," the shorter one said.

"Just the two of you?"

The girls shook their heads.

"How many girls are there?"

They both shrugged.

"Do you know Felicia Rojas?"

The shorter girl shook her head, but the taller one spoke up. "Yeah, I know her."

"She's one of you?"

A nod.

"And Slash went to get her back from Michael Banister?"

They both shrugged, but Becky didn't need them to explain things. She had worked gangs long enough to know how the various people involved were expected to act. A girl claimed by a gang wasn't supposed to fall for someone outside the gang. She had seen innocent people killed for that very reason many times. In most instances, those cases never got solved. She might know who did the deed, but tying them to the killing with evidence was difficult. The only thing harder was convincing witnesses to come forward.

She called a pair of patrol officers to escort the women up to SIU headquarters. They would be held there for questioning and, meanwhile, Becky searched the domicile. She found an expensive video game system, a closet of name-brand clothes, and cabinets full of junk food and liquor. In that aspect, it was a bachelor's apartment. But among the clothes and shoes, she also found a pouch with a set of knives made of composite materials that wouldn't set off metal detectors. Plus, a long, thick blade that was made of polished obsidian.

There was no doubt they were onto the bad guys, but they needed more information. Becky relayed her findings to the group and headed to the SIU offices to compose her report.

In the medical bay, Felicia was given a full exam, with multiple brain scans. Her only injury was the blow to her face, which had left a severe contusion on her cheekbone and caused swelling of her eye until it would no longer open. The doctors and nurses diagnosed her with a concussion and put a cold pack across her bruised face before administering a sedative to calm her nerves from the grief. Unlike law enforcement, they had no judgment of who she was. To them, she was a patient whose boyfriend had been murdered right in front of her. So, they treated her as such, before moving her into the room with Jeopardy.

The K-9 Officer was perched on her side to keep pressure off the laceration, which was recently stitched up with over a hundred sutures. She was on painkillers, which made her drowsy, but when Logan reached her, she understood the opportunity they had to get information from Felicia. It might not hold up in a court of law, but the ultimate goal was to find and stop the hacker and his associates, before they did any real damage to the ship's computer or banking systems.

When the nurse left, it was Jeopardy who struck up a conversation.

"Hey, what happened to you?"

Felicia turned and looked at Jeopardy with half-closed eyes and a blank expression on her face. Jeopardy hoped the medical staff hadn't given her too much of the sedative. They wanted to help her cope with the grief, not put her into a coma.

"My man did this," Jeopardy said, pointing to her face, which was bruised. There was still dried blood around her nostrils and along a nasty split in her lower lip. "Said I was cheating, but I ain't never cheated, not even in school."

"Bastards," Felicia said quietly.

"They can be, huh? I hear that some men don't smack their women around, but I ain't met one of those yet."

"I did," Felicia said as a fat tear escaped.

"You better hang onto him with both hands... both legs too," Jeopardy said with a drug-addled chuckle.

"Wish I could," Felicia said. "He died fighting for me."

"Oh, girl, that's terrible," Jeopardy said. "What happened?"

Felicia told her. Maybe she felt safe with the stranger in the hospital room, or maybe it was due to the drugs, but she laid out the entire story, starting with how she met Mike, right up to the savage fight in his cabin. Jeopardy wasn't wearing a wire, but the medical bay had a dictation system built in. Doctors used it to make notes about their patients, but it could also be used to allow law enforcement to listen in on a conversation. Back in SIU headquarters, Logan and Dave wore headphones to listen in. Both also made notes.

Jeopardy let Felicia talk, only making a few comments along the way to let the woman know she was listening. But when Felicia finished her story, Jeopardy probed for more information about the gang.

"So, who was Slash?"

"One of JD's lieutenants."

"He was military?"

"No," Felicia said with her own drug-fueled chuckle. "Nothin' like that. He was a GK."

"Ghetto Kings?" Jeopardy said.

"Yeah," Felicia said. "They ran the block back where my people come from. They made me a GK girl when I was sixteen years old."

"That young?"

"In my neighborhood, sixteen was full-grown. Them boys was killas, and we was hoes at sixteen."

"But you won the lottery, right? You got out of the hood."

It was the first time in their conversation that Felicia hesitated once she had started talking. Jeopardy didn't push. Logan had told her about the hackers and that a group of people were on the ship illegally. Frankly, she didn't understand it all. Her mind was still cloudy from the painkillers. What she understood was that there was more information to glean from Felicia Rojas, and as long as she could get it, Jeopardy was keen to try. She couldn't move without pain, and it would be at least a week before the cut to her back had healed sufficiently that she could try walking or get a bath. But she could talk, and it was exactly what the SI squad needed her to do.

"I did, kinda…"

"I know we were all desperate to get on the ship. I couldn't blame nobody for hustling their way on."

"That's how I felt. The shot caller for the GKs hooked some of us up. He's got a crew on board. That's why... why Slash came looking for me."

"Well, he's dead now. You saw to that."

"Don't mean I'm safe. JD won't be happy I killed his boy."

"JD's his father?"

It was the first time in the conversation that Jeopardy let it slip that she wasn't from a bad neighborhood. Fortunately, Felicia thought Jeopardy was making a joke. She laughed, and Jeopardy joined in. The drugs helped, but laughing hurt her back and she had to stop quickly.

"Girl, you okay?" Felicia said.

"Yeah," Jeopardy said. "I got some cracked ribs and..."

"And what?"

"My man cut me. I got a hundred stitches in my back. That's why I'm on my side."

"Damn!" Felicia said. "That ain't right. You need to get away from him. They's men that get rough and then they's men that kill. You got a bad one, girl."

"I know," Jeopardy said, even though she was silently thinking of Logan and feeling grateful that he was a good guy.

"JD calls the shots, always has. He'll hurt me."

"You're already hurt."

"This ain't nothing compared to what he'll do. Probably turn me over to his troll, too."

"His troll?"

"Yeah. He's got a nasty little toady that does the computer work. They call him Crank. Was him that got us all on the ship."

"He hacked into the lottery?"

"He's hacked into everything," Felicia said. "Done got

computers and such in his cabin. Stinky little troll is what he is. Ugly and weak, but he's protected."

They continued talking for nearly an hour before Felicia grew drowsy and dropped off into sleep. Jeopardy couldn't be sure, but she felt confident that she had gotten all she could from the woman. The rest was up to the team, although she had no doubt they would bring the criminals down. Jeopardy fell asleep feeling like she had done her part.

"WHAT DO WE HAVE?" Flint asked after giving a report on the killings to Commissioner Forrest.

"It's coming together," Becky said.

"Jeopardy came through," Dave added. "Got us all the information she could get. The only thing better would have been if the girl had made her a list of names and cabin numbers."

"Which I will get," Edge said.

Becky nodded and stepped closer to Flint. When she spoke, it was in a quiet voice. "She's good. If you get the chance to keep her, I would do it."

"Not sure that will be my call to make," Flint said as he glanced over at Sergeant Moya. "Continue."

"Alright, we know about Slash," Dave said, throwing a picture of the deceased thug onto the big display screen. "He was a lieutenant for the Ghetto Kings. According to Felicia, that's who infiltrated the ship. We're not sure what their reasons are, or what they're trying to do, but we've identified three more of them. Albert Brenner, Kyle Folson and Martin Vance are, we believe, the other three members of the gang."

"They all have larger-than-normal private rooms," Edge pointed out. "And none of them have a work rotation listed even though they're all on the ship's manifest as experts."

"But the real catch is this man," Dave said, bringing up a picture of a man with dark features. "Tay Mattox, we believe from Felicia's description that Tay is the hacker. We ran a check on his cabin. It's drawing more power than average, which suggests he might be running a good-sized computer in there."

"He's jacked into the network," Edge said

"Wait, what? Jacked in?"

"It means he plugged in via a hardwire connection, Sarge," Dave explained.

"Okay, thank you. Please continue, Chief Bright."

"He's jacked in, but he's also bouncing his IP. That alone is pretty sophisticated."

"And another reason to believe he's behind the hack," Becky pointed out. "But we haven't isolated their top guy."

"Felicia called him JD," Logan said.

Becky felt her blood run cold.

"You okay?" Flint asked her.

"You're sure?" Becky said. "You're absolutely positive they called him JD?"

"Holy crap," Dave said. "How did I miss that?"

"Miss what?" Edge asked.

"Take a look at a man named Julius Descartes," Becky said. "He could be the guy."

"No way," Dave said, his hands flying over his keyboard. "No way."

"Who is Julius Descarte?" Moya asked.

"You'll recall that in the attempt on Everett Goddard's life, a bystander saved him." Moya nodded but didn't say anything. "That person was Julius Descarte. There was something about the man that seemed wrong somehow. We were looking into him."

"He's in a berth on the third floor," Dave said.

"That room is reserved for families," Edge pointed out.

"He doesn't have one," Becky said. "He was pursuing me for a while."

"Doesn't mean he's a criminal," Moya said. "If anything, it would suggest he's not. Why else spend time with a law enforcement official if you don't have to?"

"Oh, that's strange," Edge said.

"Not so strange," Becky argued.

"Not that. You're lovely, any guy would be happy to have you."

"They would be lucky to have me," Becky said under her breath.

"I just found something," Edge continued. "It's not obvious at first. He mixed it in with the regular surveillance.

"Mixed what in?" Flint asked.

"This," Edge said, hitting a few keys on her control board and bringing up a video feed of the SIU squad.

They looked at the video display, then they turned. There was no camera that any of them could make out.

"Where is that coming from?" Flint asked.

Logan went over to the back corner of the bullpen. There was a rack of shotguns with non-lethal beanbag shells. They were locked in place so that only law enforcement officials could access them. Set on the foam barrel rest between two of the weapons was a small tube. Logan picked it up, and the picture on the display changed.

"That's it," Flint said.

"Can't tell what it is," Logan said.

"Let me see it," Edge told him. Dave stood up as Logan set the device onto the desk in front of the computer specialist. Dave looked over her shoulder. She gave the tube a twist. It popped apart.

"Lens, battery, and some kind of microchip," she said.

"That's a short-range bug," Dave said. "Never seen one quite like it. That lens is standard enough."

"The battery too. But it doesn't have a way to transmit the signal."

"Unless..." Dave said.

"What?" Edge asked.

"It could be that the tube is the antenna."

"Brilliant, but it wouldn't transmit far."

"You said it's dialed into the surveillance network, right?"

"So it would only have to transmit to our own wireless receiver," Edge said, her voice rising with excitement.

"Which is where?" Flint asked.

"There's one in every berth, every office," Edge said, pointing up to the ceiling where a square plate was mounted flush against the roof of the bullpen and painted to match.

"Are there more?" Becky asked.

The next hour was like a game of hide and seek. The rogue cameras were popping up everywhere. The most disturbing were the ones in Becky's own berth.

"Why aren't they in any of our cabins?" Logan asked. "Why just Becky?"

"He's obsessed with her," Moya said.

"That usually means you've been in contact with the subject," Flint said. "Do you remember him?"

"No," Becky said. "I would remember that face," she added, pointing to the picture of Tay Maddox (aka, Crank) on the video screen.

"I have a theory about that," Dave said. "We were surveilling you when you went to dinner with Julius Descarte."

"I remember," Becky said.

"Well, what if we weren't the only ones?" Dave suggested.

"You shot Descarte down," Flint said. "Maybe the hacker wanted what his boss couldn't get."

"You still have no evidence that this man, Descartes, is in any way involved," Moya said.

"She's right. But there is one way to find out," Becky said. "Permission to bring in this Tay Maddox."

"You pick him up, and the others will know we're on to them," Dave said. "Maybe we should wait."

"We can't wait," Flint said. "But you're right about alerting the others. Here's what we're going to do."

FLINT AGREED to let Becky bring in Tay Maddox. He was the smallest of their targets. She also had a pair of patrol officers backing her up, as did Logan, Dave, and Flint, who were each set to bring in one of the other GK lieutenants Edge had identified.

The squad was operating in a synchronized fashion to minimize the risk that someone else would get tipped off to the fact that law enforcement was onto the gang. It wasn't exactly cutting off the head of the snake. The man at the top, the enigmatic JD, still had not been identified , even though he would know the SIU was on his trail. JD wouldn't be able to operate, at least not very efficiently, without his underlings.

They had also made the assumption that of the nearly sixty people brought onto the *Colossus* by the Ghetto Kings, most of them were women. Once the lieutenants were secured, they would set about rounding as many of the GK girls as they could find. It would be a big operation and, while being a gang affiliate wasn't in itself a crime, hacking one's way onto the colony ship was.

"It's time," Becky said, as the order from Flint came through her cufflink.

Becky led the two patrol officers to the door and opened it without warning to the occupant inside. It wouldn't have mattered anyway. As soon as the door opened, Becky knew her suspect was dead.

"Looks like a ten-fifty-four," she said, using the police code for a dead body. "Let's clear the berth, though. Stay alert."

She made her way straight in. The cabin smelled of death. There was a coppery scent of blood in the air, along with body odor and unwashed clothing. Becky checked the body. It was unmistakably dead with a blood hole in the back of the skull. She turned the head, ignoring the fluid that leaked out the back, and studied the face. It was Tay Mattox, better known as Crank.

"Clear!" Each of the patrol officers shouted after checking the bedroom and bathroom.

Becky tapped the controls on her cufflink that sent the signal for medical help to her location.

"Detective, better take a look at this," one of the patrol officers in the tiny kitchen said.

Becky walked over and noticed the computer in the sink. It looked like a block of solid rust. She had fished computers out of water before, but never had she seen one so corroded. It looked like some ancient artifact pulled from the ocean.

"Don't touch it," Becky said. "Whatever is in that sink, it isn't just water."

Another icon sent Flint a message to contact her when he could. Just after the medical personnel arrived, he called her on the comlink.

"Nash, you good?"

"I'm fine," Becky said. "But Maddox is dead. I'd say gunshot wound to the back of the head, but there are no burns or powder marks."

"Really?"

"Oh, and his computer was cooked. I'm thinking some sort of corrosive agent in water. We'll get nothing from it."

"The leader is covering his tracks," Flint said. "We got the others, but they won't talk. You can tell at a glance they've been through the system, probably many times."

"So, we're back to square one," Becky said. "I can't believe it."

"This guy we're after is smart," Flint said. "But we have to find him."

"I'll keep searching," Becky said. "Maybe we get lucky and pick up something he missed."

The law enforcement officers in Cranks berth looked through every nook and cranny, but it wasn't until they had tried all the sneaky places that a person might hide something that Becky looked at the desk again. The medical team had removed the body. All that remained were the three monitors and some cords. Becky very nearly missed the most vital clue of all. Just as she was turning away, the flash drive caught her eye. Everything about Crank's set-up was old school. The computer itself was bulkier than she was used to. In fact, she hadn't seen a laptop like Cranks since she was a teenager. It was worthless, of course, and the monitors were no help, but as she was turning, her eye swept across the tiny thumb drive. It was the size of the fingernail on her pinky, and an eighth of an inch thick. One end was black plastic, the other was dull gray metal. She picked it up and looked at the device. There was no way to be certain what it was, not simply by looking at it. If it was a memory device, it was probably useless. No one in their right mind would leave it behind.

She slipped it into her pocket and headed out of the smelly cabin. The need for a shower and sleep was heavy on her shoulders. Her stomach growled, too, and she realized it had been a long time since her last meal. But that was the way of things with law enforcement. When a case was breaking, you pushed through until it was over. Eating and sleeping could come afterward.

After a long walk back to the office, she had just about convinced herself that what she found was nothing. It was probably a component from the display cables that had popped free when whoever killed Crank was ripping them out of his computer. But she was pleased to find Edge still at Becky's desk, working away on the big, encrypted computer she carried.

"I found this," she said, fishing the little drive out of her pocket. "Is it anything?"

Edge took the tiny drive and held it up.

"This looks old school," she said. "Could be a memory drive. Hang on."

From a compartment inside the case, she pulled out a dongle with eight short cords coming out of it, each with a different input receiver on the end. She plugged the single side in, then fished through the different cords until she found what she wanted. The little drive slid neatly into it. And on her computer screen, a video file appeared.

"What have we here?" Edge said.

"Let's hope it's something good and not just his porn collection."

"Right," Edge said as she clicked on the icon that made the video start playing.

On the screen, a group of men sat at a table. There were bottles of liquor in front of them. Most were drinking. Becky recognized the faces as those of the GK lieutenants. Then another man came into view. He pulled out a chair and sat down.

"You want a drink?" One of the lieutenants said.

"Nah, and you should stop," the newcomer said. "We got plans to make. I need you straight."

"We good," another of the lieutenants said.

Becky recognized Slash. He looked different with his skull not caved in. "What's the play?"

"Alright," the newcomer said. "Here is what it is."

Edge froze the screen with a touch of her spacebar. "This is important, isn't it?"

Becky nodded. "This is everything," she said in a quiet voice. She was in complete shock. Not just because the crucial evidence they needed had been lying on the desk in plain sight. Not just because she had nearly missed it herself. Those things were flashing in her mind like neon signs, but there was something even more crucial on the video.

"Who is that guy?" Edge asked.

Becky had to work her jaw up and down a few times to get some moisture back into her throat before she could answer. "That's Julius Descarte," she said. "We have the proof we need to bring him down."

"You were right about him," Edge said, clapping Becky on the shoulder.

But all Becky could think about was that she had sat across from a stone-cold killer and enjoyed a lavish meal, without ever once realizing who he really was.

They watched the rest of the video, which laid out the crew's plan to not only steal from the *Colossus* Bank but to insinuate themselves into the executives' lives in order to blackmail them. It was the motive and a vital piece of evidence that linked the men together. The video, along with the hacking evidence, was enough to put them all away on Racketeer Influenced and Corrupt Organization charges.

When the video ended, Becky rushed to get Flint. He was in the detention area where the three lieutenants were being held. They had one in each of their two interrogation rooms and the third was locked in the holding cell. She led him, Dave, and Logan back to the bullpen, and Edge played them the video. It wasn't long, just under ten minutes. It was obvious that none of the men knew they were being recorded.

"Mattox was a sneaky little bastard," Flint said.

"Covering his bases," Dave said. "I can't say I blame him for that."

"You were right about the identity of their shot caller," Logan told Becky. "Congrats."

"I think I'll celebrate when he's in custody," Becky said. "Think about this. Mattox was dead. Someone killed him and ruined his computer."

"They were onto the fact that we discovered what they were up to," Dave said.

"But how?" Logan asked. It wasn't so much a question as an accusation. They were all looking at Moya.

"Why do you stare at me?" She asked in her thick accent.

"Who did you tell about this?" Flint asked.

"The Commissioner," she said. "He would never be in league with criminals."

"Doesn't have to be," Flint said. "I'd bet a year's salary that he told the captain, and then one of them told Goddard."

"Wait, you think Everett Goddard is working with the Ghetto Kings?" Dave asked.

"No," Flint said. "But I think he's gotten close to the man who saved his life."

"Julius," Becky said.

Flint nodded. "He probably shared that the bank was hacked and that we were trying to find out who."

"So, Descarte shut him up before he could rat them out," Logan said.

"Tried to," Becky responded. "But obviously, he didn't recognize the thumb drive. Otherwise, it would have been dropped in the vat of acid along with Mattox's laptop."

"This is enough, right?" Dave said. "We can bring this monster in?"

"Yes," Flint said. "Check his location."

Dave bent over his computer and then straightened up. "He's in cabin zero-zero-one on deck two."

"That would be Everett Goddard's suite," Flint said. "Let's go get our man."

CHAPTER
THIRTY-SIX

THERE WAS a musician at the piano playing softly. The party goers were being treated to a seven-course tasting by a beautiful chef named Harmonia Lukid. Everyone at the table was dressed to the nines and richer than most countries back on Earth.

JD was the odd man out. He didn't come from old money and hadn't created a business empire. Yet he had caught the eye of all the women in their tight-fitting, custom-made cocktail dresses. Everyone was exquisitely groomed and the conversation was engaging. JD lifted his glass of wine and took a sip. It was some of the best he had ever tasted. The kind of wine that, no matter how much money a player on the streets could earn, he could never find wine of such exquisite taste.

Beside the man who, just hours earlier, had murdered his associate in cold blood, sat a woman with an Egyptian accent who JD could imagine as the queen of the Nile. Nearby, at the head of the table, Everett Goddard sat in a custom-made suit, having a conversation with the Captain of the *Colossus*. Captain Hastings was in his dress uniform and was also enjoying the wine. It was finer than anything he had ever tasted, and paired perfectly with the poached salmon they had just been eating.

JD thought he had arrived at the pinnacle of society. He had done it out of cunning, daring action and smooth hustle. His original plan had failed, but he pivoted expertly into the opportunity his quick action on the streets of Topdeck had earned him. Had he known the assassin's weapon was poison, he would not have intervened. JD was not the type of person to risk his life needlessly for anyone. But fate, it seemed, was smiling on the gang leader. He had juked death as expertly as a professional athlete and simultaneously earned himself the right to be Goddard's friend. He would turn that friendship into status on the new world. All that remained to do was cut off the excess baggage of his old life and JD would truly be Julius Descarte, wealthy aristocrat and businessman. No longer would anything be denied him. He could join the most prestigious clubs. He could attend the most lavish parties. The rich and famous would flatter him. And best of all, he could live wherever he wanted without fear and without the threat that someone was waiting in the shadows to put a bullet in his head.

A bell chimed and the dinner party guests all looked at their host. He smiled and lifted his hand. One of his employees, a man by the name of Briddenham, hurried from the edge of the room where he had been helping to serve the wine to Goodard's many guests. He answered the door. When he reappeared a moment later, the man looked distressed. Behind him was Becky Nash. She wasn't in a ten-thousand-dollar designer dress. She hadn't spent the day having her hair and nails done. Nor did she have the benefit of the best plastic surgeons to sculpt her body into a work of art. And yet, JD thought she looked more beautiful than any of the guests. Which was why he felt no qualms as he drew the small .38 caliber pistol that his lieutenants had secured from one of the storage warehouses on the *Colossus*. JD had tucked it neatly into a hidden pocket just inside the waistband of his slacks. He had another pistol strapped to his ankle for just such an emergency as what he saw coming for him, as JD looked in the face of the woman he had tried to win over not long ago.

"Sorry to interrupt," Flint said.

"Sergeant, what is the meaning of this?" Captain Hastings snarled. "You can't just come barging in here."

"Sir, we apologize for the inconvenience, but we're here to arrest Julius Descarte."

"What?" Goddard said. "This is preposterous. You can't do that."

"We can and will," Flint said.

He was side by side with Becky Nash. Behind them were three more law enforcement officers. JD felt a burning, seething hatred for the people who would rob him of his chance to be a great man.

"Guavanna? Is this serious?" Captain Hastings sputtered.

"I'm afraid it is, sir," she said. "The proof is irrefutable."

"Proof of what?" Goddard demanded.

"Proof of a conspiracy to defraud the banking institution on this ship and in the colony on Secundo," Flint said.

"Julius, what the devil are they talking about?" Goddard said.

It was time to pivot again and JD was the master of it. The cops hadn't seen the gun under the table. He pointed it toward Everett Goddard, thinking, *if I can't have all this, no one can.*

The report of the pistol shocked everyone. The bullet tore into Goddard's stomach and lodged in his spine. Everything happened fast after that.

Flint yelled, "Gun!"

There were screams from around the table. JD's second shot was a bit low. It hit Captain Hastings in his knee, pulverizing the joint and plowing through the muscle in his thigh. He screamed and grabbed the woman beside him. His fingers caught in what appeared to be her long, silky blonde hair. But as he toppled over, he ripped a hairpiece from her head, causing her to scream and pull away. It just happened to be right into the path of Flint's return fire.

His rubber bullet hit the woman square in the back and knocked her up onto the table. By that point, people were scrambling to get out of the way, which was a problem for the cops, but not for JD. He didn't care who got hurt or killed. He let his fury fly as he pulled the trigger again. His bullet, aimed for Flint's chest, passed through the linen tablecloth. But instead of hitting the police sergeant, Flint's subordinate threw herself in front of her boss. She had drawn her weapon, but hadn't fired. JD's bullet hit her in the chest, passed through her lung, and shattered her shoulder blade.

Flint caught her and they both fell to the ground. Flint could feel her hot blood pumping from the hole in her chest and running down her side. She seemed to him thin and delicate in that moment. He clamped his free hand over the wound and pressed hard to stop the bleeding.

In truth, none of the SIU had expected there to be a fight. Guns were not allowed on the *Colossus*. Possession of one was a major crime. There were, of course, guns in storage for the colony. It was widely believed that large predators most likely roamed the pristine new world. Although hunting would, of course, be one way the colonists provided their sustenance, especially those who planned to branch out from the main colony and explore the wilder places on Secundo.

The law enforcement officers were excellent marksmen, but none of them were gunfighters. JD was. He had already raised his left leg under the table and retrieved his second pistol. The table was made of a long piece of broad red cedar with many coats of lacquer and polish. It weighed over two hundred pounds. But JD's adrenaline was pumping hard. He shoved back from the table, toppling the high-backed chair, and then knelt below the table. With a heave, he pushed it over. The dishes and glasses, including several bottles of wine, slid to the floor, which was made of marble tiles. The VIPs had paid through the nose to be on the colony ship and many had paid extra to outfit their private accommodations in the lavish style they were accustomed to. The fine china plates, crystal glasses and bottles of wine shattered, with champagne sprayed up and glittering in the lights.

Of the remaining three cops, only two had pistols. They fired back at JD, but their rubber bullets hardly left a scuff mark on the polished surface of the expensive table. Then the gangster came up over the upper edge with a pistol in each hand.

Dave Bannon dove to help cover Becky Nash alongside Sergeant Flint. Logan threw himself in a headfirst dive toward the grand piano, which had been abandoned by the musician the moment the shooting started.

The only officer remaining was Moya Guavanna. She was shot three times by JD as he swept his weapons away from Flint and followed Logan.

Two bullets passed over Flint, who lay face down over Becky. He heard a ~zipth!~ sound as the subsonic rounds passed by over-head. And then he raised his pistol. It was not the .45 caliber auto-matic he had carried for nearly two decades as a police officer. But Flint was an excellent shot. His round hit the edge of the tabletop, splintering the wood and sending a shard of it into JD's face. He grunted, falling back onto his haunches as both of his pistols that had been tracking Logan were elevated. The bullets spewing forth from the little eight-round semi-automatic pistols hit the piano instead of Logan. The breach of one snapped open as the last bullet was fired and the other pistol jammed.

JD quickly turned and hurried down the length of the table on his hands and knees. He was close to the piano and the cops still expected him to be at the other end. That gave him a slight advan-tage over them. He came charging out, snatching up a pointed steak knife with a serrated edge as he went. Logan, coming out from under the table, met his charge. With a powerful thrust, JD expected to gut the copper. Instead, Logan spun out of JD's path. The knife missed, but Logan's punch landed square on the gangster's jaw. The bones snapped under the blow and three teeth flew from their places in his mouth as JD went sprawling across the top of the piano. The wooden support bar snapped like a dry twig, and more of the guests screamed as the wooden top slammed down with a boom like thunder.

JD slid off the piano, hit the floor on his shoulder and came rolling to his feet. But the other cops had seen him and shifted their aim. Flint and Bannon fired as one, their rubber bullets speeding through the air and hitting JD square in the chest. He flew backward into the wall and crumpled to the ground.

"Logan!"

"Got him!" Logan responded, dashing toward JD.

The gangster was hurt. His sternum was cracked and a rib was broken. He wheezed as blood bubbled at the corner of his mouth from a punctured lung but he had been shot before and always survived. As Logan rushed toward him, he prepared to fight. He drew one fist back and swung at the cop. It was slow, with barely a hint of strength. The effort sent pain roaring through his chest and back. Logan caught the gangster's fist in his hand. For a second, they were face to face, both men's eyes blazing with hatred. And then Logan twisted the gangster's hand. His arm turned, and before he knew it, Logan had him pushed against the wall with one arm pinned behind him so hard it felt as though it would either snap or his shoulder would pop from the socket.

"Don't move," Logan said, kicking JD's feet apart. "You're under arrest."

EPILOGUE

SAWYER FLINT STOOD on the observation deck on the starboard side of the *Colossus'* Topdeck. He wasn't alone.

Several thousand crew members stood around him. They were the engineers and maintenance workers, cooks, gardeners, and medical technicians who were going to make the trip back to the Sol system. In the distance, they could see Secundo. It was a huge ball of color with the system star to port and shining onto the surface of the planet.

For Flint, it was a bittersweet goodbye. A lot had happened since the Ghetto Kings were caught. The most significant was the death of Becky Nash. Flint didn't understand why she sacrificed herself for him. The bullet from JD's pistol had done too much damage to her lungs, and she had died in the operating theater a few minutes after the head of the GK's was arrested.

Nor had Becky been the only casualty of that horrible evening. Sergeant Moya Guavanna had been shot to death as well. They were both heroes in his opinion. He had never liked Moya and, at times, resented her presence, but when the chips were down, she had gone with them to arrest JD and died on her feet. He couldn't fault her for that. In fact, he hoped when his time came, he would meet it as bravely as Moya had.

Captain Hastings survived his injury, although he had to have total knee replacement and could never quite let go of the pain medication. Commander Lova Koll had replaced him, first on an interim basis, then permanently, as the captain succumbed to addiction. Everett Goddard survived as well, but was never able to walk again. He continued on as President of the bank and had joined the colonists to help guide the financial system as he had promised to do, and for that, Flint admired him.

No one knew it at the time, but one of the bullets that JD fired punched through a wall and hit the chef. There had been a time when Harmonia Lukid had pursued a relationship with Flint. But after the injury, which wasn't life-threatening, she retreated into her private space. The trauma of the dinner party had left scars on everyone, even those without physical wounds.

Feeling nostalgic, Flint left the watch party and went to the command center. He went to the top deck and found Commander Koll in her dayroom. She had been right about many of her predictions, including the fact that things would slow down once the colonists were no longer on the ship. It had taken a month to ferry everyone down to the surface who was going. Flint had said his goodbyes to the members of his team. He would find them all again one day when he decided he was ready to join the colony, but he felt like the *Colossus* held unfinished business for him. And he wasn't the type of man to leave things undone.

"Do you regret it now that we're leaving?" Commander Lova Koll asked as she put a long arm over his shoulders.

"No," Flint said. "I don't regret it. This is where you are, it's where I want to be, and my friends have lives to live down there."

"We'll join them… eventually," she said.

She had been instrumental in settling the unrest on the ship. The fact that the captain had been wounded at a lavish dinner party while his enforced curfew was still in effect didn't help the frustra-tions that several hundred thousand passengers felt. But with Commander Koll needing to step it up, the opportunity to present a new leader to the ship was just what was needed. The curfew was lifted and a full two-hour documentary was aired about the bomb threat. Six months later, a second documentary revealed the results of the riot. Both times, actual footage recorded by the security cameras on the ship helped convince the passengers that nothing was being hidden from them or denied by the ship's senior officers.

The very public trial of the Ghetto Kings was also effective at shifting the emphasis away from the people killed in the riots. Commander Koll gave the approval to have the entire thing broad-cast on the ship's network. The same officers who had saved the *Colossus* from the terrorist bomber had also brought down a crim-inal mastermind. At least that was how the passengers interpreted the arrests. Along with JD and his lieutenants, there were over fifty women charged with fraud for being on the ship. Those who coop-erated were given the chance to earn their way onto Secundo, since no one had the heart to send them back to streets that had demanded so much of their innocence to begin with. And to their credit, each and every one took the deal. They testified against the Ghetto Kings, served one hundred hours of community service on the *Colossus*, and were given a chance to learn vocational skills that would be used in the new colony.

Since then, the ship had been relatively crime-free. The SIU, while not being shut down after the riots, had little to do.

"I have to get the ship underway," Commander Koll said. "But I'll have time for dinner this evening."

"I'll be waiting," Flint told her.

She kissed his cheek, and he waited until she was gone to break down in tears. The worst part of everything was that his friend never got to see the new world she was so excited to become part of. That knowledge was almost more than he could bear.

Down on Secundo, things were busy. Big farm implements were churning fresh soil and planting crops across wide fields under a bright blue sky. In the colony proper, concrete was being mixed and poured fourteen hours a day. The colonists had massive foundations that were covered with crates of supplies and food that were stacked fifty feet in the air. They awaited the construction of metal buildings that would go up around them. Construction crews could erect the massive buildings in a single day. Meanwhile, in prefabricated, temporary buildings, new businesses were being started. There was a huge tent city on either side of the construction zone. It was a hive of activity and every former passenger of the *Colossus* was pitching in. Once all the supplies were properly stored and future harvests were planted, the colonists would be free to spread out and explore the new world.

Dave Bannon was with Logan Keys on a small rise that overlooked a beautiful river just a mile away from the colony. Big round rocks lined the shallow, but swiftly-running stream. On the far side, bushes with bright red flowers grew. Behind them, tall trees with willowy branches stood in a thick forest. The grass on Secundo was dark green and grew ankle high. The air was clear and warm.

"I don't know how we did it before," Dave said, taking a deep breath.

"The air wasn't like this on Earth," Logan said in a soft voice.

"This air is sweet."

"You think she'll like it here?" Logan asked.

"Yeah, she will," Dave said.

Behind them, Jeopardy and Edge walked with Stu, who had a slight limp, but no leash. The humans were happy on Secundo, but the dog was overjoyed. At times, he ran hard and fast in huge circles. Jeopardy said he had the zoomies. Logan had to admit he had never seen any animal as happy as Stu seemed to be on Secundo.

"This is beautiful," Jeopardy said.

"So peaceful," Edge said.

"I registered it in her name today," Dave said. "I don't know if she had relatives, but if any of them come out here, they'll find her place."

"Won't someone else take it?" Jeopardy asked.

"Edge and I are listed as co-owners. We'll make sure no one takes it."

"She would have appreciated it," Logan said. "It's still so hard to believe she's gone."

"Becky was my best friend," Jeopardy said. "This was all she wanted here. A place to call her own. Something beautiful and wild. I think she can rest in peace here."

"And maybe we can let her go now," Dave said. He took off his backpack and pulled an ornate urn from it. He opened the top, and they each took a handful as Stu dashed back and forth through the river. "I'll go first," Dave volunteered. "Becky, we've missed you every day. We hope you like your place on Secundo. This world isn't the same without your laugh and your bright smile, but we will remember you and all the incredible things that made you who you are."

He finished and held out his hand. The breeze carried some of the ashes away, and the rest he poured out onto the hillside.

"I didn't know her for very long," Edge said. "But what I saw was a brilliant detective, fearless and passionate about her job. From what I've learned about you, Becky Nash, you were also a faithful friend and dreamer. I admire that about you and I promise never to forget you."

She copied Dave's solemn release of the ashes she held.

Logan cleared his throat and held his hand up high. "God, I know you are here, loving us just as you did on Earth. We ask again that you take our friend to your eternal glory. We loved her then, we love her still. Becky, if you can hear me, thank you. I know your opinion about me in the beginning gave the Sergeant the confidence to add me to the SIU. I'll never forget what you did for me, and I'll never forget you."

He poured out the ashes in his hand. By that point, Jeopardy was crying. Stu, sensing her distress, moved to her side. As the wind picked up a little, her baggy shirt hugged the curve of her protruding belly.

"Sorry, Becky, I'm emotional. Blame it on the baby hormones," she said. "I think about you every day. You saved my life. You saved Stu, too." She gave the dog a loving caress around his tall, pointed ears. "This is the perfect place for you, but we aren't saying goodbye. We'll take you with us, in our hearts, every day. We'll share every new vista, every wonderful discovery about this place and everything we love about it with you, because you are with us. We love you. Until we meet again..."

She let the ashes go, and the wind picked them up, lifted them over the treetops, and carried them off into the vibrant new world.

As the *Colossus* began the long journey home, Sergeant Flint took the elevator down to the brig. On the ship, with only a quarter of the original crew, Flint was the sole remaining law enforcement officer. The SIU offices were closed, along with the university and the schools. Most of the office buildings were locked up. Only businesses along the main avenues were allowed to stay open, but most of the proprietors had joined the colony, even many who had agreed to stay on the colony ship for at least two trips to the new star system. Commander Koll hadn't held them to their contracts. She let everyone join the colony who wanted to. Fortunately, there were enough crew members willing to go back and make the run again.

Down in the brig, every prisoner was locked into a cell. They had solid metal doors halfway up, and then bars from there to the top. As Flint walked past them, he could see inside each one. They had a small table that came out of the wall about eighteen inches, a single stool bolted to the floor, a metal bunk with a rubber mattress, and a toilet/sink combination. Flint had gathered meals for them. Each prisoner had a spoon with a rubber handle that they were responsible for. He passed out the disposable trays of food at each door. He passed the GK lieutenants who had survived. Each one cast baleful stares at him but said nothing. He passed the terrorist Titus Russel and the man who had groomed Truman Arlington into hacking into the ship's computer system. In cells that were side by side were Henry and Johnny Miller. Unlike the others, they both looked distressed. But Flint wasn't there to see them. He passed the others and stopped at the last cell. Inside, JD lay on his bunk. The man hadn't eaten in days. He had a cough that he couldn't shake and he had fallen into a deep depression.

"Dinner," Flint said, putting the meal onto the top ledge of the metal portion of the door.

JD didn't move, but his eyes were still keen. They watched Flint.

"We're on our way back now," Flint continued. "Fourteen months, unless we run into delays. You going to live that long, Julius?"

"Screw you, man," the prisoner said in a weak voice.

"I'll admit, it was tempting to stay. Secundo is a beautiful world. But you know what made the difference? I stuck around because I wanted to watch you die."

"I ain't dying, pig," JD croaked.

"Sounds like you're dying," Flint said.

"I ain't..." his declaration was interrupted by a fit of coughing.

"Had it been up to me, we would have just put you in the airlock," Flint said. "But maybe this is better."

"Shut up."

Flint grinned. "Maybe this way you will remember what you lost. You can remember how close you came and, as you slip slowly into hell, you'll hear the sound of your many victims calling for you."

JD didn't respond; he just stared back at Flint, who watched him for a moment, then he shook off his hatred for the man who had killed his friend and left him down in the tiny detention cell. As he made his way to the elevator and rode back up through the massive ship to the senior officer's quarters that he had begun sharing with Command Koll once they reached orbit. It was a big step up from the small berth he had shared down on deck eighteen. He walked into his new life, took a deep breath to drink it all in, and accepted that it was time for him to be happy again.

AUTHOR'S NOTE

Dear reader, thank you so much for reading the SIU books. They were a dream of mine. I love a good police procedural story, but I discovered along the way that writing them is much more difficult than expected. Constantly thinking of criminals and putting myself into their mindset was onerous. It certainly took me longer to finish than it should have, mostly because I just felt the darkness in my mind. By the end, even though I knew the story, I found myself resisting the writing process. That's no place for a writer, and so the SIU books will end here.

Dead Space was my one hundred and nineteenth novel. Just saying that makes me feel a bit like Bilbo Baggins at his famous birthday party. I promise not to disappear on you. In fact, as I write this, I've already launched into my next story. Writing is what I was created to do, but not every kind of story is my forte. I'll try to stick to what I do best in the future.

Up next is the fourth book in my supernatural End Times Bible Prophecy series, *The Three Woes*. If you haven't given those books a try, I highly recommend them. The first book, End Times, is the story of Hank Downes, a regular guy caught in some supernatural circumstances. If you love a good adventure with suspense and mystery, you'll love End Times. It's only 99¢ and has a 4.6-star rating on Amazon with almost eight hundred ratings. If you think Christian Fiction isn't for you, let this book change your mind. For a universal link to End Times click here!

END TIMES 1

Let's get the obvious out of the way. You aren't going to believe me
—not at first—and that's okay. This isn't a story for the faint of
heart. It isn't a horror novel that pulls you in and lets you sleep at
night because you can tell yourself it's just a story. No—this story is
true, and the truth is bigger than many people can admit. We've
been trained to be blind. Again, I know you don't believe that, but
just because you don't believe it doesn't mean it isn't real. That's
the thing about truth that so many people get wrong these days.
There is no your truth or my truth; there's just truth. What you do
with the truth once you know it deep down in your bones—that's
where things get interesting.

My name is Henry Downes, but my friends call me Hank. It's a
bit old-fashioned, but that's what my parents liked about it. They
were sentimental people, right up until they died in a car crash. I
should have been killed too. I was eight years old, no longer in a
safety seat, and my seatbelt failed, probably because I didn't fasten
it right. Hey, I was a kid. What do you expect?

Anyway, the car hit something. I never saw it. When you're
eight and in the back seat on a dark rainy night, you don't really
pay attention to what's happening on the road. I was always in my

own head too; I still get that way sometimes. My mother said I had a world-class imagination. My teachers said I was a dreamer. Either way, I never saw what we ran into. I don't think my parents did, either, because I don't remember them shouting in alarm or hitting the brakes. One second we were traveling down the road, and the next second the car stopped. I went flying straight out the windshield, which my mother had shattered for me. Yes, I know, I should speak about their deaths with more respect, but that gets sticky. There are too many emotions that come wafting up out of the void their deaths left in the middle of my soul. So, I try to keep things light.

They died, I lived. Eight-year-old boys are incredibly resilient. I landed in the bushes on the side of the road and wasn't even found until morning. To be honest, it's all a bit of a blur now. Time has a way of softening the hard edges of those painful memories we can't shake. But I do remember riding in the ambulance, which was not at all glamorous or fun. They strapped me to a gurney and poked me with needles while the siren roared, and the ambulance shook and lurched all the way to the hospital. That wasn't fun either, mostly because I didn't have a family anymore. My parents met in their thirties after their own parents had died. If there were any distant relatives, I knew nothing about them. This meant I was suddenly a ward of the state. Losing your family is hard enough, and it's even worse when you're then forced into the homes of strangers.

I'm happy to say I wasn't abused. There are plenty of stories about that, but I was lucky. I was taken in by a temporary foster family that saw me through the funerals where I was looked at with pity by my parents' friends, but none of them were willing to take me in. That meant I was officially an orphan, completely on my own. From the temporary home, I was taken to a state-run shelter for children. Fortunately, my story appeared on the evening news and online. This was mostly because of the mystery surrounding the crash, but we'll get to that eventually. Like most of the horrible things in life, it came back around when I was older. But I'm getting ahead of myself.

I was put into a foster home fairly quickly after the shelter. Peter and Nora Soto were a kind, older couple who never had children of their own. They felt sorry for me and were kind. I went along with whatever they decided for me because I just didn't have the will to resist. And being an orphan is a bit of an oddity. I don't have to tell you that being different in public school is not a good thing. It's why the system works so well and why so many people are essentially clones. I know you probably don't agree, but give this tale a little time and you might just have to rethink some things.

I stayed with the Sotos until I was eighteen years old and graduated from high school. I wasn't a great student and college wasn't really an interest to me, so I enlisted in the Air Force, where I became a logistics specialist. In four years I reached the rank of senior airman by being good at moving things and checking lists. The mundane has always been in my wheelhouse. I think that's because I don't mind the boredom. Mentally numbing tasks were my specialty; I could move boxes all day, my body doing the repetitive task while my mind was far away. But four years in the service was enough for me, and by the time I got out of the Air Force, my foster parents were no longer around. Nora Soto had succumbed to ovarian cancer, and Peter Soto was taking a sabbatical in Japan. If I'm being honest, I wasn't close to the Sotos, anyway. After my parents died, I felt it safest not to get close to anyone; it doesn't hurt as much when you lose someone you're not close to.

My last post in the Air Force was in Spokane, Washington at the Fairchild Air Base. This is where things got a bit odd. If you're anything like me, you reach a point where it seems like life is nothing more than a series of random events. I didn't believe in anything when I was sent to the INW (that's the Inland Northwest for those of you that don't know). I didn't call myself an atheist, although technically I was one. I simply didn't think about much less believe in anything beyond what was on my duty schedule. Knowing I only had a few months left in the Air Force, I began to put some thought into what I might do next.

And that's when the world I thought I knew got ripped to shreds right before my eyes.

END TIMES 2

The thing—that's what I call it—came in late at night. I was the only person on duty in warehouse Charlie Four, and I was working on a manifest list for pallets of cargo set to go out the next morning. Like I said, not your dream job, but there I was. A group of specialists brought in a crate on a forklift. I saw them enter but didn't pay them any real attention; it was a regular sight at Fairchild. There were no fighter jets or bombers at this base, as I was in a section that shipped potatoes and other victuals to other bases. Like I said: glamorous.

Normally the specialists would have brought in their cargo, set it down in the designated area, and left without a word—but this group never made it to the area they were headed for. One man was driving the forklift, and another man and two women followed. Suddenly—and for reasons no one ever explained to me —the driver of the forklift stopped the vehicle, stepped out, and collapsed. You've probably heard stories just like this one: a healthy, active man in his early thirties with no history of health issues suddenly just collapses and dies. That's what happened to this poor guy. His friends tried to help him; two did CPR while the third ran to call for help.

Naturally, I stopped my inventory to see what the commotion was all about. Soon there were medical personnel rushing into the warehouse. They went to great pains to try to revive the dead airman. One of the emergency response people told me to take care of the cargo, and I agreed.

The group cleared out, including the dead airman's companions, leaving me alone in the warehouse. I got in the forklift and checked the paperwork. The crate was supposed to go into locker two. That's a refrigerated compartment in the rear of the warehouse. So I'm thinking I've got a crate full of produce or even meat of some kind that needed to stay cold. It had been sitting on the forklift for well over an hour by that point, and when the smell hit me, I didn't think much of it at first. I mean, it wouldn't be the first crate of victuals to go bad in transit. Plus, a man had died in the process of getting the goods to the refrigerated locker. That's what I would classify as special circumstances. It crossed my mind to make a note in the paperwork that the cargo had spoiled, but as I drove the forklift forward, I got a better whiff of the smell as it wafted back at me.

I don't want to be graphic here, but I was in the process of losing my lunch when I crashed the crate into a concrete barrier. Cursing my bad luck, I shut down the forklift, whipped the mess off my lips with the back of my sleeve, and staggered away some fifteen or twenty feet. Unfortunately, just running away wasn't an option. When I caught my breath and settled my trembling stomach, I went back to inspect the damage. A warehouse at night isn't well lit, so I always carried a flashlight. I pulled the tool from my belt, flicked it on, and inspected the crate. There was a crack in the corner. I could see the seam and the nails used to assemble the crate. I thought that a little work could get the box into reasonable shape again with no one being the wiser about my little accident. The smell was worse than ever as I got closer. It wasn't just rotten meat or decay; it was something incredibly vile—a mixture of death, body odor, and old excrement. I started to gag again, but then my light played over something I couldn't explain. Fear replaced my revulsion, and I stared into the crate.

Something inside it stared right back at me.

END TIMES 3

Okay, now I know you want to know what's in the box. That's just human nature, but you can't go down this road thinking I'm telling you a spooky story. No, that's not it at all. Think of it like you would if we were in a courtroom; this is testimony. I'm telling you what happened—not what I think or what I felt, but what I actually *saw* in that crate.

It was an eye, three quarters of the way open, staring blankly out of the crack in the side of the crate...only it wasn't like a human's eye at all. It was massive, the size of a grapefruit. I kid you not.

I think I might have screamed when I saw it, but there was no one around to hear me. The warehouses are in a row behind the hangars at Fairchild, and not every warehouse was in service at the time. There might have been a few airmen outside the warehouse, but no one came running to check on me, so I assume no one heard me. Or maybe the scream was just in my mind. I felt paralyzed in that moment; I couldn't move, and I couldn't look away. The only thing that was certain was the lifeless glaze in the eye. It didn't move, didn't blink or shift. It just stared straight ahead, out of the box, and right through me.

Now, consider for a moment what you might do in such a situation. When my senses fully returned to me, I knew that I needed to get the box to a refrigerated locker. The thing in the crate had been out too long. The smell I was gagging on would only get worse. So, I got back in the forklift, drove the crate to locker two, put it inside, checked the refrigeration settings next to the door as per our protocols, then left. I took the forklift back to its place by the big, overhead doors on the front side of the warehouse. Then I went and cleaned up the mess I had made. Finally, I went back to my inventory of the pallets set to go out in a few hours. But for the first time in my military career, I couldn't focus. All I could think about was the eye in the box. I needed to see it again. I needed to get closer and really see what it was.

My excuse was that I needed to repair the box. I got a hammer and went back to locker two. My heart was racing as I went inside. I shivered immediately—partly from the cold, and partly from fear. I was about to do something I knew was forbidden. I hadn't consciously broken a rule in years, maybe not even since my parents died. Growing up with the Sotos, I was a loner. I spent my evenings reading sci-fi novels in my bedroom. When it was time for bed, I went to bed. When my teachers assigned homework or the Sotos gave me chores, I did what was asked of me. I didn't complain. Maybe I wasn't very good at those chores, but not on purpose. I may have been an average student, but it wasn't because I didn't do the work. My problem was a lack of interest. I had no interest in generating negative attention. It was better to do my job, keep my head down, and hope that no one noticed me. After over a decade of intentional obedience, I decided to do something I knew was forbidden. I knew it because whatever was in that box wasn't human. It looked almost human, and it wasn't just the size that was strange; the thing had captivated my mind in a way that nothing else had besides Jessica Mitchells in the tenth grade.

The lights in the refrigerated locker weren't any better than those in the warehouse proper. I used my flashlight to see as I pried open the busted end of the crate. The smell was terrible, but it was less like a rotting corpse and more like the foul waste of a backed-up latrine. The cold air helped me deal with the stench and kept me from being sick. I didn't have to try very hard to get the end of the crate off, as the forklift crash had done most of the work. I popped the end off, and I could see inside.

What I found was, in a word, unbelievable.

There was a giant inside the crate. And I don't mean a big man like Shaquille O'Neal or some oddity of nature in the Wide World of Wrestling. I walked the length of the crate to get a rough measurement. The crate was ten feet long, and the thing inside the crate was lying in a fetal position. My guess was that the giant had to be fifteen to sixteen feet tall standing up. Its muscles were lank, but there didn't seem to be much fat on the body, which was mostly uncovered. The creature wore a kilt-type garment—more than a loin cloth but not by much. It was incredibly hairy. Thick hair spread over its chest, stomach, shoulders, and back. I saw thick hair on its thighs too, but the hair thinned on its lower legs.

If you've seen illustrations of orcs from the fantasy video games, you'll get the picture, but it wasn't exactly the same. This was no green-skinned video game monster. It was pale but very dirty. The jaw was wide, the beard and shaggy head of hair were both fiery red, and the strangest part was the teeth. The giant's mouth hung open in death, its tongue swollen and protruding over two rows of teeth. Again, I know, hard to believe—but this is what I saw. I recall the details all too well because I can still see that thing when I close my eyes at night. I've dreamed countless times that it came to life and killed me, and in every single dream, the giant was exactly the same.

Along with the huge body was a shield—not the shiny, decorated type that you see in movies, but a rough bunch of heavy wood planks that had been crudely nailed together, with rawhide thongs for the bearer to loop his arm through. And beside the shield were two pieces of a single wooden shaft that had been broken in two. At the end of one piece was a metal spearhead, long and tapered to a point. Again, not a clean, smooth-edged weapon, but one that looked like it was thousands of years old. The edges were ragged, worn-down, and nicked. There were traces of dried blood on it and on the giant, who had more bullet wounds than I could count without moving the body.

I stared at the corpse for a long time and then finally got up the nerve to reach out and touch it. The skin was cold and stiff. Now I'm no expert in dead bodies, but I did touch my mother at her funeral. It felt exactly the same.

END TIMES 4

If you're still reading, then there's hope for you. Morbius said it best when he offered Neo the chance to discover what the Matrix really was: *"This is your last chance. After this, there is no turning back."* I love that movie. Anyway, if you keep reading, there's no turning back. You'll never see the world the same again.

I'm not sure how long I spent with the giant in the box. Long enough to memorize what I could see, and then a few minutes more to repair the crate. When I left the refrigerated locker, my shift was nearly over. It was the first time in my short, military career that I failed to complete my assigned duty. Fortunately, my supervisor, Staff Sergeant Jennings, had heard about the airman who died.

When I got back to the little office that we logistic specialists worked out of, Jennings was already there. He never came in early, so I knew something was wrong.

"Hey there, Downy." That was the nickname my drill instructor had given me, and it had stuck. "I heard about the airmen dropping dead last night. Can you believe that shit?"

I shook my head. "No, Staff Sergeant."

"It's those damn vaccines, man. I'm telling you, they're gonna kill us all one way or another."

I didn't bother to answer. Most of the airmen I worked with resented the government telling them what to put in their bodies. I recalled getting all kinds of boosters and shots upon intake, but I wasn't the type to complain or even join in with my peers when they grumbled. And believe me, there was always something to be mad about. But like I said, I tried my best just to blend in.

"Did you see him go down?" Jennings asked.

"No, sir, but I heard the commotion. Tried to help, but there wasn't anything I could do."

"Hell of a thing. Word is, he didn't make it. They revived him for a minute in the ambulance, but he coded again. It's not official, but that's what I heard."

"It was pretty frightening to be honest," I said.

"It's a wonder you were able to finish your shift," Staff Sergeant Jennings said. "We'll complete the inventory on that shipment going out today. You've been through enough. Why don't you call it a night?"

"Yes, Staff Sergeant. Thank you."

He waved me off, propping his feet on his desk as he turned his attention back to the computer. It was the privilege of rank. He was a supervisor, and he wouldn't be caught dead actually helping us do the work we were assigned. When he said "we'll complete the inventory," what he really meant was that he would have someone else do the work that I failed to complete.

I left the warehouse feeling frightened, and yet relieved. I was fascinated by the body but repulsed by it too. The Sotos had always said there was no such thing as monsters. Clearly, they were wrong.

The moment I stepped outside the warehouse, I was met by two men in civilian clothes. One flashed an ID at me. I caught the rank of major on it but little else. The other man, a tall individual with a blank stare, never said a word.

"Airmen Downes," the major said. "A word, please."

"Yes, sir," I said, stiffening a little. I didn't salute. I wasn't sure what the protocol was with officers out of uniform.

"We're here about the cargo that Airman McCalister failed to secure," the major said. "You were on duty here last night?"

"Yes, sir. I got that crate moved to locker two," I told him.

"You moved the cargo?"

"Yes, sir. It was all I could do to help."

"I see. And did you open the crate?"

"No, sir," I lied.

To this day, I'm not sure why I lied. But if I'm being honest with myself, I think it was because the giant was so terrible and so hard to accept as real, that in that moment I didn't want to talk about it. So I lied, hoping the major wouldn't press me too hard. There were cameras all over the base, although I didn't know of any in the warehouse I was working in all night. But that didn't mean I hadn't been seen peeking into the cargo crate.

"You did well, Airman," the major said. "We'll take it from here."

I started to ask them where they were going to take the giant, but I caught myself. Keeping my mouth shut was a habit, and to be honest I was surprised at how close I had come to asking a very, very stupid question.

They left me standing on the street that ran between the hangars and the warehouses. I felt stiff and uncertain. Part of me wanted to go back inside and see what the two officers in civies were going to do. But I forced myself to start walking. Soon, I reached the on-base-housing and the apartment I shared with Senior Airman Wendy F. Presley. We were friendly, but nothing more than room-mates. She worked days, I worked nights. There wasn't much over-lap. She was eating cereal and watching the morning news when I came in.

"Hey! Did you hear that someone collapsed?" she asked.

"Yes," I said, then quoted Staff Sergeant Jennings. "Hell of a thing."

"He just fell over dead, like that football player not long ago."

"The football player didn't die," I pointed out.

"Only because they keep medical staff on standby at all those games," she said. "There are news stories every single day about athletes dying. They haven't said a damn thing on the news about this guy."

"Maybe they haven't heard," I said.

"More likely they just don't care," she said.

She dumped the rest of her cereal and milk down the sink. "Do you mind if I brush my teeth before you take a shower?"

"Sure," I told her.

She hurried off. I stared at the television for a moment and wondered what they would think if they had seen the giant in the box. Then I pushed the memory out of my head and fixed myself a sandwich. I ate, then washed the grime from a long night in a dirty warehouse from my body. As soon as I got out of the shower, I went to bed and fell asleep.

But the giant was there, waiting for me.

9 781968 189204